Dear J,

Thanks ~~~~~~~~~~~~~ gh
this proce~~

Happy rea~~~
D/

emerge 17

ABOUT *emerge*

In its seventeenth year, *emerge* is an annual publication produced by students, alumni, faculty, and industry guests of the Writer's Studio. Students are assigned to teams and, over a four-month period, work with the publisher, editors, designers, our printer, and local booksellers to produce, market, and sell this anthology.

ABOUT THE WRITER'S STUDIO

The Writer's Studio is an award-winning creative writing program at Simon Fraser University that provides writers with mentorship, instruction, and hands-on book publishing experience. Over the course of a year, students work alongside a community of writers with a mentor, developing their writing through regular manuscript workshops and readings. Many of our alumni have become successful authors, and have gone on to careers in the publishing industry.

The Writer's Studio 2017 mentors:
Hiromi Goto—*Speculative Fiction and Writing for Young Adults*
Kevin Chong—*Fiction*
Betsy Warland—*Poetry and Lyric Prose*
JJ Lee—*Narrative Non-Fiction*

The Writer's Studio Online & Whistler 2016–2017 mentors:
Eileen Cook—*Speculative Fiction and Writing for Young Adults*
Jen Sookfong Lee—*Fiction*
Fiona Tinwei Lam—*Poetry and Lyric Prose*
Claudia Cornwall—*Narrative Non-Fiction*
Stella Harvey—*Fiction and Personal Narrative*

sfu.ca/write

emerge 17
THE WRITER'S STUDIO ANTHOLOGY

Gurjinder Basran
Foreword

THE WRITER'S STUDIO
CREATIVE WRITING PROGRAM

SFU SFU
PUBLICATIONS

Simon Fraser University, Vancouver, B.C.

Cover Design: Solo Corps Creative
Cover Illustration: Suzy Baker
Typesetting and Interior Design: Solo Corps Creative
Printing: Friesens Corporation

Printed in Canada

LIBRARY AND ARCHIVES CANADA CATALOGUING IN PUBLICATION

emerge 17: The Writer's Studio anthology /
Foreword by Gurjinder Basran

ISSN 1925-8267
ISBN 978-1-77287-021-3 (paperback)
ISBN 978-1-77287-022-0 (ebook)

A cataloging record for this publication is available
from Library and Archives Canada.

Creative Writing | SFU Continuing Studies
Simon Fraser University
515 West Hastings Street
Vancouver, B.C., Canada, v6B 5K3
sfu.ca/write

SFU Publications
1300 West Mall Centre
8888 University Drive
Burnaby, B.C., Canada, v5A 1S6

To our friend and colleague in multiple years of the
Writer's Studio and co-host of the TWS Reading Series,
Cullene Evelyn Bryant
June 4, 1941 – April 23, 2017

"She was talented, thoughtful, and always generous with
those around her. Her writing, and her public readings,
could be alternately hilarious and heartbreaking, and
they were always insightful.... She entered our community
without excessive pride, happy to be a student learning new forms."

—Wayde Compton, Director, Creative Writing Program, SFU

"I saw that I could become a writer if
I paid attention, if I was careful, if I observed the rules,
and then, just as carefully, broke them."

—Carol Shields

Contents

Foreword

The term *emerging writer* has often been used to describe a writer in early stages of their career. It has also been used to describe a writer who is learning their craft through practical study and application. Either of these descriptions may be suitable for the sixty-two writers you will meet in the following pages, and yet, in my estimation, neither description is wholly accurate.

To emerge is to rise up. To emerge is to move out of or away from something, to be seen. Regardless of their experience, all writers are emerging. They are all evolving and coming into being. They are all discovering themselves through their work. The established writer and the novice differ only in their backstory—the place or circumstance from which they emerge and the motivation for doing so.

I have often thought that writing is simultaneously an act of rebellion and an act of self-actualization. It is to make visible the unseen and articulate the unsaid. It is a quest to make the unknowable known, and a desire to challenge and change long-held beliefs. The writers in this anthology intend to do just that. Through their work, they strive to show what is hidden, they ask you to witness an idea or a moment, and invite you to *see what they see*. Through their prose and poetry, you will see them in the moment that a mother sees herself in her child, you will see them remember love on the end of an apron string, you will see them recall their youth, you will see them in the experience of loss, and you will see them in worlds still being imagined. Through story comes revelation.

As a writer, I have long struggled with the idea of "revealing" and "emerging." When I was in the Writer's Studio in 2006, I spent much of my time wrestling with meaning, view, proximity, and perspective. I wanted to claim my narrative intent and know the purpose or meaning of the story before it was ever complete. Over time, I realized that my own thoughts on the subject mattered little, and that meaning was derived through the writing process, not before; even then, meaning often changed over time. Through the Studio workshops and the generous feedback sessions, I learned that readers are also emerging. They too are rising up, coming into view. Each person brings their own history to a reading: how they assign meaning is rooted in their own experiences, and in that way, writing and reading are two halves of a whole. This may seem obvious, but for the solitary writer the idea of considered or varied interpretation is a foreign one. My time at the Writer's Studio was transformative. It gave me community, mentorship, and the courage to evolve my own writing. It gave me permission to have a voice in much the same way it has given voice to these sixty-two emerging writers.

As you begin this anthology, I encourage you to bring your own sensibilities and experience to your reading and interpretations; through story we are all revealed.

—*Gurjinder Basran*, Delta, B.C., 2017

Speculative and
YA Fiction

T. M. Baldwin

Becoming Crow

AN EXCERPT

I stared at the ceiling, tracing shapes between the irregular dots that littered the mineral fibre boards. I'd always hated ceilings like this. They were cheap nuisances, good for nothing but attracting the sharp ends of pencils tossed skyward for target practice by mischievous students. As a teacher, I wager I spent at least a few days' worth of my life clearing the classroom ceiling of HBs, watching those small holes overhead become mighty chasms.

Now here I was, staring up at another pierced ceiling board, looking for answers. What I saw was a rabbit. Orion, the hunter. Three horse heads. A dragon, if I squinted.

Sandra came in, hands in the pockets of her pastel tunic. The scent of sanitizer and rubbing alcohol drifted into the room on her wake. I raised a hand in greeting, and for a moment my mottled skin seemed to blend in with the ceiling. Was that a bird on the back of my hand?

"Ready to start the day?" she asked.

"Yes," I replied half-heartedly.

"Do you want to go to the bathroom first?"

My insides tightened and the hand I'd lifted in greeting now closed the distance to my chest, pulling the blankets up until the wool scratched the underside of my chin. "No, I'm okay."

"All right," she said, not unkindly, her gaze steadfast. She looked down at her white-sneakered foot, chewing the inside of her cheek as she tapped her toes methodically, up and down, soft rubber to aged linoleum.

The silence dragged. Sandra's ponytail ticked side to side, a pendulum of thought. I knew she was trying, and I hadn't been giving her much to work with. It wasn't her fault, any of it. The doctors said my MS was progressing. That the loss of function in my legs was probably related. They said I was lucky not to have broken any bones when I fell. That the bird-like foot I'd seen in place of my own was just a hallucination. They said it might be a sign of early onset dementia. That I was senile.

Of course, that last bit wasn't spoken, only implied, but I supposed it to be true. Sometimes the world felt distant to me, like I was sitting at the back of a theatre watching my own descent into invalidity play out on stage. But Sandra, she sat right there at the back with me, the annoying audience member who refused to let the standing ovation die because she believed there was an encore coming.

Sandra rattled off some morning activity options, each with a smile or the hike of an eyebrow that suggested there was some fun to be found in the banality of playing chess with Margaret or watching television in the common area, where Jim Phillips would no doubt inch his way over, fancying himself lithe despite the jade-green walker that steadied him, to make a pass at me. Jim was in his late eighties, widowed, still possessed of most of his wits. I was more than ten years his junior; he called me a "spring chicken" and "the prettiest lady in this joint." I would roll my eyes, he would persist with pleasantries, and thus our relationship had continued for the past six months. His last great effort at romancing had included a joke gleaned from his grandson.

Morning, Aggie, he'd said after his slow approach. I hate being called Aggie. Jim knew that. *I've got a new one for you today.* I smiled thinly, watching the cigarette lines pucker and pull around his lips as he asked, *What time did the man go to the dentist?* He smiled. His gums, spotted with age, had run so far away from his teeth that the thin yellow stalks were left holding on for dear life. I shook my head politely, wondering when the last time was that he'd gone to the dentist himself. *When?* I'd indulged. *Tooth thirty,* he replied, a small splash of spittle escaping between the gaps of his teeth along with the double *th*. There was a time I might have laughed, even told that joke myself, but all I could muster was a soft snort.

"Agnes?"

My eyes snapped back to Sandra. "What?"

"What do you think? Some time outside? The sun is out. It's warm."

Sandra offered this option last because it ran contrary to her mission of getting me to socialize more with the other residents. She also knew it was the option I would choose and, in point of fact, had chosen, again and again over the past months. I nodded my consent to the outing, figuring it was a fair compromise. I got to be stubbornly predictable, she got to be relentlessly motivational. We both won.

Sandra's cheeks dimpled in triumph. "I'll get your things ready. It won't take long," she said.

"I'm not going anywhere."

Sandra chuckled and began to pull sweaters and blankets from drawers, kitting out my wheelchair until it looked like a poor man's palanquin. She manoeuvred it close, raised my bed from reclined to fully upright, and lowered the railing guard, the metallic clang sharp in my ears. Sandra pulled the covers back, exposing the skinny legs she'd dressed in maroon slacks a few hours earlier. Her hands slipped beneath my ankles. "Are you ready?"

I pressed my hands to the bed, fingers sinking only slightly into its firmness, and tried to support some of my weight. I nodded, and Sandra swung my legs around. I wanted to assist, but in reality all I could do was ensure the top half of me didn't topple over. The bottom half didn't speak to me much anymore. Facing me, Sandra slid her arms under mine, clasped her wrists securely beneath my shoulder blades, and with feet firmly planted on either side of mine, lifted me from the bed. My arms splayed out, shoulders climbing to my ears as Sandra's upward lift fought gravity's downward pull. A dull ache spread through my lower back as I hung in the air, the compression in my hips and spine slackening only to return in a moment when, in one fluid swing, Sandra shifted me from cushioned slab to blanketed hearse.

"You're getting a little light, Agnes. Better gain some weight or I won't get enough exercise."

"Maybe you're just not lifting enough at that gym of yours," I said. "What did you tell me you were—what is it, *deadlifting*?—the other day? Apart from me, that is."

"Two hundred pounds," she replied, swathing me in blankets.

I shook my head. Girls weightlifting was an oddity in my day, something reserved for high-performance athletes. We praised them as powerful, berated them as unladylike. But here was Sandra, wispy brown bangs and French-manicured nails softening the sharp line of muscular arms, and I could hardly call her unladylike in appearance, let alone in manner. Perhaps it was better to be a stone than a feather in the face of a fierce wind.

It was a short trip down the hall, with only a few nods to the other attendants and residents before we reached the double door leading out to the yard. The panelled glass slid aside on our approach and we emerged into the mid-morning sun, the glimmer stinging my eyes. As I raised a hand to shade my view, Sandra wheeled me across the lawn to my favourite spot at the far edge of the property—a patch of flattened earth between two thick roots of the old willow tree. The willow was the first I saw of Haven Estate, and probably the reason I agreed to stay. From the passenger-side window of my granddaughter's red Ford station wagon, its forty-foot umbrella had loomed into view as we came up the drive, imposing even at a distance, grand and lonely. This willow, without a brook, seemed out of place in a place where nobody really belonged, at least not for long.

"I'll come back for you in an hour?" Sandra asked as she secured the wheel brakes.

I nodded. She gave my shoulder a squeeze and padded away.

I closed my eyes and let the breath fall from me, a sigh into the breeze.

Around me the willow fronds danced, the gentle touching of leaf to leaf a murmuring chime that prickled across my skin like a dry fall of rain. The early summer sun teased just beyond the veiled canopy, fringing the edge of each long leaf in gold. Like a familiar poem, the tree was all line and symmetry: five thick roots reached down into the earth while five slender trunks reached up into the sky. I reached out to rest my hand on the nearest tree root, its grey skin smooth and cracked, like mine.

—*He took it from you, didn't he?*

I jerked in surprise. The wheelchair rocked beneath me. "Who's there?"

Only the wind answered. I was alone.

"Excellent," I sighed to myself. "First seeing things, now hearing things."

At least senility wouldn't be boring. I wondered what Dr. Madden would make of this. Perhaps I wouldn't tell him. After all, everybody heard voices sometimes, didn't they? The voice that tells you what to do and what not to do, or gives you the unsolicited opinion you know a family member would have. Still, there was something . . .

—*You're not hearing things.*

The voice ran like a shiver down my spine. I could feel it. A slight rumble in the earth, a shifting of the dirt beneath me. And I could hear it. A faint crackling, like wood on a fire or the snap of dry twigs. A crackling that was somehow words. Old words. Not my words, but words I knew.

The voice ran like a shiver down my spine. I could feel it. A slight rumble in the earth, a shifting of the dirt beneath me. And I could hear it. A faint crackling, like wood on a fire or the snap of dry twigs. A crackling that was somehow words. Old words. Not my words, but words I knew. The voice ran like a shiver down my spine. I could feel it. A slight rumble in the earth, a shifting of the dirt beneath me. And I could hear it. A faint crackling, like wood on a fire or the snap of dry twigs. A crackling that was somehow words. Old words. Not my words, but words I knew.

Lis Jakobsen

The Golden Scarab of Bloor Street

Polly gave her head a covert shake, like she'd been jangled out of a secret sleep. Her sister Lillian's charm bracelet rattled, keeping time with the ends of her sentences. Murmuring drifted with cigarette smoke across the kitchen table, ash and words settling far too lightly to grab onto.

Lillian ground out her cigarette in the *Miami: The Magic City* souvenir ashtray. "... And so there's a caring and intelligent universe out there that's constantly messaging us. If only we'd listen."

Huh? Somewhere after agreeing their cousin Celina was a flapping idiot for wearing flip-flops to a family wedding, Polly had lost contact with her chair. Her sister's sudden pause made her aware of her bum, squashed hard onto one of the mismatched chairs that framed the thrift store table.

She nodded, faking comprehension, but was overcome with a need to examine the table and recognize something new in it. *How about that. It's exactly like the one we had when we were kids.* She ran a finger over its fake marble grain, mining it for a clue as to what Lillian was on about.

"... So Jung was trying to convince his patient, this Viennese woman—a real Cartesian-driven extremist—to embrace the concept of synchronicity ..."

Polly glanced out the window at Bloor Street, twelve floors below. How to escape what was likely to be a long—really long—holding-forth on Dr. Jung? "Hey, Lil, how about some more coffee?" She sprang into the narrow galley kitchen like it was a doorway in a rainstorm, opening one cupboard and then another, searching for the coffee filters.

7

For some reason she'd become incapable of putting anything in the same place twice. Not since coming back to Toronto feeling like she and her things were about as stably rooted as the contents of a confetti cannon. She pulled another drawer. Stuck. She yanked harder.

Lillian's head snapped up. "Christ on a cracker!"

The drawer hung from Polly's hand as she surveyed the floor, now scattered with a bunch of God-knew-what from the previous tenant, a travel writer who'd gone on a trip and never come back, according to the super.

She started cramming stuff back in. About fifty hotel and restaurant matchbooks from around the world, two dried-up Sharpies, possible mouse droppings, a few rheumy evil eyes, an Australian beer bottle opener, an Eiffel Tower fridge magnet, and a large assortment of cheap Egyptian tourist trinkets.

Polly twirled one of the Cheops key chains on her finger. "No idea where the coffee filters are." She laughed. "But these six pyramids might work great with your bracelet."

This inspired a G-force eye roll from Lillian, who'd already helped tote out the rest of the ex-tenant's abandoned junk. Polly had lived there for six months, never dealing with a dozen or so boxes—not hers—and two half-unpacked suitcases—hers.

As usual, Lillian had taken charge the morning after her arrival. "You've got to claim this place. Settle in." She shoved a carton out into the hallway. "Geez, Pol. It's more than time."

Leaning on the counter while the coffee brewed, Polly studied her sister. California colouring played on her clear complexion, only faintly lined even now and framed by a neat blond bob turning to grey. At fifty-one, she'd entered a PhD program in philosophy at a Bay Area college and was jazzed about "massive ideas," living near the Pacific Ocean, and all that damned golly-gee tree-ripened fruit.

Even so, all the sun-kissed guava in the world couldn't stop Lillian from snoring like an old hyena. Over her visit, insomnia had prowled the one-bedroom apartment, stalking Polly on a nightly basis. A gnawing and uneven sleep had set eddying, tired lines around her eyes and deeper marionette tracks around her mouth.

"... No matter how Jung tried to convince her that there was miraculous healing in looking for clues, that is, by listening to what the universe had to tell her ..."

Polly struggled to look benignly interested. *Might have been a lot easier if Jung had just told that lady to move to California.*

Polly poured milk into her coffee, researched the beige results like it was a new shade she'd invented, and then noticed it matched the colour of the worn linoleum perfectly.

"And, you know, synchronicity means things that seem like coincidence are really the universe's way of giving guidance."

Polly flashed back to last week when she'd suddenly thought about an acquaintance she hadn't seen in years. The next day she'd ditched her AA meeting when she spotted the same woman there, reciting the Serenity Prayer.

Lillian stirred her coffee. "And lots of synchronicity adherents say, rightly, everything happens for a reason."

Polly made fists under the table, wishing they were jammed at her ears as a corroborating story was hauled out. A young man about to graduate was walking down the street trying to decide if he should go into the family business or become a physician. Suddenly a woman fell in front of him, stricken by a heart attack. The student was able to use his basic CPR skills to save her. Question answered by the universe.

Right. I suppose next she'll say it's God's way of travelling incognito.

"Doris Lessing says coincidence is God's way of being anonymous," Lillian added.

Polly's shoulders sagged. *Is this God's way of doing a little showboating in my kitchen? Playing the synchronicity card just for the heck of it?*

9

And really, she hardly needed Him to tell her that a Nobel laureate had already outdone her; but there, there, that's okay. *No actually, it isn't okay.* Absolutely nothing was okay when she really came down to it.

"... Anyway, this woman refused to be open to all that and started telling him again about a recurring dream about a golden scarab ..."

Polly thought about another woman, one who made the Viennese lady and Flip-Flops Celina seem like paragons of good judgment and intellectual flexibility. A woman of advanced middle age who'd been such an idiot that she'd put her Forest Hill house up for sale, sold or given away nearly all her belongings, quit her job, and gone to Belize to live with a man she now couldn't even flatter herself to call a gigolo. At least gigolos took you dancing.

Had the universe been hurling unheeded communiqués at her as she gave away her mid-century Danish modern sofa? Where were the warning texts from Alpha Centauri as she listened to his stories about how his money was tied up in a complex real estate deal in Miami? Or the one about how his big trust fund would loosen up when his family in Sydney—or was it Melbourne?—stopped disputing it, any day now. Money was always somewhere ... just out of reach.

Where had the intergalactic Lassie been when she could've been barking messages to potential rescuers? "Little Polly has fallen down the well! Get off your asses and send her down some rope before she pays for another meal, set of airline tickets, new suit, engraved watch, or house rental on a Belize beach!"

Her friends had told her he was shifty. One had even used the words "flimflam artist." But she'd simply cut them out. Lillian had been part of the chorus, and the two were only now reconciling after a year.

And worse, there had been whisperings from her own cranial universe, swatted away like a constant, buzzing insect in her ear.

"... As she was telling him about the dream, there was a tapping at the window, and when Jung looked up he saw a glittering scarab—well, what we'd call a beetle—rapping insistently against the window pane."

Lillian got up, charging for the kitchen drawer. "Jung went to the window and caught it." She rooted around until she found what she wanted. Crossed the room again. "He held it out to her and said, 'Polly. Here is your scarab.'" She put it gently in her sister's hand. "Take it."

S. L. Shields
Cedar
AN EXCERPT

The orange pickup moved along rough terrain, kicking up gravel. Sid enjoyed the sound of earth against the windscreen and the mid-morning sunlight reflecting off the silver casing of the driver's side mirror. The first days of November brought a crispness to the air, hinting at the cold that was to come.

The ride into Derby took just over ten minutes, giving him enough time to sing "Jackson" to himself twice before crossing the township line. The first road signs appeared just as he was failing to layer the voices of Johnny and June Cash. His arm hung out the open window and cold air travelled up the sleeve of his tartan coat, tingling in a familiar way as the dark hairs stood at attention along the length of his forearm. Sid breathed deep, in through his nose and out through his mouth. On a day like today, not much of anything seemed to matter.

It was the first Tuesday of the month, the only day out of thirty that was worth a damn, according to his wife. On this day every month a small package arrived from an overpriced book club, stamped with the name Mrs. Louise Jenzen. Sid never could understand the appeal, but then again he had never been a reader.

The post office was nestled between a stationery store and a Tourism Maine booth. The teller window was small, covered in a thick layer of plastic cut with several air holes and an aluminum drop tray. The place had come a long way since its humble origins as a Spud Shack. Ruth often joked that on summer days you could still smell the residual tones of french fries.

"Ruth!" he called.

"Just a minute!" It was Ruth's voice but disembodied. A series of clunks and shuffled steps announced her arrival at the window. "Hiya, Sid. Didn't expect to see you."

Sid focused on her words, digging deep for the charm that came so unnaturally to him. "You sound disappointed," he said, laying a hand over his heart.

Ruth smiled, stretching back her lips, exposing her smoker's teeth. She had aged in exactly the way that all women fear to, looking closer to ninety than her near-seventy. Ruth was a widower once and a grandmother three times over, red-headed and so friendly it was nearly nauseating.

"No! No, jeeze, no," she said. "That's not it at all. It's just that it's the first Tuesday and I thought Lou would be coming in."

"She's a little under the weather. Just call me Errand Boy."

Ruth paused for a moment, caught by the unexpected answer. Sid imagined her features pooling, heaping over themselves as if they were made of milk.

"You are just the sweetest thing," she said. "Real thoughtful." She laid her hand on the counter between them, her fingers outstretched, leaving a large print. Her blue eyes met his directly. It caused an uncontrollable itch. The longer the two of them maintained the stare, the more uncomfortable Sid became.

What the fuck does Ruth see? he thought. "Can I grab the book, Ruthie?" he asked, thankful for a distraction. It felt good to call her that, and he wondered why he hadn't done it before.

"Coming right up," she replied over her shoulder as she made her way back into the stacks.

Sid was still singing when the truck crested the final hill on the road home. The tires made an odd sound as they crossed the wooden planks that bridged the gap over a narrow creek. Ascension Bridge had received its name due to the steep incline at its end, marking the end of the public road and the beginning of Sid's driveway. The aging truck seemed to hesitate against the angle, but Sid leaned down on the accelerator.

It reminded him of his youth and the sound of playing cards bouncing off the moving spokes of his bicycle. His mother had attached them for him. Other kids had baseball cards, but these were cheaper and sounded the same.

Sid pushed down on the accelerator, giving the old truck the final burst it needed to clear the incline separating the outer edges of his property and the thin creek that surrounded it.

A clearing cut through the tree line, the ground levelled save for the protrusion of the main house, garage, and shed. A metal gate blocked off the final stretch to the house. Sid threw open the driver's-side door with a noticeable rust-induced creak. A single metal chain held the two sides of the gate together, scraping as it came undone. The sound of it, that metal on metal, left a vibration in his teeth.

The orange pickup passed along the road, the gate left swinging behind him. Sid refused to get out of the car again. An open gate was not the end of the world, he reasoned.

"Hello!" he called into the house.

Silence.

No voices. No groans or creaking floors. Just pure and absolute quiet. Sid dropped the box onto the kitchen table and moved toward the sink. The gate had left marks of grease and dirt along his fingers. His eyes scanned the yard through the uncovered windows. The grass had become that crunchy yellowish-brown reminiscent of first frosts and snowfalls that don't stick to the ground. The property line of the yard was encased in trees.

The proximity to these woods was one of the main selling points of the house. They were his woods. Sid's eyes scanned the space between the front door and the garage. Somewhere nearby, he knew, he would find a speckled, greying lump by the name of Chase, snoring in the sunshine. Chase had been brought home to act as a shop dog but did little to protect his home. More than swinging gates and moving vehicles, the only thing that could wake Chase was the sound of kibble hitting the empty metal of a food bowl.

Sid moved his attention back to the table and the thin box that sat on it. He could hear the book sliding around as he shifted the parcel from side to side.

The box produced a hollow sound as it bounced against the sides of the plastic bin before settling in as recycling. Sid pulled bubble wrap away from Lou's newest smut read. *I'll save this for later,* he said to himself as he popped several of the thin bubbles.

This month's cover was less risqué than some of the others. Two darkened silhouettes, a pink setting sun. A plywood bookshelf occupied a small corner of the living room. Rows of pastel spines lined the shelves, but it would be out of space soon.

Sid surveyed the room from the narrow doorway that led to the kitchen. He could not remember a time when the house had seemed so quiet. The setting sun lit the room. The hardwood floor seemed to reflect an almost orange light, altering the normally familiar space. Sid took in the shadows forming on the walls. The room was silent save for a low growl coming up from his stomach.

He had turned on his heel to leave, when the evening light illuminated a piece of the wall next to him. A large handprint stuck out against the matte paint. Its fingers were large and splayed out, looking as though it had been left there under considerable pressure. Sid took a step closer to it, examining the life and love lines imprinted on the wall. Near the bottom of the palm, the prints were coloured with red.

Rust, he thought. *No, it's darker than rust.*

Tatiana Lee

Fisherman's Friend

AN EXCERPT

I remember when we used to haul in the nets hand over hand. Now I watch those gill nets spool in and out on the drum, like the thread on Nancy's sewing machine when she's really in the zone. I imagine she's probably on to her second quilt since I left port.

We'd been talking about going on a vacation, her and I—Tampa, to see her sister. Not much of a vacation if you ask me, but I'd go, for Nancy. She'd love the flea markets, the beach, and chattin' it up with Kathy. Me, I'd probably sit in the shade with a beer. Maybe go big-game fishin' once or twice. Nancy always laughs when I "fish while I'm not fishin'." Fishin', it's not work, it's just a parta who I am whether ye pay me or not.

But I do like gettin' paid when I'm supposed to be. This captain, he ain't so good at the payin'. The fishin' and the workin', he's top notch— never skimps on that. Last week, the boys were at it on the aft deck somethin' like twenty hours a day all week long. They look like the walkin' dead about now, but they know the payout this time should be worth it.

Least now the crew knows I am on their side. I may be the bosun, but lemme tell you, there ain't no love lost between the cap and me. We worked it all out last trip; now he gives me a wide berth. Trouble is, I also lost all the perks o' being the bosun, like being inside for a spell on days like today.

Standin' under the overhang of the wheelhouse, I huddle to keep warm and try to stay dry. From here I can keep an eye on the rest of the crew sortin' out the fish, detanglin' corpses from the nets before they get crushed. If only the cap would let us smoke 'n work like the good ol' days, it would take the stench and monotony out of it. Rain's peltin' down so hard now I guess a smoke would get soggy before you even got it lit. I look over the crew and notice a greenlin', out on his first trip, pukin' over the side.

"Hang on, Kai, or you'll get pitched over," I call. I s'pose he's just gettin' his sea legs, or maybe it's the smell of fishy death. Maybe both.

The boat heaves to and fro as the storm reaches its height. Nothin' out of the ordinary, but the boys still have to hang on to slippery hand-rails to keep from fallin'—or worse. No one wants to be the guy swept overboard and never found.

Our catch is just about in the boat's hold when, abruptly, everythin' is still. It's almost worse than the storm, because it comes on so fast. The sudden lack of movement makes me nauseous. I look around and notice the net is jammed in the drum. Even the boat, usually so loud with activity, is quiet. The only sound is the rain and the jammed motor.

I hear the radio fillin' the aft deck with screechin' feedback and then the captain's voice: "What the hell is going on down there?"

It's then that I see somethin' huggin' the boat's gunwales. It's the colour of a cadaver that's been in the water too long, just like you'd see on one of those cop shows. I wonder who the jokester is playin' today's prank. Not a funny joke if you ask me. I seen a few boys fall into the drink and done enough rescues for that kinda thing to bring back bad memories, not laughs. I look around and realize the whole crew is on the aft deck starin' at the same spot I am. The captain is glarin' out from the wheelhouse window. No one seems to be holdin' in any guffaws or belly laughs. It feels different. Then I realize there's a growin' smoochin' sound, like what you'd hope to hear if that Marilyn Monroe photo was happenin' in front of you for real, or like Nancy does when she blows me a kiss from the dock as the boat heads out.

Kai sees the creature and goes apeshit and, of course, is the first one to go overboard. Stupid kid lost it, ran, slipped, and then slid right off, past that *thing* and into the water. The rest of the crew stands frozen in

17

place waitin' for the punch line—no one moves to throw a life ring to Kai, includin' me. Instead, we are frozen in place by what we see: tentacles advancin' up and over the railin' where Kai went over. The ensuing crunchin' and screamin' in the water tells us it's no joke.

Gerry starts for the spare anchor. Tyler falls to his knees and pukes. Tentacles keep spillin' onto the deck and into the openin' in the floor that leads to the fish hold. I find it funny how the hold, minus-twenty degrees Celsius, doesn't seem to bother this thing. I'll admit, I've seen a lot. But this, this I never seen.

The tentacles keep comin' without a body in sight. They seem to be embracin' the *Betty Jean*. I hear metal creak. Tyler and Gerry are pinned in place at the stern, tentacles blocking their escape. At the other end of the boat, I'm stock-still in horror.

Frozen, just watchin' the scene like I'm at a movie theatre.

Thomas Onstott
Banshee's Tale
AN EXCERPT

Banshee sat in a café, sipping her coffee and watching the world bustle by. America was a strange place, always on the move, always trying to accomplish something. It was never quiet; there was always a truck screeching past, or a television set blaring. Compared to the Irish countryside, it had been disorienting, but now she had come to enjoy the chaos. She was desperately grasping the fleeting feeling of happiness before it inevitably slipped away.

The small tables on either side of her remained vacant, but she didn't mind. Her crimson hood and its noxious odour drove people away. A small child stopped and stared before being ushered away by her mother. She'd learned to ignore the small, insignificant people, especially the children. Every time, the ritual was the same: kill the child, treat herself to a drink, find a bog and rest.

The killing of the child had remained relatively unchanged, although the invention of the gun had made things more interesting. Certainly cleaner than with a knife or a sword, but quicker and less personal. With the progression of time came new drinks, and she was forced to adapt. Mead to beer, beer to whisky, whisky to tea—the drinks had marched along with her and the generations.

In April of 1916, she had found herself in the midst of a dust-up on the streets of Dublin. It took the unexpected killing of twenty-three young Irish lads before she finally found the correct one. This extra work left her parched.

All the cafés near the General Post Office had been boarded up, but

19

after some searching she found one still open several blocks off O'Connell Street. In desperation, she tried a cup of coffee; all the tea had been requisitioned by the British soldiers. The cup and saucer clattered as the little man's hands trembled uncontrollably, his wife whimpering softly from her position of assumed safety behind the bar. Banshee was indifferent to their terror as she sat in the café alone, enjoying this fantastic new beverage. The new smell flitted in her nostrils, and the bitter taste lingered in her mouth. She had not felt true warmth in such a long time. Deciding it was far superior to tea, she spared the little man's life and from then on ordered coffee.

Having never been to America, she was afraid they wouldn't have her cherished drink. Much to her relief, she had stumbled upon a small corner store which was open twenty-four hours a day. Oh, the possibilities and options this country presented: iced coffee, latte, mocha … she didn't know what a pumpkin was, but even that could be added to her coffee, for a price.

Finding a place in which to rest would be the most challenging part. Having never been outside Ireland, she quickly realized America was sparse on bogs. It seemed Louisiana and Florida had swamps, which could suffice, despite the water being too warm for her liking. The Bogville Mall outside Syracuse had potential but would need further investigation. If she could find a fairy ring, she could fly back to Ireland, but that was difficult for someone of her notoriety. She had a few friends, or at least informants, but an even larger number of enemies.

She sipped her coffee and grew tired. She wanted to sink down, to be enveloped in the cold murky waters, to sleep for another fifty years. How many times had she curled up in a different place to sleep? How much longer would she be doing this? As she finished her coffee, she thought about her future and dwelled on her past, and the last bit of happiness and warmth slipped from her grasp.

The sun was shining and she was in love! Well, the sun wasn't exactly shining, but occasionally there were breaks from the rain and the black clouds would lighten for a little while. It was almost spring, and no late cloudy days could hold back the joy bursting from within. She wasn't really in love, just bursting with life—exuberant, her father would say. She had just turned sixteen and had caught the fancy of a strapping young lad two farms over. He had a handsome face, which made up for his being a tad pudgy. When he worked, he would sing, and if the wind was right, Mara would catch the odd note. None of Papa's stories about falling in love with dashing young princes had happened yet, but there was still time.

She was strolling leisurely down the road to the market, a little goat in tow, when she spotted him. At first, she thought it was the neighbour's son, but as she got closer, it turned out to be a stranger. He was sitting, back against the stone wall, strumming his lute and singing, without a care in the world. Even from a distance, he was striking. Tall, lean, strong, a full head of sandy blond hair.

When their eyes met, he took off his hat, smiled, and bowed his head in an overdramatic, almost comical fashion.

"Well hello, young traveler," he sang with a strum of his lute. "And where ye be headed this fine marnin'?"

She giggled and covered her face. "I'm off to Ennis. 'Tis market day."

He struck up a melody on his lute and sang along.

"The young lass went to market, little goat in tow.
The only thing she missing was a bonny bow.
Her hair so fair and eyes so bright.
Who will buy my goat tonight?
I'm selling goats for ribbons and bows.
How much will he fetch, anyone knows."

She listened and giggled, while the goat let out a bleat of protest and gently pulled on the rope. The man was on his feet now, walking toward her, still strumming his lute and singing.

"I'm not buying ribbons and bows," she said. "We need seeds."

"Every night she sang some words so sweet and kind.
The oats grew more than any farm ye would find.

"And what do they call you?" he asked with a grin and a drink from his flagon. The wine mixed with rain dripped from his beard. He smelled intoxicating and sweet, but revolting at the same time.

"Mara," she said and pointed to the goat. "And this is Bartleby."

"A beautiful name," he said with a smile. "Did another share it?"

"My ma, before she died," Mara answered.

"I was talking about the goat." He broke into a song.

"Bartleby went to market, bleating all the way.
Little did he know, he would be traded for oats and hay."

She giggled again. "And what do they call you, fine minstrel?"

"I'm a poet, my child." He put down his lute. "And they call me many things, but mostly Ciaran."

"I'm not a child," Mara answered quickly. "I'm sixteen, and you don't look much older yourself."

"And from where did you come?" Ciaran asked.

"The farm down that way," she said, pointing behind her. "And you?"

"All places, everywhere and nowhere in particular."

"And what kind of answer is that?" Mara looked up at him and flashed a quick smile.

"I'm a man of mystery," he said with a smile. "Do you like mysteries?" He stepped closer. His eyes looked wild, and she was suddenly scared.

Mara moved away from him; the goat had stopped bleating and was munching on a bush beside the road. She remembered Papa's stories about little girls snatched from the road by evil spirits. The hair on the back of her neck lifted, and her heart pounded. "No," she said as she pulled on the rope tied around the goat's neck. "And I don't like games either. Farewell, poet."

Bartleby made a noise of protest and reluctantly left the bush to follow Mara down the road. She didn't have time for mysterious strangers;

she was late to market already. She knew from experience the best prices came early in the morning.

But the man was so lovely, with his long blond hair, his green eyes, his voice. He made Mara laugh, and even made her happy. She shook her head to clear the image. He was vile, and smelled of wine and dampness.

He was still on her mind as she rounded the bend, and there he was again, standing in the middle of the road. He swung his lute from side to side in such a way that Mara could not tell if he was beckoning or threatening her. "Come here girl," he said, the sweetness in his voice replaced with cold, sterile command.

Any conflicted feelings Mara had were replaced by fear. She tried to hustle past him without looking up, and had nearly succeeded when he grabbed her hair and pulled her roughly to the ground. She kicked and struggled as he dragged her off the road to a ditch beneath a large gnarled oak.

He grabbed her tightly by the wrist and yanked her roughly to her feet. She couldn't breathe. She struggled, but he held her wrist tightly. She heard her tunic rip, and she felt the cold, damp air on her legs.

She hesitated for a fraction of a second before launching her attack. She rolled her wrist, forcing his grip to break, while simultaneously bringing her other arm across his face. He stepped back, stunned, and she used the opportunity to land a kick squarely in his crotch.

Michael Zibauer

The Barmaid's Adventure

AN EXCERPT

The quartet of Loki, Nemitz, Mithandus, and Mona have left the
town of Casterbridge Wilds to find Mona's mother.

LOKI

They walked for what seemed like days to the tired and sore thief. His
ankle was still tender after the fall from Bad Knees' second-floor window, but he was able to walk without much of a noticeable falter. He
wished that he had a horse like the wizard and was marginally put off
that the wizard had neglected to offer to let Loki ride rather than him.
Then he remembered that the wizard too had twisted his ankle in the
fall from the second floor of the inn. It still pissed him off that he had
to walk. He had to remind himself that the wizard's horse was not his
horse—not yet, at least.

Loki was glad to be away from Casterbridge Wilds. He had not travelled outside the city for many years, and the farthest he had been from his
home city was just a day's journey north to visit some family when he was
a child. Though his relatives were long since gone from the north, he did
have a fond memory of visiting cousins when he was a kid. This was before
his mother and father were killed by the plague that ripped through the
city when he was twelve. After that there was no contact with other family
members, and Loki and his brother, Rolf, were forced to steal to survive.

At first, it was just a couple of tarts or apples from local hawkers.
Then they moved up to stealing horses and breaking into buildings in

the rich neighbourhoods of Casterbridge Wilds. Loki and Rolf had worked as a team. One would keep an eye out for the city watch while the other ransacked whatever passed as an opportunity for advancement for the duo. That was, until his brother got caught.

Loki had been fifteen. Both he and his brother were robbing a well-to-do family in an outlying neighbourhood near the Singing Soul. Loki was watching the street for the city watch while his brother rummaged through the house looking for valuables. As Loki watched the street, he thought his brother was taking way too long to get out of the house. Then he saw two of the city watch coming toward him.

Loki made the loud whistle that was the brothers' signal for trouble and ran down the street to hide behind a building. He watched the guards come closer to the house. Just as they arrived at the building, Rolf came out onto the street with a candelabra and a bag of valuables. The watchmen instantly raised the alarm. Rolf dropped the booty and ran, but it was too late. The watchmen had the jump on him, and just as he ducked down an alley, they were upon him.

Loki ran to help his brother, but by the time he rounded the corner all he was able to see was his brother being attacked by the two guards. The first guard pinned Rolf to the wall with his sword while the other managed to place cuffs on him. They took him alive to the central square. Loki followed, intending to get his brother out of the mess, but he was only able to watch as Rolf had his hands lopped off by the guard and then was hanged from the gallows in the middle of Casterbridge Wilds.

"How far do we have to travel to reach the village proper? I thought we would already be there by now," Loki asked.

"Not far now. If we were all on horseback, we would have been there an hour ago," Mona answered.

Loki felt like a fish out of water. The countryside was strange to him and foreign. As they passed small groves, he thought someone might jump out and attack him with every step. The country was a lot different than the familiar buildings of Casterbridge Wilds. For comfort, he fingered the gold in his pockets and remembered that he still had that strange book in his possession. For sure, he would keep the book secret from his travelling companions. No need to tell them anything. He thought he wouldn't be with them for much longer anyway, but he debated whether or not he should kill them. He entertained the idea, but he realized too that it might be more difficult to do in practice. They all seemed to have their wits about them.

After another half hour or so, the warrior Nemitz called out. On the road were the bodies of several soldiers, stripped naked. Loki watched as Mona walked a little closer then stepped back and turned away. The wizard walked up to one of the bodies.

MITHANDUS

Mithandus knelt at the first body and carefully touched the skin of the dead man. The body was covered in bites and gashes, as if someone or something had taken very large hunks of flesh from it. The men had served as dinner.

The blood on the dirt road had already dried, so it appeared that they had been out there for quite some time. Also, there were flies frantically buzzing and feeding upon the remains. Though the men had been purposefully stripped of their armour, their clothing included the padding required to support it. Though trashed, their gauntlets and shields were strewn around the scene.

"These were no ordinary men," Mithandus announced to both the group and to himself. "They were veteran soldiers."

Nemitz came over and knelt down by another body. He turned a broken skull, and as he did a penis fell out of its mouth. Mithandus saw Mona turn her head violently away in order to shield herself from the sight.

Nemitz touched one of the wounds. "Who could have done this?" he asked.

"I think I know. We must be careful from this point on," Mithandus answered.

"Obviously," Loki said sarcastically. "But we already knew that, didn't we?"

Mithandus had taken a dislike to Loki. It wasn't so much that they had rescued him from the situation back at the inn. It was more that he was always watching everything, and Mithandus could almost feel him calculating every move he made and keeping score of something. He was determined to watch the man.

"Yes, but this assures us that the road is much more dangerous than they told us back in Casterbridge Wilds. They aren't getting information back there because no one is returning from the East," the wizard surmised.

"Yes," Nemitz affirmed. "But who would do this hideous act?"

"Gnolls," Mithandus said.

Gnolls were evil descendants of hyenas. They acted in all manners with the viciousness and savagery of their dog cousins. It was said that a demon lord had transformed the dogs into humanoid creatures bent on evil and destruction. Mithandus could tell the bite marks in the flesh were canine in origin. Since the bodies had been stripped, half-eaten, and left to rot, all signs pointed to gnolls. The dog-men took only what was valuable, dined on the bodies for a time, and mutilated what was left to rot along the road.

Mithandus rose, leaving Nemitz still examining the bodies, and walked over to where a short sword had been left lying on the ground. He picked it up and approached Mona. "Here, take this," he said, handing her the sword.

"What? What can I do with this? I don't know how to use a sword," she said.

"You need to arm yourself. I know you have no skill, but at least if trouble comes up you should be able to defend yourself."

"I don't know," Mona said, but as she did she took the weapon. "How will I wear it?"

Nemitz rose and picked up an old scabbard that was lying on the road. "Use this," he said.

Stephanie Gray

Lockhart and Teague

AN EXCERPT

Lockhart scanned the crowd for the warlock and found him shadowed beneath the purple awning of a nearby tea shop, hanging back from the crowd as if he didn't want to be noticed. Lockhart watched him calmly, while the warlock's own eyes were glued to the front of the crowd as his former lover dropped, the sound of her neck snapping audible even across the distance.

The assembled onlookers murmured with disappointment when Katrina died with comparative quiet, spared the protracted indignity of a death by slow strangulation. They compensated for the lack of spectacle by picking up stones and dried clumps of horse shit from the street and hurling them haphazardly at the dangling corpse.

The warlock watched all this with apparent apathy, his hands moving with glacial slowness as he took out and lit a cigarette.

When the crowd finally began to disperse and Teague had still not moved, Lockhart approached him.

"They'll leave the body there until nightfall," he offered. "If you planned on waiting around."

Teague turned his head slowly, his mouth slack. The tinted spectacles he wore didn't quite hide the dark circles underneath his eyes.

"What do you want?" he asked.

"Your help."

Teague scoffed, turned, and began to walk away. Lockhart followed.

"I did save your life, you know," Lockhart said slyly, keeping pace with Teague's slow strides. "Some people might feel obligated."

"Some people can—what was the charming turn of phrase you used?—lick me." He kept walking. Lockhart kept following.

Teague approached his coach, where Viola stood brushing the grey mane of one of the horses. She tensed when she saw him, her hands sliding pointedly toward the long knives sheathed at her waist.

"Just hear what I have to say," Lockhart said.

Viola opened the carriage door for her employer and lowered the steps. Teague placed one foot on the lowest step, then seemed to hesitate. Without turning back he said quietly, in an almost regretful tone, "Now is not a good time."

Leo Lockhart had it in his clockwork heart to be a subtle man, when it suited him. He chose not to be. "Whenever you're free," he said simply, "there is a murderer on the loose somewhere."

Teague turned slowly and stepped back down onto the ground. His eyes had lost some of their vacancy, yet Lockhart did not fail to notice the way his hand hovered above Viola's shoulder as he descended the steel steps.

"I think I'd like a cup of tea," he said, nodding at Viola. Quite casually, he sidestepped into a tea shop with a wooden sign over the door that read *Pot of Eden Confectionery and Tea House.*

Lockhart followed him in, looking around warily. It was a small, intimate room with white lace doilies on all the tables, sparrow's-egg cushions on the wicker chairs, and turreted palaces of bite-sized pastries waiting luxuriously behind polished glass.

Teague sat down heavily at one of the rear tables. Lockhart sat across from him. A girl in a blue-and-white striped dress brought a pair of china teacups and saucers, cream and sugar, and a plate of complimentary heart-shaped sugar cookies.

Teague took off his tinted spectacles. Behind them his eyes were bloodshot. His face looked thinner, sharper than it had a month ago. "What do you want from me?"

Lockhart picked up his tiny flowered teacup by its stem-shaped handle and lowered it to his lap. Beneath the table, he fished Jessamine Carstairs's eyeball out of his pocket and dropped it into the cup. Then he placed the cup back on the table and slid it across to Teague.

Teague looked into the cup, his face registering dull surprise. "Now?" he asked incredulously. "Right here in the tea shop?"

"Who's going to stop you?" Lockhart asked. He drew the knife out of his boot and held it out, handle first, for Teague to take.

With some reluctance, Teague took the knife. He picked up the eyeball using a cloth napkin and held it tightly in his fist as he made a small incision in the sclera. He took a quick look around the nearly empty room before squeezing the small, rubbery lens, awash in viscera, into the cup.

"Gin?" Lockhart offered, holding out the small glass bottle he'd picked up on the way over.

Teague gave him a perturbed look but took the bottle and poured a small splash into the cup, submerging the lens.

He put his spectacles back on and raised the teacup to his mouth. With a slight grimace, he tilted the cup back and swallowed the contents. Lockhart couldn't see if Teague's eyes changed colour behind the tinted glass. But he could see the familiar shudder running through him as the vision took him, and he could hear his choking cough. A server turned her head at the sound but quickly looked away again.

A few minutes later Teague coughed, raised his napkin to his mouth, and discreetly spat out the regurgitated lens. His eyes were squeezed shut. He rocked forward, pressing the heels of his palms against his temples.

"What did you see?" Lockhart asked.

Teague opened his eyes and for a moment just stared at him, awestruck. "You're a cunt," he finally said.

Lockhart raised an eyebrow.

"You could have warned me she was hacked apart by her own father."

In the pause that followed, Lockhart counted three beats of his clockwork heart. "It *was* her father, then?" he finally asked.

Teague was about to answer when the waitress came to pour their tea. Lockhart contemplated asking for a clean cup, then decided not to bother.

"She was still alive when he killed the other girl," Teague said weakly, spooning sugar into his tea. "And you ..." he added wonderingly. "You tried to save her."

"You saw all that?"

"I did," Teague confirmed, taking one of the heart-shaped cookies and biting off a ventricle.

Lockhart frowned. Nothing about the murders made sense, and it irritated him to no end that everyone—the Dogmen, even Six—seemed content with that.

"Who was he?" Teague asked, dipping a cookie into his tea. "Was he crazy?"

"Why? Do you know a lot of perfectly sane people who hack apart their children with wood axes?"

Teague shook his head. "Not intimately. Did you know him?"

Lockhart shook his head dismissively. "I didn't think he did it. I was wrong."

"That doesn't seem like you."

"It's not."

Eager to change the subject, Lockhart asked, "Why were none of your kind here today to see one of their own put to death?"

Teague's blue eyes refused to meet anything but the glassy surface of his tea. "From the moment she broke the covenant, Katrina wasn't one of us anymore, she was a heretic. She was filth."

"But *you* came," said Lockhart.

"Yes," Teague confirmed. "I came."

"Did you love her?"

Teague put the teacup down and ran his fingers through his hair, sighing deeply. "I'll always love her," he said. "It is a betrayal of my God."

"You believe that?" Lockhart asked skeptically.

Teague looked at him with an endless sadness in his eyes that Lockhart didn't understand. "With every fibre of my soul," he said. Then he picked up a cookie and bit it in half.

Robyn Drage
The Gift
AN EXCERPT

A sliver of moonlight snuck in through the gap in the curtains, played along the top of the typewriter, and brushed the folds of a mound of blankets that was rising and falling with a gentle snore. Max the cat scaled the bookcase and climbed into the empty typewriter box, watching the desk intently, eyes bright in the shadows. A few minutes passed. Max cocked his head to one side and tensed.

At first it was just a tendril, a tiny lick of dark mist testing the air, curling up from the shadow in the centre of the old machine, a suggestion of a sharp black claw at its tip. But soon one black ribbon became three, then ten, as black smoke curled up from under the keys, thickening and solidifying as it swirled between the typebars, ribbon spools, and paper. It floated there, gathering form as its edges hardened, building into a squarish head with powerful jaws and a compact body.

Megan snorted and rolled over to face the desk, and the mist scattered. She murmured something and her eyelids fluttered, then her breathing slowed, relaxing back back into the rhythm of deep sleep.

On the bookshelf in the corner, an old clock rescued from an estate sale down the street ticked its way through most of a minute. The smoke poured out quickly this time, flowing up along the back of the typewriter and hovering over the metal band that pressed down a fresh sheet of paper. Two slits of burnt orange opened slowly, blinked a few times, then flared wide, turning bright red, before narrowing and fading to a dull rust. They pulsed gently, black catlike irises burnt into each centre. Two clawed hands unfurled, closing over the metal bar, and arms solidified, rising into powerful shoulders. It stretched, closed its eyes, and inhaled deeply. After holding its breath for a moment, it exhaled and let its shoulders relax. It ducked its head and shook itself like a dog, definition rippling down its stocky body, short muscular legs, and scaly tail.

The eyes flicked open, trained on the cat. Max crouched lower and returned the stare, the bubble wrap in the box creaking slightly. Red eyes narrowed as the shadow dropped backwards off the typewriter onto the desk and slipped toward the window as a silhouette. It pulled the curtain aside with one claw, and the moonlight lit its face with sharp blue highlights. Twisting its face into a grin, it dove through the window and was gone.

The creature slid down the slanted porch roof and dropped silently onto the grass. A muffled bark came from inside a nearby house, but otherwise the neighbourhood was still, silent. The creature zipped across the lawn, dove between some small shrubs, and disappeared under the porch.

In the inky shadows, it relaxed against a pile of loosely stacked wood, and a cigarette appeared in its fingers. It struck a match on a rotting plank, cupping a claw around the flame, and nodded at a spider that emerged a few feet away, yellow-orange glinting in eight obsidian globes. The creature inhaled sharply, puffing to get the cigarette to catch. A small bush at the base of the porch steps burst into flame.

"Jeez, Harold," said the creature, "cut it out. That joke is old. Plus someone in this respectable neighbourhood might notice a spontaneously combusting bush and come charging at us with a water sprinkler."

The fire winked out. "No one is awake. And Dante always laughs. You just have no sense of humour, Frank." A figure ambled forward, grinning widely. He had broad eyes in a thin face, a thin awkward neck, and a narrow upper body that expanded into a perfectly round belly over thin legs. His oversized claws, similar to his friend's, looked out of place on his gangly frame. "I thought you'd never get out of that closet."

35

"No thanks to you. How long was I in there?"

"Twenty-five years, six months, four days, fifteen hours, thirty-seven minutes, and a couple 'a seconds, in case anyone's counting."

Frank grimaced. "I was starting to wonder if you'd left me there for good. I know I was stretching the rules, but come on. That was just petty."

"The higher-ups were starting to doubt your commitment. They thought you were stretching it out unnecessarily, maybe getting a little soft, a little too attached to your prey."

Frank held out the cigarette to Harold. "There's no trust these days. Why is everyone in such a rush? There's no time to savour a well-constructed downfall. It was a slow burn, but I had him exactly where I wanted him. Then that cocky little upstart showed up."

"Wasn't my decision, man." Harold held up his hands.

"You know, I'm starting to doubt your loyalty. Dave was committed to being a failed writer until your guys decided to meddle. He was content, probably happy, and I would have crushed him when the time was right."

"I know. I tried to reason with them." Harold took a long pull of the cigarette.

"And suddenly there was this new crap about running off to Panama or Costa Rica or wherever to open an ice cream stand. He's so suggestible—he *believes* he's living the dream. That's what those assholes don't understand. The beauty of the job was keeping his dream alive as long as possible then watching the destruction on his face when he realized it was all a lie."

Harold shook his head, eyes wide and sympathetic.

"That other guy, what's his name, Anthony? He's pure evil, the young kind of evil. The kind that has no patience, no appreciation for artistry or subtlety. And was he there to torture Dave or me?" Frank growled.

"He's climbing the ranks pretty fast. I bet he'll be elected to the Senate in a few hundred years."

"The Senate? When did we get a senate?" Frank said, taking back the smoke.

"Oh, things have changed around here. Last month they tried to ban cigarettes! I can't tell who's on which side anymore, honestly."

Frank shook his head. "I told you, right? I figured that with this new flood of politicians into our ranks, it was going to get weird. Priorities would be changing."

Harold nodded. "You should see all these new motions and proposals. And memos, God, so many memos. And committees, and committees to investigate the other committees. I miss the days when we just settled things with a good smiting."

Frank grinned. "So. This new gig. I got started already. They don't usually take to it so quickly, but she's got the fire for it. You can tell the big boss was improvising, being creative."

"But not too creative, right? I just got out of a fifteen-year seminar on Finding Your Voice," Harold said, "emphasis on the Importance of Understanding Your Place in the Chain of Command. You could've joined us, but you were indisposed."

"So maybe I should thank you for stranding me in that closet," Frank smirked.

"Yeah, you owe me one! Anyway, here are the details." Harold produced an ancient manila file folder.

Subject: Megan Kingsley was typed on a white label at the top, letters blurred and jumbled as if the label maker had jammed while printing. Torn bits of old labels poked through underneath. He flipped it open. "Says here she's twenty-five, showed early promise in the arts, but her teachers squashed that crap early. She coasted through coffee-shop jobs et cetera after dropping out of pre-law liberal arts at the local college. She's had this bookstore job for six months, doesn't hate it. Parents defined 'helicopter parenting' and live on the other side of town, nice and easy driving distance. Mother, Ruth, sells real estate and Mark, her father, is an accountant and very proud of his successful local business.

Her being a lawyer was their idea, and they believe sustained, concentrated disapproval could still force her down the right path. Holiday family dinners don't end well. Her younger brother is a smug little brat working on his MBA."

"Good. So ... she's floating, directionless. I can work with that. Anger ready and waiting to be stoked, and she'll realize how much it could piss off her parents if she throws it all away to follow in her uncle's footsteps. She has a new dream. She's going to be *A Writer.* "

"Something like that," Harold said, flipping the envelope closed and handing it to Frank.

"So if I get through this, you promise to break me out of this Failed Writer gig and get me a real job, right? It used to be fun, feeding the exhilaration, getting them addicted to the high, then smashing them them down to that awful, staring, swallowing blank page. And then finding just the right amount of hope to push them through the despair to do it all again. It's an important craft, but I think I've lost the passion for it. I'm ready to try new things," Frank said, stubbing out the cigarette.

"The boss has a few ideas brewing, so I'll tell you what. Get through this one fast and I'll put in a good word. Now, make sure to read the supporting documentation all the way through. This new generation is something else."

"Hah! I got this kid. It's all human nature. So let's get to work," Frank said. "This one's gonna be easy."

Cynthia C. Huijgens

The Novice Collector

AN EXCERPT

Max closed his eyes and tried to recall the era and origin of every object on the shelf. "Pharaoh's toe, Upper Egypt; Mameluke sabre, Ottoman Empire; WWII tankard, North Africa; 2,000-year-old papyrus, Ptolemaic Dynasty, Roman city of Herculaneum."

The collection was vast and varied, and Max could have easily continued, but an unfamiliar sound caught his attention. It reminded him of air escaping through the pinched opening of an overstretched balloon. His eyes scanned the room for the source. He heard a sorrowful yowl coming from the floor next to his bed, where his dog lay. He rolled over until he was hovering just above her stomach. "Poor Ramses, I think you've eaten something you shouldn't have, like maybe one of my socks?" He stretched out a sympathetic hand and gently rubbed her bloated belly.

Ramses the labradoodle from Chichester, England, had been a Christmas gift to Max from his parents when he was ten years old. She had been about the size of a rugby ball then. Her glossy black coat, a thick mass of wispy curls, was the softest thing Max had ever felt. When Ramses was six months old, Max took her to obedience training, where she learned to walk with a lead, stop on command, and sit and stand according to hand signals. Max taught her to catch a Frisbee and fetch a ball. In a very short time Ramses grew tall, her long thin legs giving her the elegant walk of a show dog.

As Max listened to Ramses' twisted gastronomic cries, he longed for some aspects of his old life in England. Time with Granddad, and the comforting familiarity of his old neighbourhood and school friends. Max watched Ramses squirm and slowly kick out a hind leg. "Hooh, Ramses. What did you eat?" An odour something like rotten meat commingled with stinky cheese swept up his nose. "Grrrooosssss!" he laughed, pinching his nostrils and rolling as far away from the dog as possible.

Max stood and did an entire body stretch, popping the knuckles on each hand one by one. A kink in the side of his neck sprang free with a slow half-circle twist of his head. He made a start for the desk, clumsily twisting away at the last minute. Max couldn't bring himself to sit in the chair. He needed some new excitement for the old material he couldn't muster any feelings for. He began walking the perimeter of his room, dragging a finger along the wall as he went. Four steps along he came to the built-in wooden wardrobe where he kept his clothes and shoes and a few items not worthy of a place on the shelves. The wardrobe, with its handles like heavy brass knockers and its stylized corner carvings of stems and leaves, was not something Max would have chosen for his room. But as it was an original feature of the villa dating back to 1915, he knew it had value.

Stepping heel to toe around the wardrobe, Max came face to face with one of four English Premiere League football posters he had hastily hung his first week in an attempt to make his new room feel a bit more, well, like his room. Brown greasy spots blotted each corner where sticky putty residue had bled through, but the images were as clear as ever. The entire Manchester City team, clad in their sky-blue Etihad uniforms, stood nearly eye level with him now. Max gave two thumbs-up as he recalled the joy he felt the day Man City beat Sunderland to win the Capital One Cup. His smile turned cold at the realization that he hadn't seen his favourite striker, Sergio Aguero, in over six months. Since moving to Egypt Max had stopped watching football matches live, opting instead to follow his favourite teams on the Internet. The time he'd once spent watching football with his mates was now taken up with exploring the streets of Cairo, canvassing for treasures, and dealing with the never-ending demands of Grade 9.

He was desperate to catch up on schoolwork and wished he had a tutor, or better still, someone who would complete the work for him. He recalled the old days when Granddad had helped him with homework. Granddad made it seem fun, like it wasn't work at all. Sometimes he would pull a small object from his pocket—like a tarnished half-dime coin two centuries old, or a miniature stone figurine from an ancient civilization—and tell Max the most incredible story. Objects gave Granddad passage into the past, glimpses into moments in people's lives and periods in history that felt so real, it was as if Granddad had been there himself. The stories fascinated and delighted Max and gave rise to his early fascination with antiquities. If it hadn't been for Granddad, Max probably wouldn't be a collector at all.

In England most of Max's classmates had been focused on collecting sports memorabilia and old metal cars, stamps and rare coins—the sort of collectibles with clubs in every town. But not Max. His interests stretched further back, to things like a 2,000-year-old papyrus buried during the eruption of Mount Vesuvius. A novice observer might think the scroll on his shelf looked like a large lump of charcoal, but Max knew what lay within the tightly wound layers of delicate carbon sheeting. It was impossible to unroll the charred texts without breaking them into a million pieces, but one day new methods like 3-D x-ray imaging or a super-advanced laser reader might reveal its hidden secrets.

Max stood back and admired his life's work—well, more like six years of it. Most of his objects had been acquired scouring antiques shops, specialty traders, obscure street vendors, and fairs. The collection had been methodically catalogued, photographed, and documented in an acquisition registry which Max kept in the top drawer of his desk. His treasures were displayed along two deep shelves just inside his bedroom door. He never tired of them, but one day he hoped to bring home an object he'd excavated himself.

Max lifted his arms as if to embrace the entire collection in a group hug. "Aren't you glad you're not in a stuffy old museum someplace?

Displayed next to an object you can't stand, having total strangers stare at you all day, wondering what's so exceptional about you?" Max laughed, hearing himself talk to objects as if they were human. "At least here, you're loved. And you're part of a family. I'd show people how exceptional you are, but I've only got one friend at the moment."

Max's shoulders dropped a couple of notches as he realized how dorky he sounded, even to himself. Mostly he realized how lonely he'd become. He wanted friends, but so far Youssef was the only kid to express any interest in him. Most of the kids at school appeared too busy with friends they already had, or maybe Max just wasn't cool enough to attract attention? Whatever the reason, making new friends in Egypt had proven more difficult than he had anticipated.

Feeling a bit nostalgic, Max reached for the WWII tankard. It was against his protocols to handle artifacts without gloves, but today felt like an exception. He was surprised to find the wooden handle, with its silky finish, warm to the touch. Max lifted the tankard and cradled the cold brassy bottom, pulling it close to his heart. The tankard was not by any stretch of the imagination his favourite object—that honour belonged to the pharaoh's toe. However, as part of a small number of artifacts Max had inherited from Granddad, it held special meaning. Max spun around, raising the tankard to the light for a better look. "This'll do," he said.

Max returned to the bed and nestled into an oversized pillow. He raised the tankard to his lips and imagined drinking an enchanted brew, some ancient tribal extract which would somehow miraculously provide answers to the remaining questions of Mrs. Marjorie's assignment. As he swallowed down the very last remnants of magical thinking, the tankard came to rest sideways on his chest. An inscription close to the rim, so worn and tarnished it was nearly impossible to decipher, read: "Desert Campaign 1940–1942." Max ran a finger along the faded contour line where Egypt met the Mediterranean Sea, and down along the Suez Canal into the Red Sea, which neighboured Saudi Arabia. With a little imagination, Max thought he could see topographical details. Toward the bottom he came upon more writing: "British v Corps, British x Corps, British xiii Corps . . ." His muscles twitched, and a feeling of intense struggle surged through his body. He was bombarded, as though by a ferocious attack, with thoughts of the thousands of men who had lost their lives fighting from Tripoli to Cairo and beyond. Along the base were the words, "Before Alamein we never had victory. After Alamein we never had defeat. —Winston Churchill."

As Max conjured images of heavy artillery and battle-weary troops advancing on a hostile enemy, the muscles in his body went limp. His breathing became slow and shallow. He lay motionless, watching the tankard disappear, burrowing itself into his chest like a soldier taking refuge in the sand. He blinked in disbelief and blinked again just to be sure he was awake. As he tried to find the tankard, an eerie sort of quiet enveloped him, and his mind evaporated into a starless sky somewhere between twilight and total darkness. He hung there for a while, suspended like a kite at the end of a long string, held afloat by a very warm breeze.

Samantha Balliet

Bridge World

AN EXCERPT

The lengths one could be pushed to when motivated by the memory of home were both funny and depressing. Isra mulled over this unfair truth as she followed Michael down the well-trodden path to the plum plantation. The plantation was situated at the base of a grassy hill just outside the city, and the air lacked its usual loud chatter and clatter of citizen life. The sun loomed high in the late afternoon, and though the sweet scent of plum trees should have calmed Isra, she couldn't help but feel nervous.

A small cottage sat at the edge of the orchard. Michael and Isra hesitated at the entrance for a few seconds before Michael shook his hands out and knocked on the door with three quick raps. Isra took a deep breath. Finish the jobs, collect the payments, and eventually go home. She could do it one step at a time.

The door was thrown open and a mogling man with impressive eyebrows and biceps came forward to peer down at them. Isra couldn't help but trace his long, wiry fingers—the mogling trademark and the only characteristic distinguishing them from humans. This mogling's fingers in particular stretched to nearly double a human's, and the mere sight caused her to shrink back.

"Humans?" the mogling muttered to himself, his voice scratchy and low. "What are you doing here?"

Michael coughed into his fist. "Sir, we're here for a job that you posted in City Square. About removing the … carnavens?" Isra held out the flyer without a word. The mogling snatched the paper and read it carefully. Isra put her hands behind her back and tried her best not to cower.

"I should have known only humans would respond to this." The mogling scratched his long nose with a forefinger. "Very well. Follow me to the back."

The mogling walked with heavy steps through the rows of plum trees, his thick leather boots skidding roughly across the grass. The leaves of the trees clashed nicely against the dark bark with its rosy magentas and indigoes. Plump fruit of all sizes peeked out of the leaves in clumps, shining with a delectable beauty in the sunlight.

Michael and Isra followed the mogling deeper. An unpleasant odour of mould and rotting meat wafted to Isra's nose. The stench grew stronger, and Isra cupped both hands over her face, choosing to breathe through her mouth. Ahead of them, a single tree with metal buckets set beneath it stood out like a stain among the other flora. A black substance like hot tar covered the wood and seemed to be spreading across the entire tree like a disease. Where it had reached several branches, it dripped thickly into the buckets below.

"Have you ever seen a carnaven?" the mogling asked them. Isra shook her head and Michael leaned forward, eyes sparkling with interest.

"Disgusting things, they are. One carnaven turns into two, two into four, and they pile onto each other until they form a clog—an *infestation*. By law, we have to get rid of clogs manually. They are a terrible thing to deal with." The mogling reached into one of the buckets and pulled out a large, knotted sack. He tossed it to the ground in front of them. "This is powdered vinegar. It breaks down carnavens. Dust it over the entire clog and get rid of the remains. And *don't* make a mess." He eyed the two for a second before turning around and grumpily walking back through the trees.

Michael, with his lips pursed and eyes narrowed, stepped across the grass and inspected the dripping carnaven.

Isra gasped. "Michael, how can you stand that smell?" she whispered.

45

"It is awful, isn't it?" the blond boy agreed. "I just wonder what it's made of ..." He stretched out a finger and poked at the tainted wood. His forefinger pressed into the foul, inky substance, which fizzled at his touch. The thick goo shifted, latching onto his finger and rising. He gasped and freed his hand, shaking it and wiping it off on his overalls. He stared at his finger a moment before a grin spread across his face. "That's so *cool*," he said.

Isra stood back and watched as he reached into the sack, grabbing a pinch of powder. He inspected the white, grainy powder, then suddenly tossed it onto the bark in front of him. A large lump bubbled and opened up like a mouth, then began to cry out. It was a strange sight, Isra thought.

The white powder muddled itself into the carnaven and began to fizz. Steam rose, and the powder, once thoroughly mixed with the carnaven, turned into a rough, grey, layered aggregate that looked suspiciously like an ordinary rock. It dropped from the tree with a thump, and Michael, using a hand shovel, scooped it up and dropped it into an unused bucket. "I can see why that guy didn't want to do this himself," he said, frowning.

The pair spent the next half hour that way. Isra would toss the powdered vinegar onto an affected portion of the tree and, after it had done its job, Michael would scoop up the remaining rocks and put them in the waste bucket. A lot of the task involved waiting, but ever so slowly the plum tree was returning back to its normal form. Eventually, however, Michael began feeling impatient, and he called forth a dozen field mice to help speed up the process by picking up the rocks. They came forth from the grasses in a flurry as they always did, eager to please their master.

Isra stood back and watched as the mice picked up the smallest of the rocks with either their front paws or their teeth and dragged them to a second bucket that Michael had laid on its side for easy access. She couldn't help but feel envious at her friend's strange power. With the added speed, they were almost done.

A tiny squeak from below stole Isra's attention. She squatted down and found two mice fighting over a rock. "Hey, hey, hey," she said softly. "We don't need to fight. There's plenty of rocks for every—"

The mice rolled on top of one another, tumbling in a lump of fur until they accidentally fell into the carnaven clog with a resounding slap. The clog bubbled up and formed several mouths with razor-sharp teeth, latching onto the mice viciously. The mice cried out and writhed.

Isra gasped, leaping forward. Without thinking, she shoved her left hand into the thickening clog, frantically reaching for the mice. The wailing carnavens felt slippery, almost like a viscous oil, until they latched onto her arms with their teeth. Pain shot up her forearm and she yelped, shutting her eyes.

The pain disappeared. As did the wailing and the godawful smell of the clog. Disoriented, Isra opened her eyes and looked around.

She was sitting on her knees with her arms stretched out, just below the infected tree—exactly where she had been before. Only now, it seemed like she had been transported to a twilight zone of black and white. The setting around her was an echo of what it used to be. All the plum trees were stripped bare, and the grass that had looked so lush was now a dry yellow. The sky had lost its life as well, and grey, unshifting clouds loomed above. The air was cold, *so* cold, and she was alone in the ash. Everything was dead.

Distant wails reached her ears. Shaking, she whipped her head around and saw black marks begin to appear on the other trees. Gaining size and crying louder, the carnavens began to form and multiply, taking over all the trees. The horrid stench hit her nose at last, and she covered it with one hand, the other shielding one of her ears from the wailing. Her eyes began to tear and she shut them in fear—a feeble attempt at escape.

The wailing ceased. The stench gave way to fresh air. Isra opened her eyes again. The plum trees swayed peacefully in the wind. Finches chirped at each other, and the sky had returned to its peachy glory.

"Isra, are you okay?" Michael asked worriedly, waving a hand in front of her face. "You've been spacing out more than usual today."

"I'm fine," Isra mumbled, rubbing her eyes with the backs of her hands. Nausea roiled in her stomach when she thought about the strange vision.

Michael held his hand out in front of her, and she found herself face to face with two shamefaced mice. "I talked to them. They're really sorry that you had to save them."

She looked down at her arm at the reminder. The skin was clean and undamaged. Had she imagined the entire episode with the carnavens? She forced a smile onto her face and moved to comfort the guilt-ridden mice. She would worry about the vision later, as she always did.

As she and Michael cleaned up, the mogling returned and gave their work a once-over. He reached into his pocket, huffing, before tossing a small pouch that clinked as it flew to Michael. He stalked back to his hut without a word.

"How much did we make?" Isra asked.

"Three tokens. Each." Michael kicked at the dirt, head down.

"And how much are the tickets, again? For the ferry back home?"

"Eight hundred and seventy-five tokens … each."

Elecia Chrunik

How the Earth Went from Flat to Round

AN EXCERPT

Me and the sun are barely up, groggy in the kitchen with Ma humming softly as she packs our bags for the day. Last night's dreams drip out, making room for the birds' chirping outside to ring and ping and bounce around my brain. Pa slipped away early again this morning, down to the shore, long gone before I opened my eyes. What he's doing exactly is anyone's guess.

All I know is that Ma and I are off again today to round up some more cactus juice. More and more and more, and Pa won't say much about it, not to me at least. It must be something special though, 'cause it's like he's got lightning bolts in his pockets when he comes home. When I ask what he's up to, he lifts me up and swings me around and rubs his nose against mine. "I will show you soon," is all he says, with bright teeth and happy eyes.

The sun starts to creep in over the window ledge, spreading warmth along the dirt floor and up through me. Ma thinks I'm not looking, but I see her slip some extra dried fruit into her bag. She'll try to surprise me with it later, up on the cliffs, when my arms are tired and the high sun is baking us. I'll still pretend like I wasn't expecting it. I turn my back to her and practise lifting my eyebrows and opening my eyes wide.

Ma hands me my bag; she made it light for the walk. Hers has the food, the water, and the sharp blades. Mine has only the two empty containers of smooth wood that Uncle carved. They're simple compared to the animals that line the shelf by my bed. Just the other day he showed up with a new one, a strange creature with four legs and a long neck.

Ma gives me a crooked smile as she takes a hat from the hook on the wall and crunches it down on my head. She's trying to make it stick so she doesn't have to weave yet another one. She slips on her own hat and we step outside. The birds in the mango tree flitter up and chirp in a ruckus before settling down again. The morning is still quiet, but we can hear the waves lick the shore. The air smells fresh and alive. The stars have all gone, but the white moon still sits low in the sky, small and curved like the pieces of fingernail I chew off and spit out and get in trouble for. When I was little, Uncle taught me how to wink, and I send a quick one to the moon.

I look up at Ma. She's staring toward the cliffs that stick up on the edge of the island like the tall, bored towers I used to make in the sand. She looks down at me and reaches out her hand, and I take it with both of mine and press it against my cheek. Her hands used to feel soft as clouds, but since we started skinning cactuses the clouds have turned tough.

We leave our yard through the opening in the low stone fence, onto the path that spreads out like a web around the island. The old, worn roads get tangled up with roots, and vines try to close in on them from above. Pa and the others chop them back with big blades, but that's a race they'll never win.

Ma and I set out, our footsteps silent on the dark dirt. Her hand wraps tight around mine, her thumb pressing just enough into the back of it to make me feel settled. Ma and Pa have given up on trying to make me wear the clunky sandals that strangle my ankles and choke me from the feet up. My bare toes feel good on the dirt.

We turn left and pass old man Reeshe's place, with all his seashell wind chimes barely jangling in the morning quiet, then my friend Suna's place, whose ma just had another baby. A few days ago, we left a basket for her with fresh, bitter greens and bright flowers from our garden, and

Suna's ma came by that evening with the babe and some of her special herbs that she ground to a paste and rubbed on our sore, raw hands.

Finally the trail comes to an end. The cool shade of the leafy trees stops too, and the cliffs rise high above us. Ma lets go of my hand and faces me. She puts her hands on my shoulders and pauses to look deep into my eyes, then steps ahead to lead the way. It's easier for me to keep up now than when we started. Twenty trips now? Maybe thirty?

The ground starts going up and up and up. We climb this way then that, the path barely there and steeper with every step. It's a different world already, the air turning drier the higher we go. We step over jagged rocks and carefully walk through a few spots of prickly bushes. Up and up and up we go, and the bright green life of the island below withers to dry, pale brown. I need to keep my mind off the tired feeling building in my legs, so, like always, I think about the first time we came up the cliffs.

I was smaller then and needed stories to fall asleep. Ma and Pa would cuddle up with me, and their tales always started the same: "One day, we found a secret path . . ." They whispered in quiet voices about the hidden trail that winds along and around the edge of the cliffs, high above the rest of the island. A path so small and skinny that one wrong step or blast of wind would send you tumbling from the sky. My favourite stories were about how they and Uncle spent nights under the stars and how they were high enough that the sky settled down on them like a blanket while they slept. I always fought to stay awake for the best part, how once you got to the top, you could see all the way to the end of the world, and that's when I would slip off into dreams, floating up, high as the clouds.

One day we were pulling roots out of the garden for dinner, and I saw by the way Ma and Pa were looking at each other that they had a secret. Ma's crooked smile and Pa's crinkled eyes meant good news. Finally Ma said it: the three of us, plus Uncle, would head up the cliffs for a picnic and a sleep like they used to do.

We got ready for the climb that night, and I didn't sleep a wink. As bad as I wanted it, the thought of being so high up scared me stiff. The next morning I tried to hide that I was shaking like a leaf, but Pa could see. He wrapped me in his strong arms. "Don't be afraid," he said.

Pa led the way with blankets and firewood, Ma next with a basket of food, and then Uncle with me tied in snug against his chest. I remember the bones in Uncle's shoulders that stuck out like stubby wings, and the way the ones in his ribs felt lumpy against my legs every time he bounced me back up when I started to slide.

As we started up the trails, waves of panic rippled through me, and I clung tighter to Uncle. I'd tried so many times to imagine what the edge of the world looked like, if it would be anything like it was in my dreams. But with the thump, thump, thump, thump of Uncle's footsteps and no sleep the night before, I was fast asleep when we reached the top.

I woke up under a tent they'd made for shade, my tongue dry and fat, thinking that the air had somehow caught fire. Then Ma grabbed my hand and held it tight as we walked toward the cliff's edge.

I shake my head to bring me back. Ma and I are finally at the tough part, just as the sky is turning bright blue and the air is heating up. We're breathing hard; the air whistles through our lungs, mixing with the sound of wind and roaring water below. The sheer rock wall rises straight up in front of us, and the rest of the path disappears around the side of the cliff. Ma passes me some water, and the coolness slides down my throat and shocks my belly. She looks at me and lifts her eyebrows. "Ready?" she asks.

I wink back and she smiles. We shift our bags to the front of our bodies and step carefully toward the ledge.

Even on the calmest day, the wind on the cliffs whips up and swirls dust into our eyes. The path narrows even more, until we're forced to press our backs and hands against the smooth rock and start doing the sideways walk. I'm already getting dizzy, but as long as I can feel my hands on the rock wall, I don't think I'll fall. Left foot to the side, right foot to it. Left foot to the side, right foot to it, and on and on we crawl like slow little crabs. The ledge twists up and around the cliff, winding higher still. We're two little specks, step-by-stepping along, the wind so strong I choke on it. The wind blasts again, so I have to clamp my hat down onto my head and try to blink the tears away.

The same thing happens every time, ever since I first stood on the edge of the cliff holding on to Ma's hand, looking out over the huge distance of forever into nothing. My brain goes bad, like suddenly it no longer knows my body, and I can't tell up from down or this way from that. I try to breathe deep in the lashing wind. Somehow holding my hat on my head helps, like then my brain knows it can't escape.

I fight to stay calm, though; if Ma knew how I felt, she'd leave me at home and come on her own. Maybe she hears my thoughts, because she puts her rough hand on my shoulder. "Are you okay?" she yells over the howling wind.

I force a nod, trying to slow the swirling inside.

"Only a little longer."

A big blast of wind hits us from below. I gasp and try to stop my legs from trembling. We stop and press back into the stone wall until it calms. Just a few more steps. A few more steps.

Finally, the path widens again and we can step off the ledge and onto safer ground. And from there, the rest is easy.

Shilpa Raju
Ties

The grille of the balcony felt like bars on a cage to eleven-year-old Tara, yet it was her favourite spot in the whole house. It offered her the freedom, however limited, to be a part of nature, at least vicariously.

The railing was four feet high and her chin barely touched the steel fence. The grille blocked out the openness, lending her a gridded view of everything outside. The inconvenience did annoy her, but it didn't make the balcony any less desirable. She would sit on the chair and lean against the metal rods, breathing in the fresh air and taking in the scenes of nature.

She knew everything about everyone in the street. She knew that the hunchbacked old man limping toward the neighbour's house worked for them as a gardener. She knew that the dhobi living in the shack at the end of the street drank almost every day and occasionally beat his wife. She also knew the names of the kids who played cricket on the street every evening. She regretted that she wasn't one of them.

The air in the balcony was often redolent with a mixture of aromas from the dishes cooked in the neighbourhood. Tara's mouth would instantly water and her stomach would rumble in hunger. But then she'd realize that she had to rely on store-bought grub in the refrigerator instead of homemade delicacies.

Tara's parents were both working professionals who rarely had time for their daughter. Neelam, their maid, acted as a babysitter until they returned home from work.

Tara got so used to the solitary lifestyle that she dreaded weekends. Her parents would take her shopping and to movies and restaurants, but all she craved was her room. She was drifting further and further away from her parents and they didn't realize it.

Tara's room smelled of books—all kinds, from children's magazines, encyclopedias, and dictionaries to fairy tales, novels, and comics. Books were a solace to her. They offered an escape from the lonely world where no one ever asked her how her day went, no one ever checked whether she had finished her homework, and no one ever bothered to ask what her favourite subject was. She felt like a piece of furniture that's well fed and taken care of but never acknowledged.

Tara customized her room to match her likes, sticking up posters of her favourite Power Rangers on the walls and hanging superhero action figures from the curtain rods. The mahogany study table in the left corner was filled with precarious heaps of volumes she had borrowed from the local library.

That evening her parents were at work as usual. Neelam made herself comfortable and sat down in the living room to watch soap operas, as usual. During ad breaks, she would perform a perfunctory act of checking up on Tara.

Tara carefully picked one book from the table without disturbing the pile and walked past the queen-sized bed onto the balcony. The storage space behind the headboard was stowed with soft toys that had remained untouched ever since they were put there.

Tara began reading *The Chronicles of Narnia* from where she had stopped the previous day. She loved the novel because it had talking animal characters. She was an animal lover and had longed for a pet ever since she was born. Her fondness resulted in numerous fights with her dad. She begged for a hamster at least, but he was strong on the no-pets policy. He had his reasons, of course. "Who would take care of the animal while you are at school?" he asked.

It was four in the afternoon and the sun shone bright, soaking everyone exposed in vitamin D. The air was filled with the hollers of amateur cricket players on the street. Around the curve, a street dog dug a pit in the sand and settled in comfortably. Sparrows and pigeons still hovered in the sky.

Despite the din, Tara's ears were sharp enough to detect some faint chirps coming from inside the house. Her ears were erect with attention and were angled toward the room. The sound was specifically coming from under the bed. Slowly, she placed the book on the chair and walked toward the source. The chirps, sounding more like cries, were continuous now. She bent to her knees and peeked underneath to find an injured sparrow.

Mixed emotions ran through Tara. First, surprise; second, happiness; and third, sadness on seeing its condition. Tiny droplets of blood trickled from under its wing and it barely moved. She extended her hand and carefully took the bird into her palms. "Oh, you poor thing," she said. "I will take care of you. Don't you worry. Stay calm."

Tara placed it on her cushion and went to search for a cardboard box. She didn't dare make a noise as she tiptoed into the kitchen. Neelam lay sprawled on the floor, busily gobbling peanuts as she watched TV. Tara found a shoebox in the kitchen cupboard and quietly toted it to her room. She punched holes into the box and spread layers of cotton inside. Then she cleared her study table hastily and placed a tray over it. She set down the sparrow and examined the wound.

The bleeding had stopped by then, but the bird still seemed to be in pain. Tara found a gash just above its leg, hidden beneath the feathers. She cleaned the abrasion with cotton and water. Then she snuck a bandage cloth from her parents' room and tied it around the bird's wound.

After she was done tending it, Tara wondered what to feed her little pet. She remembered reading in a book that sparrows mostly eat grains. In a flash, she ran into the kitchen and came back with a bowl of oats. She placed a small basin in the corner of the shoebox, within the sparrow's reach, and poured some grains into it. The tiny creature started pecking greedily, as if it had been starving for days. Then she closed the lid and allowed it to rest for a while.

Tara tried to read for a bit, but her mind wandered toward the shoe-box. She couldn't keep her eyes off it. After one hour of suppressing the urge, she removed the lid and checked on the bird. The creature, proba-bly asleep, woke up with a start and let out a loud chirp.

"You sleeping? Sorry!" Tara apologized. "How are you feeling now? Do you want some water?" She spoke as she would do to a human.

The sparrow stared blankly at her, occasionally moving its head, probably to survey the strange creature making sounds and looking at it.

"Here, have some." Tara held an eyedropper filled with water to the bird's beak. It stared into space, having no idea what the human was do-ing. When Tara didn't budge, the sparrow just pecked at the bulb in-stead of putting it in its mouth.

After thinking, she brought a flat plate filled with water and placed it in the box. The sparrow hesitated for a few seconds, then hopped its way toward the plate. This time, Tara's attempt turned out to be successful, and the sparrow got some water into its system.

"Hmm. What shall I name you?" Tara mused as she watched the bird twittering with renewed energy. "Birdie? Spar?" She moved along her room, ruminating, before resolving to call it Birdie. Quite an innovative moniker for a bird, don't you think?

Tara's parents didn't notice the sudden change in her demeanor. She confined herself to her room more and more and showed herself to her parents less and less.

Tara became quite attached to Birdie. Birdie too lost its fear of hu-mans and interacted with its savior in its own way, by pecking at her fingers or rubbing its head against her palm. Tara replaced books with Birdie and talked to it like she would to a close friend. Her new pet would respond with an enthusiastic tweet, and that was enough to make her heart swell with happiness.

Birdie's wound healed quickly, although it still couldn't fly very well. Every evening after returning from school, Tara fed the bird, perched it on her finger, and carried it to her favourite spot in order to have a heart to heart.

"I wish I could take you to school, Birdie. You would be my best friend. You know, my friends at school are upset with me because I don't go on play dates with them. I want to play and joke around with my friends, but what can I do? Mom and Dad never let me step out of the house. I feel so lonely. I think you're the only one who listens to me, Birdie. Don't ever leave me," Tara said and kissed it on the beak. A single tear trickled down her cheek.

"Chirp," Birdie replied in a futile attempt to cheer its friend up.

Days went by and Tara looked forward to coming home, thanks to the newest, not to mention secret, addition to the family. All she wanted was to spend time with her friend, talk to it, love it, and keep it forever.

Leslee Silverman
If It Weren't For You Kids

I ran away from home for the first time when I was six. No one told me that I was from a dysfunctional family, or I would have left sooner.

"If it weren't for you kids, I would have left him a long time ago." The bedroom door slams and my mother is wailing behind it. My father has retreated to his workshop in the basement, and I am on the floor above in the deserted kitchen.

I see that little girl. She is braiding the fringe of the plastic tablecloth while maniacally pumping her knees up and down. There is no adult there to yell "Stop that right now!" and she is left alone to kick all she likes and to decipher the "if it weren't for you kids" equation.

She goes to the fridge and looks at the pictures held in place by her dad's industrial-strength CNR magnets. Her mom looks so happy in all the pictures with just her father and big sister, before the little girl was born. "It must be me," she reasons. "Mom is saying 'if it weren't for you kids' because it was good when there was a kid but not so good when there were kid-z."

She hears the evening train whistle. The familiar sound subliminally suggests a plan: she will leave and then her mom won't have to, because she will only have one kid again, not "kid-z."

That settled, she opens the fridge and takes a little red box of raisins with the sun maiden on the front and goes to get her stuff from the bedroom. Her sister and her sister's friend Alexis are lying on her sister's bed. They ignore her, as usual, as she collects her pyjamas, *The Blue Book of Fairy Tales*, and Peter Penguin, her stuffed animal for sleeping.

"What is she doing?" her big sister says disdainfully when she sees her filling the little suitcase for dolls that lives under the bed.

Alexis shrugs, not interested. She has two dumb sisters of her own at her house.

"Get out of here," says her big sister.

"I am. I am getting out of here," she tells her, neither of them appreciating then that each will repeat those very words many times over in their lives to come.

Her winter boots are easy-peasy to get from the floor in the hall closet, but she has to tug and yank to get her winter jacket off the hanger. Happily, her mitts are waiting for her in the pockets. She empties the raisins from the little red box into her mitts like her sister taught her, so that she can pour them straight into her mouth without freezing her fingers off. And she leaves, out the back door into a Winnipeg winter's night.

No one stops her. No one calls out. It will become apparent as the years progress that no one, particularly the "significant" others, will ever try to stop her when she leaves.

What a clever little thing! She goes to the side door of the stucco garage with the blue paint that matches the wood trim on the house. And luckily the beach pail and the shovel are next to the barbecue briquette bag in the summer-stuff pile on the floor. Then she takes ten steps to the back gate, lifts the metal latch with two hands, checks for big dogs in the lane, and—*shh!*—is as quiet as a mouse when she shuts the gate.

The light from their kitchen window pours moon-coloured onto the snow. She looks up to see if anyone is watching. Years later, the girl will often dream about the faces in the kitchen windows she passes hundreds of times during her childhood: Mrs. Atkinson, Mrs. Lenowski, Kayla, the nice crabapple tree lady, and the priest's wife. All the mothers, all the same in the kitchen windows, singing Frank Sinatra songs as they wash the dishes and gaze out unguardedly, looking so different than their front-yard faces. But the little girl sees no mothers in the windows tonight.

Crunch, crunch—the sound of your boots on the hard-packed snow in the back lane imprints on the visceral memory. It is as eerie as the inside of a candlelit church.

Crunch, crunch—a sound like a prayer that asks God to notice: "I exist, I exist."

The little girl is not frightened. She is headed to the ditch next to the railway crossing, her secret place. She goes there in the spring to catch tadpoles and collect pussy willows for her mom's old pink vase that lives on the piano.

Her nose is running and her cheeks are beginning to tingle from the clingy frost that makes her scarf wet when she breathes out. The railway crossing is clear because a man with a big shovel comes to keep it clean. She knows this and the other kids don't because her father works on the trains. He has a blue-striped cap which she got to wear to kindergarten last year on Parents Day.

She looks both ways for trains like she is supposed to do before she stands right in the middle. Nope. No train coming yet. "But when it does," she thinks, "I will flag it down like a school patrol." She drops her suitcase and pail to practise the arm-waving to stop the train, but, oops, she has to eat the raisins first before they all run out of her mitt.

The little girl sits on her suitcase and pours the raisins into her mouth. They are frozen as hard as rocks and need way more chews than the unfrozen kind, so she has time to think of what to tell the caboose man when the train stops. "I will tell him I only need to go to Toronto, where my Aunty Ada lives. Uncle Morris is a little scary, though. He has joined-up eyebrows. He probably just goes to work and listens to hockey, like all the dads." She gets up to look as far down the track as she can, but still no train. Then she takes off her mitten and puts the few remaining raisins on the tracks to see how flat they will be after the train squashes them.

That night the little girl learns that anything is possible by the railway tracks. Whether it is as small as a pebble or a Hemingway-sized problem, she will always bring her grief and fatigue from the living world and the racket from the skeletons in the closet to the sanctuary of this place, and other railways in other places. In the future, she will smoke cigarettes and drink bourbon out of the bottle by train tracks, hear the saddest stories in the world and be dumbstruck by fresh love near a railway crossing at night. But not this night.

This night, she is only six years old, and the night begins to crack open. She knows she should dig a snow fort, but her fingers are burning, even when she sits on them. What if she gets there and her Auntie wants a boy, not a girl? What if her toes freeze and fall right off into her boots?

She knows, even at six, all she has to do is get up and go home. But she can't.

She abandons herself to the pain and the aloneness. That way, it can't eat her up. That way, it is she who has chosen to leave, not they who have abandoned her.

Eventually, the little girl's father comes.

It might have been an hour or it might have been three. She hears him calling her name. She hesitates but in the end answers. She does it for him, because she doesn't want him to fail her mother again by not finding her, like all the other things her mother says he hasn't done or should have.

"I'm here, Daddy, waiting for the train. Right here!" And she raises her patrol-crossing arms high in the air so he can find her.

He picks the little girl up and holds her close. He says nothing—he isn't the talking kind of father—just lifts her up. But he makes sounds, like aches from the inside coming out.

He carries the little girl home, just him and her, and there is the crunch of his big boots on the snow and the smoke of his breath in the air, trailing behind his head. She hears the gate opening. She sees the light from the kitchen window on the snow in her backyard.

That is the end of the story of the little girl in a prairie town one winter's night. Another night in the future, she and her mother will be in a hospital room as her father is dying. She will remember him lying there, breathing away chunks of himself as the heart machine beeps and beeps like a warning signal at a train crossing.

"Please. Please," he will say to her, his eyes suddenly open and impossibly wide. *Please, please* will be his last words ever. He left it to the girl to complete the sentence. And she knows that he is asking for her to remember him as the one who lifted her up from the darkness and the cold, and carried her home.

Michelle Stack

Circle Time from Hell

AN EXCERPT

I wish I had fucking stolen a chocolate bar and ended up in juvie instead
of this hellhole. Every morning starts with circle time. You know, like
we had in kindergarten? We sit in a circle, and the therapists sit in chairs
looking down at us.

Head Honcho Dr. Fuckwad starts. "What choices do you want to
make today?" The suck-ups twitch away and yell out, "I will make a
choice to be grateful for all I have." Or "I'll make a choice to accept who
I am." My ass. They just want points so they can graduate and get out
of this hellhole. This sorry state of affairs goes on for ninety pathetic
minutes from Monday to Friday. I get through it by daydreaming about
all the ways I could die a quick and definitive death.

Next, the adult patients go to occupational therapy. The new adults
bring an old sock and stick lavender-scented flax seed in it because some
genius decided this would make them feel relaxed and accomplished—
maybe it's like being a baby. I don't want to know. Once they've finished
their sock pillow, the newbies are ready to join the line for the microwave.
We've got the twirlers, who fling their sock around while waiting for the
microwave (a.k.a. manic); the clutchers, who hold their pillow like it's Jesus himself (a.k.a. generalized anxiety); and the zombies (a.k.a. clinically
depressed). Sometimes the twirlers become zombies. Fifty seconds in
the antique microwave and if you're delusional you think that sock pillow
is a sign someone gives a shit about you.

Youth can't be trusted with flax seed or, God forbid, making tiles
with our initials. We get Life Skills instead, and this means every day

eight of us—Porno Tom the time bomb; withdrawn, tall, Aboriginal John, thrown around from foster home to foster home; Charlotte, the 15-year-old mother forced to give up her baby; Serena, the anorexic told by Ratched she'd be sent for electric shock if she didn't start talking; Lori, who lost her mother and adoptive mother but had a super-rich dad; and tiny, loud, twitchy, acne-ridden Fred—file into the next part of our prison day. I go for the stained, vomit-coloured chair—at least it has metal arms on it. There are windows, but if you close your eyes, or, shit, even keep them open, you can smell the ghostly farts of the TB patients who died here before it was the University of Alberta Psychiatric Day Hospital for village fuck-ups.

⌒

MY LIFESAVER AND WHY MOST THERAPISTS ARE SCREWED UP

My big sister Francine is my number one lifesaver. Before I started at this hellhole, she heard about an all-marching band that included a trip to Pasadena to march in the Rose Bowl Parade. At the day hospital they said I would be given a pass to go for one week. I play the baritone horn and we have practice three times a week. The horn teacher is nice but gets frustrated because I go left when he says right and right when he says left. I don't mean to, but anyway it makes people bash into each other, and we're all supposed to do things at the same time. He said I could just hold the horn up to my mouth and focus on right, left, right, left. I'm definitely the worst in the band. I'd quit, but I really need to get the fuck out of day hospital for a week. Nobody knows I'm in day hospital and they treat me like I'm normal, except that I don't have a sense of beat or rhythm or right and left.

On break I practise my left-right marching in the huge hospital bathroom. They promised me I'd still be able to go running, but now they won't let me go, even at lunch. I'm worried I'm going to get fat and won't be able to run fast. I want to run marathons. Josephine suggested taking laxatives because I can't make myself throw up. She says it'll keep me from getting fat.

To bug the therapists, sometimes I play my horn during the break between groups. I know I'm not good, but if they grimace I say, "I'm trying to develop a hobby. Isn't that important?"

Therapist Earl starts Life Skills with the same question every day: "What's the feeling behind what you are thinking?" What's hard about understanding the feeling behind "I hate this place and I wish my asshole father hadn't taken me to the hospital after I overdosed"? You told me I'm learning disabled, so help me communicate better that I hate this place.

Therapist Bates, I swear, thinks he's a sexpot, with a moustache he strokes in place of playing with his 100% Alberta weenie. He asks template question two: "What are you really trying to say?" Okay, let me spell it out for you: I HATE THIS PLACE. Did you flunk out of Psychology at university and get a Counselling 101 course-participation certificate? My dad was a psychiatric nurse on a kids' ward, but he got called a therapist. I think he only had a year of training, but thankfully for the children of the world, his focus is now messing with adults.

Template question three goes to Nurse Ratched, a.k.a. Denise, who I swear is a serial killer, and paranoia is not in my suite of diagnoses. Ratched gives us teenagers a reason to succeed next time we attempt suicide. She asks, "Why did you make that choice?" Why not have a cardboard box with a bunch of random questions to ask, so we don't all end up dying from boredom? But since that's not going to happen, I pass the time by figuring out the therapists' triggers.

Nurse Ratched and Little Cathy turn red if you ask them how much training they have. "How did you do in your courses on helping kids? Did you take any classes on how to help us?" Therapist Bates's veins pop out when I ask him if he's here because people wouldn't pay for his services. My favourite is to sweetly ask if they became therapists to find themselves and when they think that'll happen.

Therapist Abby sometimes talks to me one on one and laughs at my questions and tells me I have guts. Tall Cathy saw me at the art gallery. I begged her not to report this to the big group. My visits to the art gallery are my secret, and I don't want it to be something else they can screw with. She didn't tell on me. I like her, but I don't say much to Abby and Tall Cathy because everything you say to anyone is supposed to be reported in the big group, and that has like forty people in it.

If you give Nurse Ratched an honest answer, you get the template response: "You know you're here by choice. You can leave anytime." Charlotte said, "Okay, I will." She started to walk out and I followed, but it was too easy.

"You're making a choice. We're required to have you committed for your own protection."

Committed means you can't even take a piss on your own. Serena left and got committed because she has anorexia and she wouldn't eat at lunch. I mean, I wonder why. The food is disgusting. I found a used Band-Aid and hair in my shepherd's pie today. Oh, and if you don't look, Wally spits in everyone's food. He has anger issues. No shit.

Another thing: what is it with therapists who sound like they sucked in too much helium before asking you "How is Michelle today?" I'm slouching in front of you and I told you my psycho orthodontist tightened my braces so it hurts to talk and eat. Also, I'm not a fucking genius, but how about "How are you today?" Do they think I'm so bonkers that I don't know my name?

Life Skills—cuz we're all village screw-ups—teaches us things we've done since kindergarten. They think because we tell them to get stuffed, we do this to everyone. But no, I give up my seat for old people on the bus, I like to chat with people. I just don't like talking to Therapist Earl or Nurse Ratched.

Neda Tanha

Mother's Day

AN EXCERPT

Photos, old and new, with different settings and scenery, were jam-packed on top of the mahogany china cabinet in the living room. The same four women appeared in all the pictures, two aging and two blossoming into young women. My father bought his first camera years before I was born. Since then, Mother's Day photos had been a tradition at our house.

In one of them, my mother and grandmother were sitting in short dresses on wooden chairs. Sama, ten years old, her hair in braids, stood behind them with her hands resting on their shoulders. I was a little girl in a pink dress on my mother's knees, looking at my grandmother, who pointed to the camera with her index finger.

On the Mother's Day when I was ten, I deliberately braided my hair to the side, posing behind my mother and my *modar joon* exactly as my sister had. But before my father could count to three I said, "This is the first year we're taking the picture without Sama."

Mother lowered her head. Tears dripped on her cheeks, as though she had been holding them back until someone else confirmed what was already on her mind. I bit my lip, and Father gave me a pointed look. Modar Joon put her hand on my mother's shoulders and said, "Be patient, my dear, be patient."

My father stepped out of the living room and returned a minute later with a picture of Sama in his hand. He handed the picture to my mother. "Hold it in your hand, then she will be in the photo too."

My mother's tears mixed with laughter. She wiped her eyes with her fingers and held the picture close to her heart.

The last time we took the picture with all four of us, Mother cried then too, and Father hid his tears. Sama had been nineteen; she left three weeks later.

Home was quiet without her. I used to crawl into her bed in the middle of the night. She used to braid my hair, read stories for me, and pick me up from school. But her trip disturbed everything. For years I blamed Modar Joon because she planted the idea in Sama's head.

It was a rainy day in the fall. Sama had been reading a book on her bed while I was doing homework on the floor of her room. Modar Joon peeked her head into the room. "What are you guys doing?" She walked in.

Sama shrugged her shoulders. "What can I do? I'm reading the same book for the fourth time."

Modar Joon heaved a big sigh and sat on her bed. "Maybe it's time that you leave."

Sama closed her book, sat up straight, and crossed her legs. "Really, do you think so?"

Modar Joon nodded, kissed Sama's cheek, and said, "Think about it."

She kissed me too and left the room. Sama leaned back, fixed her gaze on the ceiling.

Two nights later when I walked to the kitchen, my parents' and Sama's conversation stopped, but my mother's concerned eyes stayed on Sama. More whispers followed in the days after, and Father had a few strange phone calls. Mother became quiet and restless, but Sama became more elated.

One afternoon, my father came home with a strange man. He had a black beard, a great contrast to the clean-shaven face of my father. They went straight to the living room. Mother and Sama joined them shortly. Mother pointed to me to go upstairs, but I didn't. I sat on the sofa and watched cartoons on mute. Twenty minutes later, the stranger left. My father walked him out to the front gate. When Father came back through the doorway, he had a thoughtful look on his face.

"Who was he?" I asked.

"Nobody."

Sama sat down by my side on the sofa. Her face had lost its colour. Father sank into a chair and lowered his head into the newspaper. Mother, quiet, kept herself busy cooking in the kitchen. Modar Joon showed up for dinner. Eventually, she opened the subject. "How much was he asking?"

Father smirked. "A lot. It's a growing business for them." He rubbed his hand on his chin. "But it seems he is the more trusted one. A few people recommended him."

After dinner when Sama left the room, Mother turned to Modar Joon. "I'm not sure we're doing the right thing."

"Don't be selfish. How long are you planning to keep her by your side? Don't you see that her life is wasted here? There is no future for her."

Mother cried. Father patted her shoulder. "She is a brave girl. Don't worry." But his words came out shakily, as though he didn't believe it himself.

Sama was leaving. The realization felt like a slap. I ran upstairs and opened her bedroom door without knocking. She jumped, turned to me. "Hoda, you scared me." She wiped her tears quickly.

"Why are you leaving?" I asked.

Sama patted the space next to her on the bed. I walked in and sat beside her. "There's nothing here for me, no education, no work. I don't have any future here." She put her arm around my shoulders and leaned her head to mine.

It was hard to comprehend not having a future. But I knew one thing for certain: I shouldn't breathe a word about it. Everybody reminded me, over and over.

The next day, I saw my mother hugging Sama in the kitchen, telling her, "I don't know how I'm going to live without you."

My chin trembled, and I left the room. She loved Sama more than me. Sama was getting all the attention from everyone and I had become the forgotten one. That night I went to her room to sleep next her, only to find that my mother was already in my spot. I went back to my room and cried.

On Sama's last night, I promised myself to stay awake until she left. Even when she kissed me and held me tightly in her arms, I didn't kiss her back. I wanted to be the last person to hug and kiss her goodbye.

I opened my eyes. I was in my bed, and daylight brightened my room. I ran downstairs to the kitchen. Mother and Modar Joon both sat at the kitchen table in silence, holding each other's hands on the table as though they were praying. Modar Joon turned to me, her eyes red and puffy. I ran upstairs to Sama's room. Her bedsheets were untouched since the day before, and the two backpacks she had packed were gone.

My heart felt heavy. I ran to the window. Rain was lightly falling, forming bubbles on the small pool in the courtyard. On the verge of tears, I dragged myself downstairs. Mother slowly lifted her head, looked into my eyes. Her voice was so quiet I could hardly hear her. "Get ready for school. You don't want to be late."

I put on my grey school uniform, pants and a long-sleeved tunic. By the time I went back downstairs, Modar Joon was asleep on the sofa. Mother forgot to make breakfast for me; she just handed me my rain jacket. "Don't forget," she whispered, "don't say anything about Sama to anyone."

I nodded and took the jacket from her. She watched me put it on. Before I left, I wrapped my arms around her waist. She gently stroked my hair.

At recess, I sat beside my friend Maryam on the stairs of the schoolyard. She shared some of her chocolate biscuits, asking, "How come you don't have a snack today?"

"I forgot."

Maryam offered more. Her kindness made my secret lie more heavily on my chest. I couldn't keep it to myself any longer. "If I tell you a secret, do you promise not to say anything to anyone?"

Her eyes widened. "I promise!" She nodded.

"Do you swear?"

"Yes, I swear on my mother's life."

I nodded. She brought her head closer to mine. I cupped my hands around my mouth, bringing it close to her ear. "Sama left," I whispered. "She went out of the country!"

"Why?"

"Because she doesn't have a future here."

That was all I knew. I hoped she wouldn't ask me what it meant. She looked puzzled, but then she nodded. She took a bite of her biscuit and straightened her posture. I wished I could ask her the meaning of it.

Tanya Boteju

Naya in Costume

AN EXCERPT

"Take this ... and these."

A baseball cap and sunglasses landed in my hands.

"And go change into this shirt and pants."

Deidre produced these items from another cabinet in the sideboard. A ribbed tank top and striped Adidas athletics pants. Apparently, I was the Sporty Spice of drag kings.

"We'll start you off easy—you probably wear this outfit on the weekends, don't you, girl?" Deidre said, playfully tugging my ponytail.

I let out a weak laugh. "Ha ... yeah, how'd you know?" No part of me was completely on board with this yet. Least of all my legs, which seemed to be re-forming into Jell-O.

"Just woman's intuition," she said, drifting toward a wicker basket that had been tucked away under the round table in the corner. From this basket, she pulled a selection of makeup cases and cylinders.

"What's that for?" I asked, knowing the answer. Dreading the answer. But intrigued just the same.

"This is for after you get changed." I looked at the pants and tank top in my hands. "Get going." She gave my arm a loose pinch.

While Deidre fussed over multiple CDs, I undressed and then pulled on each item of clothing in slow motion, trying to moderate my racing heartbeat. The pants sagged comfortably around my bum and crotch, but the tank top hugged me tighter than I was used to. I pulled my ponytail through the opening in the hat and secured the ball cap on my head. For now, I hung the sunglasses from the neck of my shirt.

When Deidre turned to look at me, her face did that thing faces do when they think you're adorable, like a puppy. "Oh-my-cute-as-a-god-damn-button. Get over here," she said, waving me over.

She adjusted my hat a little to the side and tried to push the tank top up a bit to reveal my midriff, which I promptly put a stop to. "Don't push it, Scary Spice," I said.

That set off one of her spectacular cackles, and I felt a tiny bit better.

"Now it's makeup time. Come with me," she said.

⟫

She led me up the staircase to a two-stall bathroom on the main floor. From what I could tell, this floor housed a large gathering space with rows of foldable chairs and a raised stage. A small kitchen with a cut-out counter opened into the bigger space. It was exactly the kind of setting in which I could imagine a church potluck or post-baptism celebration taking place—had it not been for the bright purple walls and billowing rainbow flag strung across the back of the stage.

In the bathroom, Deidre placed the makeup containers on the sink ledge and positioned me in front of the mirror. She stood behind me and we both looked into our reflections.

"What kind of facial hair do you want, sugar?"

Well, there was a question I'd never been asked before. "Um. I have no idea?" I said, staring at her through the mirror.

"Long sideburns? Short? Moustache? No moustache? Beard? The sideburns really help sell the boy part."

I'd only seen Luce's work briefly last night before madly scrubbing the makeup off after the show. I hadn't really felt like looking at myself at the time. I shrugged my shoulders in mild defeat.

Deidre crouched a significant distance to wrap her arms around my waist and lay her chin on my shoulder. I didn't think I'd ever get tired of having her arms pull me in. "Sweetheart, you are a gorgeous girl and I'm about to make you into a gorgeous boy. Tell me what you want and I'll make it happen, I promise."

I gazed at her face, then at my own. Chewing on my lower lip for a few moments, I pictured the drag kings I'd seen so far and decided that the subtle look might be more my style. "Maybe slim sideburns and a thin beard and moustache? Or something like that ..."

Deidre's cheek pressed into mine as her mouth spread into a giant grin. "Done and done."

"Now, usually," she said, as she turned me to face her, "we'd use hair clippings and spirit gum, but I'll go easy on you today." She carefully pulled off my ball cap and replaced it on my head backwards, then looked at me. "Ready?"

"As ready as I'll ever be."

She began by lightly dipping a soft sponge into a circular container of dark, creamy makeup, then brushing the sponge gently along the contours of my face—above my eyebrows, down either side of my nose, across my cheekbones, and along my jawline. After, she used her finger to blend the makeup into my skin.

"This is just to emphasize your features—make them a little sharper, a little more masculine." She leaned back repeatedly as she worked, checking her craft.

Once she seemed happy with this initial phase, she used a thick brush to apply a powdery substance over the work she'd just completed.

"What's that for?"

"This, my beginner boy, is concealer. It'll keep your new face from falling off." She crossed her eyes at me as she said this, making me smile.

"How do you know what to do for drag kings? Is it the same as what you do for your own face?" I asked.

"Mmm ... not the same, but there are similarities. The only reason I know what to do with girl faces is I wanted to make sure my side business catered to all types."

"Who taught you?"

She made a smacking sound with her lips. "Girl, Dee Dee taught her damn self. Now hush for this next bit."

Deidre picked up a compact with dark eyeshadow and a makeup brush that looked like a little fan. Beginning by overlapping the bottom of my natural sideburns, she applied the makeup down along my jaw, to my chin, and then back up along the other side of my face. She added a simple sketch across the top of my lip as well.

Her strokes were firm and swift, and every so often they sent pleasant shivers across my neck.

Next, she used an eyeliner pencil to make quick, light touches over-top of my new beard and sideburns, to mimic hair, I supposed.

She continued working, topping up my eyebrows with the pencil, then smudging and lengthening until she was satisfied that my facial hair looked natural enough.

Finally content, she placed the makeup back onto the sink edge and pressed my chin between her thumb and pointer finger, gently turning my head from side to side to survey her work. "Mm, mm, mm. You are handsome, girl."

I shook my head at her. "Do I get to see now?"

She guided my hips around so I faced the mirror. The first thing that lured my eyes was the manicured beard and moustache she'd given me, like a trim, tight frame around my mouth. She'd somehow made it look like real hair, like I could touch it and feel actual bristles. When I automatically raised my arm to do just that, Deidre patted my hand away. "Don't touch. You'll smudge it. What d'you think, lovey?"

She'd been right. The moustache and beard made a significant difference, but the sideburns added a masculinity I would never have imagined possible on my own face. They somehow created an edge to my cheeks and the edge made me feel kind of ... sexy.

"I love it."

Over my shoulder, Deidre smiled. She swung me back around to face her. "Come on. This is just the first stage."

"Okay, just give me a minute and I'll be right there."

She floated out of the bathroom and I turned back to the mirror. Peering closer at Deidre's handiwork, I marvelled at the difference, but somehow I was equally transfixed by what felt recognizable, if that made any sense. My face, like this, felt ... familiar.

Fiction

Neha Puntambekar

Smoke Rings

AN EXCERPT

What a colossal shitfest life was turning into. Jiya drew the joint, a re-furbished, hollowed-out Marlboro Gold she wielded like a pen, to her lips; a slow, long drag and the thick, hazy sweetness hit the roof of her mouth. An equally long exhale, and out went some of the grime coating the inside of her head.

A mellow wave swept across her body, from her lips, to the back of her eyes, along her shoulders, down to her toes. Jiya had never been much of a smoker, and yet, here she was, smoking up the last of her stash. It had been a rough week. Between her insomnia and having to recount details of that afternoon over and over again—to her friends, her father, the lawyer, the cops—she just needed a minute of quiet. Of no thinking. Of not remembering. She took another drag.

Since that day, her first thought every morning was: leave. Pack up, forget about Mumbai, go home. She could start over, write an unsoiled story. And in that better life, if she came across his writing, his name— as she was bound to—she'd simply look the other way. Turn the page. Close the browser. It could be done. But then a tendril of anger would snake past the numbness that wrapped around her frame like a strait-jacket. Heart racing, fists clenched, she'd whisper, "You don't quit. You are stronger than this bullshit. You don't quit. You kick ass."

It was a daily battle. Leave, start over. Stay, fight. Her mind oscillated between the two relentlessly. One then the other, until she found herself reaching for the little baggie hidden between Tolstoy and Tagore on the sprawling bookshelf. These last few weeks, she had gone from partaking occasionally to lighting up twice, even three times a day. Inhale and exhale, until the red, burning tip ate into the edges of the cigarette, leaving only a heap of ash behind.

Confiding in Anita and Kunal, her closest friends in the city, had been excruciating, a salt rub over open wounds. But telling her father that first time, that had been much worse. A root canal without anaesthesia. Where Anita had supplied a soft but unrelenting stream of support, Kunal, Anita's boyfriend, offered up guttural curses, words she didn't understand and yet whose meaning she felt in her bones. But her father, Ravi Ray, had gone deathly quiet. In those few tense minutes Jiya had felt every inch of distance between Mumbai and Long Island.

⌒

"Dad?

"Dad? Say something. Please," Jiya's voice was fragile, full of cracks waiting to shatter. She checked her phone to make sure she hadn't lost connection. "Dad," she tried again. Dread, thick and putrid, pooled at the base of her throat.

When he did finally speak, his voice was arranged carefully, neutral. Not a wrinkle out of place. "You should have told me. Why didn't you? Why did you wait so long?"

"Dad ... I ..."

"You should come home," he said when she faltered. "It'll all be fine. Give me a minute to find you the first flight out of there. Once you're back here and safe, we'll figure out the rest."

"Dad ... I can't," she said softly. "Not yet. I can't let the bastard get away with it."

"Why did I know you'd say something like that?" Ravi sighed. "Fine. I don't understand, but alright—but Jiya, if you won't come home, then I'm coming to you."

"Dad! Look, I know this isn't easy, but please give me a little time, okay? Everything is so complicated at the moment, and it'll only get worse going forward. I need a few days. For myself. For my sanity."

He didn't reply immediately and, when he spoke, his voice shook with grief, or maybe anger. "Ten days. That's the best I can do. Then I'm coming." Just before the call ended he added, "I should have never let you go, J Bear. Should have never let you leave home."

That had been three days ago. In another week, he'd be here.

Jiya stood up and stretched, to shake off the memory as much as anything else. She was still in her pyjamas. The yellow ones with tiny green apples scattered across them. Her oldest pair, but also her most comfortable. It had become increasingly difficult to find a reason to change out of them. Her hair was wild, a nest of anxiety. The house was quiet, eerily so. She savoured it.

Her meal still sat on the table; guilt clawed at her chest. Anita had taken to preparing lunch before she left for work. Today it was a Thai green curry and jasmine rice.

"You better eat," she'd said before leaving that morning. "And don't make me nag you throughout the day about it, please!"

"I wish you'd stop with all the cooking," Jiya mumbled.

"You need to eat." Anita shrugged her bony shoulders and added, "I need to eat too. If I leave it to you, we'll be at the mercy of your sugary cereals. So really, I'm just being selfish here."

Jiya caught a fleeting glimpse of Anita's bright, mischievous smile just before the door shut.

So she had tried. She'd pulled out a plate from the cabinet and a fork, like an adult. She sat at the table and willed the munchies to come to her aid. But it only took a few spoonfuls to make her stomach lurch. Jiya sighed. She turned away. She still had a few hours to cook up a suitable excuse before her roommate returned and began her nutritional interrogation.

⌒

Jiya sank into the soft cushions of the living room window alcove; she cracked the windows open, allowing the late April heat to come rushing in. Downstairs in the driveway a few kids from the building, oblivious to the rising mercury, were in the midst of a cricket game. The boys, some still in uniform, their orphaned backpacks slumped against the old banyan tree at the corner of the yard, raced around, shouting frantic instructions to their teammates, chasing after the ball. Occasionally, they stopped to wipe sweat out of their eyes.

She followed the game, or as much of it as she could follow anyway. As the batsman hit a lofted shot over the bowler's head, Jiya took one last drag and tried to blow a smoke ring out the window. She rounded her lips like Kunal had taught her, then she blew. A weak, wavering blob floated out. In the background, the boys laughed. Jiya did too, but the sound she made was empty and bitter.

Adriana Louis

Gilded

AN EXCERPT

The bright red Post Bus charged down the Kampala-Gulu Highway. Zoe sat stiff as the driver overtook yet another car on the single-lane carriageway. The worn red fabric that covered the armrest of her chair was stained with something brown, but she held onto it tightly, palms sweating. She was almost glad for the potholes and the frequent mail drop-offs, which forced the driver to slow down.

She couldn't imagine what the other buses were like if this was described as the safest option. The Post Bus was exactly what it sounded like: it dropped and collected mail as well as human passengers. It ran at set times—instead of waiting for the bus to fill up—and was therefore a relatively reliable mode of transportation, albeit slower than most due to its many mail stops.

An hour into the journey, Zoe relaxed a little and dared turn her attention to the landscape flitting past while she bumped in her seat. The land was dry and the villages dusty, eagerly awaiting the rains that were soon to come. Village after village rushed by. Many roadside shopfronts were painted in telecom company colours: MTN yellow or Airtel red. Small markets buzzed with activity under the bright sun; men pushed bikes along, carrying heavy bundles of sugarcane. Brief as flashes of countryside passing by, Max's face appeared and disappeared again. She blinked a few times and pushed the thought of him away.

At each stop, Zoe witnessed mayhem descend upon them: local vendors surrounded the stationary vehicle and pushed sticks of sizzling *choma* and cold bottles of water and soda up to the windows to make a quick sale. Well aware the bus rested for no more than a couple of minutes, the merchants shouted as hard as they could, shoving their wares as close to the few willing customers as possible. She avoided those trying to catch her gaze. At nine in the morning, several fellow passengers opened their windows and exchanged 1,000 Ugandan shillings for a couple of sticks of meat straight off the grill. Some of the vendors ran with the bus as it picked up speed to make one last transaction before going back to their posts to wait for the next bus. Seeing the woman across the aisle rip the blackened meat from the stick, Zoe's stomach churned. She turned her attention back to the road.

Zoe soon got drowsy from the hum of the air conditioning and grumbling engine. She closed her eyes, her head bobbing softly against her headrest. As they entered the dense banana tree-covered grounds of Luweero, the early morning peace was disrupted by a preacher who hopped on, Bible in hand. His suit was several sizes too big, his white collar stained yellow. He spoke in a local language—Luganda, Zoe guessed—but he threw in some English terms for good measure. Devil. Soul. Saviour. This guy was not kidding around. Zoe plugged in her headphones, desperate to drown out his undoubtedly passionate counsel against the devil's tricks and the incessant call for penance.

Several small monkeys greeted them as they crossed the Victoria Nile by Karuma Falls. The bridge, set against this beautiful backdrop, had once signified something much less appealing, her guidebook told her: the gateway to Lord's Resistance Army-dominated territory. Northbound crossings had inspired fear, whereas southbound travellers were considerably relieved. Zoe's present-day crossing caused her insides to perform a double somersault.

"I'm so glad you made it," Agnes greeted Zoe when she stepped out of the cool bus and into the already sweltering streets of Gulu. "Let's go grab a cool drink. Aaysha is waiting. It's been crazy hot the past few days." Her purple kaftan swooshed as she turned to cross the road.

After a quick catch up, the three colleagues agreed to meet up at San-kofa Café after Zoe dropped her things off at Agnes's house.

Agnes unlocked the gate to her compound. Down a stretch of grass, covered in brown spots, a concrete structure had been erected. The only embellishments were the wooden window frames and doors.

"So it's not much, but everything I need is here," Agnes said, pushing open the door that revealed her concrete bedroom. The bunk bed, little desk and four shelves crowded the small space. Agnes had tried to liven up the sombre grey with a small rug and colourful sarongs that were repurposed as curtains and wall decorations. A lone bulb hung from a wire.

"I like the colours," Zoe offered.

"Through here is the shower and the bathroom." Agnes led the way to the outside facilities. The tiny structure was cool, grey concrete, like the main building, with square holes where windows should have been.

Zoe paused and peeked inside the tiny rooms; one housed the shower, the other the bathroom. A questionably clean squat toilet. *Fuck*, she thought.

"So, that's everything. Hope it's okay for you?" Agnes said. She had moved to the kitchen.

"Yes, of course," Zoe said. "Thank you so much for your hospitality."

"Don't be silly, I'm glad to have you here." Agnes squeezed Zoe's arm.

Left alone in the bedroom for a minute while Agnes was getting them water, Zoe took a deep breath. *This will be fine.*

"It's warm. I hope you don't mind?" Agnes handed her a bottle and settled down on the lower bunk. "The power is out so often that there is no point in having a fridge."

"Sounds like it's much worse than Kampala."

"Oh definitely. It's not even comparable. Whenever I get a chance to go to Kampala, it's such a treat."

Zoe smiled a little. She had thought that with the power outages and cold showers in Kampala she'd been roughing it. Child's play apparently.

A change of clothes and a quick splash of water on her face refreshed Zoe from the morning bus journey. She looked at herself in the mirror that hung above the washbasin, tightly enclosed in slabs of grey; a crack ran across her face. The glass was foggy and stained, comfortably obfuscating the reality of her reflection.

With nothing to do in Agnes's room, they decided to take a walk around town before meeting Aaysha.

After strolling around for a good hour, Zoe realised how ordinary the town was. What else did she expect? A war-stricken ghost town marked by bullet holes? Instead, it felt like any other ordinary Ugandan town: dusty, potholed, cracked sidewalks overtaken by food stands and wares from the little shops by the main roads, a beehive of cars, motorcycle taxis, and people. And yet, it had only been some years ago that this was considered a high-risk region. Not many outsiders dared venture here. Gulu and several other towns in the North had once seen a nightly influx of thousands of children. *Night commuters.* They had ventured into cities like Gulu every night from the rural areas to avoid the LRA's nightly abductions. Now, the white NGO Land Rovers which drove past were the most visible reminders of Gulu's past.

☙

A week later, Zoe and Aaysha sat sipping coffee at Sankofa Café. An unexpected afternoon shower created white noise on the corrugated sheet roof.

"Am I a terrible person for not being able to deal with this toilet situation?" Zoe looked at Aaysha for confirmation. "A frog, Aaysha. A bloody green, ribbiting frog. I thought I was cool about the whole thing, roughing it or whatever. But I draw the line at frogs in the toilet. What if it has friends?"

Aaysha's mouthful of coffee shot in all directions. She leaned forward to grab a napkin from the heavy wooden coffee table. Her short black bob momentarily hid her face from view. Her parents hated the short hair, Aaysha had told Zoe, but she loved the cool wind on her neck.

"I'm glad you find this so amusing, but I'd like to see you holding your balance while you try not to pee all over yourself and squat over a toilet while a dirty frog is ogling you, ready to pounce," Zoe continued.

"Was it a particularly aggressive frog then?" Aaysha laughed. Her bangles clinked as she dabbed her face and the worn purple cushions of the wooden sofa. The generator hummed in the background. "I have a room available in my apartment if you really can't stand it anymore."

"Regular toilet?" Zoe asked.

"And no frogs," Aaysha promised.

Lorna Carley

Love Again

AN EXCERPT

At the airport, Lexi feels her mother clutch her forearm. She tries to shake off her tight little claw, so inured she's become to this neediness, the continual requests for help that eat up all of her time and occupy so much space in her brain. But her mother has her in a death grip. The airport is hot and crowded and Lexi wishes she had brought a lighter coat. It's taking forever for her mother's luggage to appear, and she checks her phone to see if Donny has texted her from the road (he has not). Gawd, but could she use a drink.

Lexi never manages to pack the right stuff. All this access to information, there's a weather app right there on her stupid phone, and she still never bothered to check the Calgary forecast. Who expected thirty-fricken-degrees on Thanksgiving weekend? Certainly not the airport HVAC people, because, clearly, they've left the building. She starts texting Donny, telling him she's sorry, *just so sorry*, then stops. He's driving across the prairies and wouldn't see it anyway. Or he would, and that's distracted driving, which everyone knows is dangerous but carries on doing regardless. He's got the kids with him, too, saving on the cost of airfare times four, and, besides, it's his turn to apologize. She's always the one sucking up. Well, after this weekend, after mommy dearest marries slippery old van der Meer, those kiss-ass days will be history.

How old must van der Meer be now? Eighty if he's a day. One foot in the grave and the other on a banana peel, a quick fall into oblivion. Even his driver, Harold—standing sentry behind the luggage trolley, an iPad with her mother's name in all caps, IRINA KLASSEN, tucked under his arm—looks ancient. Rubber-soled shoes, pleated trousers, white tufts sprouting from his ears, progressive lenses, and that suit jacket. What is that, rayon? His friends probably call him Harry.

There are no words from her mother. No other warnings, just the hand on her arm, insistent, cloying, *motherly*. Without looking, Lexi asks, "What now?"

There's been a lifetime of these needy moments, strung together like beads on a gaudy dime-store necklace no one would be caught dead wearing. Meals out, mother-daughter weekends, family vacations with Grandma, all guilt-laden stand-ins for the life Irina should have had, the life she had every right to have, except she married the wrong guy. She married Lexi's father: professor emeritus, world expert in nanoparticle filtration systems, hardened departmental administrator, and inveterate chaser of skirts. Dead at sixty-seven of esophageal cancer.

When he was alive, Irina was forever calling about her father, late night mewlings that wiped out any chance of sleep. This, when Lexi had to work the next day, teaching and corralling no fewer than twenty-seven Grade 2ers for hours on end. The calls began: "Your father's out with one of his tootsie rolls again." And carried on downhill from there. Since his death, her mother's needs had become bigger, more insistent and, generally speaking, required Donny: Donny, replace my car's brake light. Donny, trim the caragana. Donny, fix my dishwasher. Donny, do back flips. What her mother really wanted was Lexi's life. All of it, gobbled down for herself.

Now, here's poor spineless Donny driving more than six hundred kilometres across the provinces with kids. The man who only yesterday declared he'd had all he could take. Like this was something new.

"How many kids have I got? Four, counting you. I'm the one who does all the work around here." All this because she had a few too many with dinner and couldn't just then find it in her person to deal with the ironing or whatever. More words were exchanged, barbed hooks embedded and tearing at the flesh of their marriage. Lexi barricaded herself in the bathroom with a double vodka tonic (a definite go-to) and a *People* magazine. She eventually came out for a refill, knowing he'd put the kids to bed and was now in the garage, performing an oil change on the Aerostar. He didn't mean what he'd said, no more than her mother meant it when she said her heart was acting wonky these days and she'd have to look into finding a good GP once she settled into life with Carleton.

Imagine settling into life with Carleton van der Meer. Even she'd do it. Pretty much anyone would, given all his dough. Her biggest misery would be hanging off his feeble arm and brushing dandruff off his shoulders at all the charity dinners in trade for his ginormous ranch with the unobstructed view of the Rockies, the condo in St. Bart's, the fancy-dancy cars and hired help, and all of his cash when he kicked the bucket in the not too distant future. Completely doable.

Lexi faces Irina. She's straining to say something. Taut ropes of muscle bulge like cordwood in her neck. There's no colour to her face. Her pink lips open and close without sound, without air, and it's then that Lexi understands. It's then that Irina's knees give out and she collapses on the concrete with a soft whump, leaving Lexi standing alone and stock-still. She hears the silence of everyone turning to stare, and there's the smell of sweat, of her own rising panic. And that's when Harold springs to life, yelling, "Someone call 911!"

He turns Irina onto her back and tears her silk scarf away from her neck. His thick fingers feel at her wrist, paw at her jugular, his ear held to her lipsticked mouth.

"Defibrillator?" he hollers over his shoulder.

And Lexi stands there, as if frozen in another time and place, her phone now ringing. It's Donny, and for a split second she thinks about answering, she thinks about letting him know that truly she is smack in the middle of a serious ordeal here, but it could be one of the kids. It could be one of the twins, Hayden or Noah, or worse, Amelia, her gentle, impressionable four-year-old. And how to explain that Mommy is unavailable right now, that Mommy is busy going through hell with their dear, sweet grandmother? Their grandmother who is so close to the van der Meer jackpot that Lexi can almost taste the caviar. Their grandmother who is now, once again, singularly fucking everything up.

Harold pushes on her mother's chest. One thump, two thumps, three. He seals her mouth with his, forcing oxygen into her lungs. He's thrown off his coat, exposing the worn seams of his dress shirt, the yellow circles of sweat beneath his armpits, the uneven fold of his collar. It's obvious he is alone and, for some reason, this thought lodges in Lexi's throat until it contracts as if she might cry. She sees Harold's sad little apartment, its dusty lampshades and tired cabinetry, the bathtub with a ring of filth at the three-quarter mark, and she wonders why sometimes life is so fucking hard. Why nothing ever comes easy. She drops her phone into her purse and kneels next to Harold and her mother, who is not dying, who can't be dying, not yet.

"Somebody help," she says, almost audibly.

Maureen Butler

The Dance

AN EXCERPT

*In this excerpt, Marion, the novel's protagonist, has
inflammatory bowel disease, a serious autoimmune disorder.
She decides to take a one-week cruise to Alaska on her own.*

Marion stood in the bathroom and assessed the facilities. The best public washrooms were single-stalled, little private rooms with thick doors. Starbucks and newer restaurants had three or four of these. Ideal for privacy and pain, they prevented smells and sounds from escaping. Costco bathrooms had ten stalls in a large room, but the powerful hand dryers fired up like a 737 engine, obliterating any unwanted noises. And that was good.

This bathroom, in the corner of the Spinnaker Lounge, had only three adjacent beige metal stalls. One paper towel dispenser near the sinks. Definitely not ideal. On Marion's public washroom rating scale, this rated only a four out of ten. She worried that the dancers and drinkers in the lounge would take up all the stalls and she'd have to run frantically to the nearest hallway bathroom. And where was that? She'd already gotten lost coming here. Her map of the ship, toilets marked with little green icons, was back in her stateroom. As beads of sweat formed on the nape of her neck, she took a deep breath. *Everything will be okay*, she said to herself as she marched out.

She motored toward one of the brown, leather-ish booths, delighted to see a teardrop-shaped crystal chandelier in the middle of the room. Most of the tables and booths in the lounge were already filled: older couples, small groups of women dressed in long shimmery skirts and sequined tops. A woman with blonde hair walked by wearing a stunning three-tiered chiffon skirt and, as she moved, the colours of her skirt changed from burgundy to electric blue and back. A slight young woman stood at the bar in a purple silk gown trimmed with gold. It was just like the dance world she used to know, where men and women were glamorous and graceful.

Marion sat at a high table, ordered a sparkling water with lemon, and watched. A waltz. A few senior women danced with geriatric partners. Two women danced together. And suddenly she teared up, overwhelmed by the music and the chandelier and the elegance—the twinkling dresses, smart suits, and happy couples, everything she had loved and lost. Dancing. It was like being royalty for a day.

She remembered the dance club in university, where she had learned. The travelling dances—foxtrot, waltz, quickstep, and Viennese waltz—were her favourites. It felt so good to know enough steps to move all the way across a ballroom floor. To follow, which really wasn't following at all but responding, being in sync with a partner while holding her frame. Dancing at its best was like being alone together, mirroring each other's movements. Funny how a structured group of steps and positions had made her feel so free.

That was before Peter. He knew she wanted to dance. Decades ago, she had asked him to take lessons with her, and he said he'd think about it. Then one day she came home to a new pair of men's dance shoes on the kitchen table, his way of saying yes. Over many months, they tried every class. Music was not his thing, timing a struggle. He said he enjoyed learning, yet he usually looked like he had just swallowed poison. She finally said, "You don't like this at all, do you?" And he shook his head weakly, like a guilty dog. After that, they didn't sign up for any more classes.

Then there was teaching, babies, running a household; a dozen years passed in a blink. When the girls were older, she took a few dance classes with a female colleague. Always the same: too many women, not enough men. On the dance party evenings, she sat in a corner, watching, lucky to get one or two dances with the teachers.

Then she got sick, and five years of her life disappeared.

But here she was. The music shifted. Couples stood up enthusiastically. Marion was busy squeezing slices of lemon into her sparkling water when Greg, the gentleman host, appeared. He looked so handsome in his tuxedo, and he'd even applied some gel to the front of his salt and pepper hair.

"May I have this dance?" he asked.

"Oh," she said, wiping her hands on a whole stack of napkins. "I'm sort of ... lemony." She cringed. *Stupid comment!* He smiled and waited. She stood up and took his hand.

There were a few bars of instrumental intro, strings and horns, but she knew the song right away. "The Way You Look Tonight," first sung by Fred Astaire to Ginger Rogers in the movie *Swing Time.* Marion had listened to many versions over the years, by Sinatra, Tony Bennett, even Rod Stewart, but Astaire's was the best. In the movie, as Ginger washes her hair in another room, Fred sits down at the piano and starts singing in the most tender, sweet voice.

Greg gently placed his hand in hers in dance position and whispered, "It's a foxtrot." They started to move.

"Fred Astaire," she blurted out.

Greg laughed. "I think it's Harry Connick Jr. Or did you mean my dancing?"

Marion felt herself blush. *Oh well.* Foxtrot: slow, slow, quick, quick, with variations. Box step. Promenade walks. Reverse turn. Harry sang: *Someday, when I'm awfully low ...*

"Nice to see you here," Greg said as he led her in basic step, then underarm turn. As they grapevined in a zigzag motion around the room, she tried to match the size of her steps to his. Greg skillfully navigated the dance floor traffic. His hands were soft and warm. Probably hadn't

95

done many dishes. *Oh, Marion*, she thought. *Concentrate! Feel your hand in his. Keep the frame. Head to the left. Stand up really tall. Follow his lead.* She let herself feel the music and respond to his moves. It was a lot to do.

"Wow. You can hold your own," he said, sounding surprised. And then they just danced. He held her close, as he was supposed to do in foxtrot. Well, maybe he wanted to do that? *Just be present*, she thought, as she felt her one hand on his jacket lapel, her other hand connected to his. There. She noticed his neck smelled subtly like oatmeal. Probably soap. She liked that. She liked being close to him, moving in sync as if they were the only two people on the dance floor. And for a moment, the pain and loneliness melted away.

Lovely, don't you ever change …

Soon the song ended, and Greg bowed. He led her back to her booth, one hand holding hers and the other steady on the small of her back. Okay, he was supposed to do that, but it was still lovely.

"Thank you," she said.

"My pleasure, Marion. You're a good dancer. Let's do it again."

And in an instant, he was gone to fulfill his duties, rotating around asking lonely hearts for one dance. So many lonely hearts, who were widowed or single or whose husbands preferred the casino and sports bar. She might not get another turn. But she had done it. She felt exhausted, that familiar energy crash, like air seeping out of her, a slow leak. So much work to hold her frame, to remember the steps, to listen to the rhythm of the music. To dance.

She watched the dancers for a few minutes. Suddenly, she had to dash to the bathroom, a combination of nerves and Crohn's disease. In the beige stall, she bent over in pain and breathed a long sigh, thankful no one else was there. When she quietly returned to her seat, the magic was gone. Or was it? No, it still lingered, in the music, in the shimmering dresses, and in the memory of Greg's smiling, expectant face.

And that was enough.

She had done one new thing. She gathered herself up and left the Spinnaker Lounge, followed the orange and purple carpet road home, put her arms around herself, and danced alone in her tiny, windowless stateroom until she couldn't stand up any more. Marion collapsed on her bed, stared at the ceiling, and thought about the lyrics to that song.

Wouldn't life be easy if we never changed?

Kathryn Lee

Interval

AN EXCERPT

My sister Nancy and I cluster around the water fountain with our aging father and aunts. Each Christmas they're a little frailer, a little more forgetful. They no longer venture into the main foyer at intermission in search of old friends, or climb up the winding staircases to gaze down on the crowd.

The largely female audience streams past us: two, three, even four generations of women and girls out for the touring production of *The Nutcracker*. Grandmas and aunts smile as granddaughters and nieces twirl about them in shiny taffeta dresses, imitating the ballerinas they just saw on stage.

As we step closer to the wall a familiar voice bursts out from the other side of the lobby: "Boys! Down now!"

I jerk my head but my view is blocked by a group of passing teens, their feet turned out in distinct dancers' gaits. *Mike? At the ballet? He can't afford it.* But I'd know his voice anywhere.

The crowd parts and I spot Mike's twin sons, Cole and Brody, scrubbed clean in their Sunday best, balancing on either side of a large potted plant. The trunk and leaves shake above them as they turn the base into a makeshift teeter-totter. I catch my breath. *They've grown so much.* A further gap reveals Mike, in a black shirt and slacks, gesturing madly for them to get down.

Next to Mike is Simone, and the tableau is complete. Her wavy black hair falls—no, cascades—over her bare shoulders. *Of course.* She paid for the tickets, like she no doubt pays for everything—the house, Mike's new clothes, the lawyers.

Simone crouches in front of the plant; her dark green cocktail dress moves effortlessly with her curves. She says something to Mike's sons and they let go of the tree, jump to the floor, and grin at her with freckle-faced adoration. They stand still as she tucks in their collars, licks the ends of her fingers, and straightens their hair—with her spit.

That was supposed to be me, full of patient ministrations, before Mike withdrew his offer, before Simone—his high school sweetheart—moved back to town and I became invisible. I look away and focus on my eighty-three-year-old Aunt Bea, a former school teacher. *Oh no …*

Then several things happen in slow motion: Simone stands up, takes in my little group, and beams. But she's not interested in me. With her eyes on Aunt Bea, she touches Mike's arm, points, and walks toward us, deterred by neither her three-inch heels nor the look of horror on Mike's face. All she sees is my aunt—her old teacher.

Mike turns to me and, just like that, we're gazing at each other across a crowded room. His brown eyes are pleading, as if he thinks I'm about to holler, "Where's my money?" Or maybe he thinks I'm going to grab Simone and tell her it was me who bailed him out of the debilitating legal charges and his subsequent Scotch-induced coma, me who set him back on his feet, only to watch him spin around and make a beeline to Simone's door.

I had convinced myself that if Simone hadn't come back and reminded Mike of his glory days, he and I would still be together. Now I see myself as Mike sees me: someone who knew him at his lowest, someone he clung to. Someone he owes.

Simone's approach is slowed by a swirling blur of red velvet dresses and black patent shoes. I clutch my sister's arm and choke out, "One o'clock, incoming!" Nancy catches on immediately. She was by my side as Mike and Simone's romance rekindled on Facebook—a courtship that began weeks before I realized my usefulness had run out. I was a lifeboat, but Simone was Mike's RMS *Carpathia*.

"Go!" Nancy places her hand on my lower back and pushes hard, sending me skidding down the wheelchair ramp and toward the foyer.

And not a moment too soon. Simone's sing-song voice rings out behind me, "Mrs. McKillop! You taught me Home Ec. at Franklin High!"

I take cover behind the kiosk of over-priced ballet swag and peer back. With the adults preoccupied, the twins have rolled their programs into lightsabres and are duelling by the bar. Mike, his mouth slightly open, is staring at Simone, who is saying something to Aunt Bea. Bea looks at Aunt Ruth, who points to her ears, indicating she has forgotten her hearing aids. My father ogles Simone, his one working eye appreciating her alabaster skin and plunging neckline.

Simone's face is animated, as if she's announcing, "You were my favourite teacher!" Maybe she's telling Aunt Bea how her domestic teachings led Simone to her current pinnacle: dressing her screenwriter "life partner" in black and styling his kids' hair with her saliva.

Nancy sweeps in and says something to Simone. I hope it's "I hear Mike has a very big dick." Or "I hear Mike *is* a very big dick." From Simone's doe-eyed expression, I can tell Nancy is saying the usual: "Aunt Bea's memory isn't what it was. It's so nice of you to say hello. We know how much she loved her students."

When Nancy stops talking, Simone reaches in and actually hugs my aunt. I gasp and look back at Mike. His eyes are darting from Simone to me, to the empty spot on the carpet where his children once stood. I want to walk over and say, "Relax, dude. The old folks don't remember you." Mike is vain enough to think that picking up Aunt Bea's birthday cake from the French bakery and helping her cut it—three years ago—is the centre of everyone's universe.

Simone releases my aunt and I study my ancient family: deaf Aunt Ruth, dementia-ridden Bea, and Dad, who gripes daily about losing his license on a "rubbish visual-impairment technicality." Mike's charges are full of life and promise, while I hold a protective vigil around mine. Is it any wonder I grabbed on to Mike and the youth that surrounds him?

Three chimes echo through the foyer. Cole and Brody barrel down the ramp, barely missing terrified seniors heading back to their seats.

The boys storm past me, knocking lanyards and pointe shoe keychains to the floor.

"Cole! Brody!" Mike tears after them, probably wishing they were all at a Canucks game or a monster truck rally. But he's sold himself to the highest bidder, so he'd better get used to the finer things in life.

The mini-Mikes with their blonde curls and bow-legged swaggers don't notice me. Neither does Simone. And then I realize: *She doesn't know about me. He has erased me from his story.*

Simone circles down, places a firm hand on the boys' shoulders, and marches them back to their dad. She links her arm through Mike's and sighs, "She doesn't remember me, poor old thing."

As she steers Mike toward the theatre he glances back at me and, with his free arm, shrugs his shoulder as if to say, "What can I do?"

Nothing, Dickhead. You've already done it.

Back in the theatre, the five of us settle into our seats. The whining sound of violins being tuned floats up from the orchestra pit. Nancy leans in and whispers, "Did you know Simone went to Franklin?"

I nod. "So did Mike. But he didn't take Home Ec."

"No kidding. He took Home Wreck."

"Ha, ha." I roll my eyes.

"I know someone who works in the box office," Nancy says. "Do you want me to find out who paid for their tickets?"

"Fuhgettaboutit," I joke lamely. The lights dim and someone shushes us. No one—not my friends, not Nancy, not Mike—gets that it's not about the money. He made promises and I fell for them. *At my age.*

On the other side of me, Aunt Bea starts to unwrap a candy as slowly and as noisily as is humanly possible. I reach over, ease the caramel out of the crinkly cellophane, and return the candy. I place my hand on hers in case she's agitated by my interference. She winds her long cool fingers through mine and squeezes. In that moment, I imagine my tell-it-as-it-is Aunt Bea, the aunt who never let anyone sulk too long, is saying: "Buck up, kiddo, you dodged a bullet. That boy never was very bright."

Scott Lear

A First Year in High School

AN EXCERPT

After science class Stephen and I head to the RPG Club proudly carrying our books, dice, and figures. The classroom is set up in groups of tables and Mr. Jacobs tells us to sit at one. We see Tommy with two other kids so we go and join them.

Mr. Jacobs hands us the adventure for the session, "The Secrets of Stone Able." He tells us the goal is to enter the ruined mines of Desporya outside of the town of Gillunton and retrieve the Scroll of Narsist to return to Stone Able.

Stephen is elected Dungeon Master. As he reads over the adventure, we pull out our characters: me as Jiweldaren, my Level 6 Elf Ranger; Tommy as Thorek, his Level 8 Dwarf Fighter; Brayden as Braytoo, his Level 8 Human Wizard, and Natel as Nataliya, her Level 4 Cleric/Level 3 Elf Rogue.

Stephen grabs our attention and begins the adventure, telling us, "The four of you find yourselves in the Black Dragon tavern in Stone Able. Stone Able is the capital of the Rangrin region and known for its blacksmith and tannery economies as well as the centre of government for Rangrin ..."

The tavern is dense with smoke and filled with the sounds of laughter and arguments. The four of us sit in a dimly lit corner drinking mead when a traveller stumbles in. Water from the storm outside drips from his dark hat and overcoat making his white face look even more pale. With widened eyes, he looks around.

He mentions something to the bartender, who shakes his head while handing him wine. The traveller's hand shakes as he brings it to his mouth. Wiping the excess wine from his chin, he looks around until his gaze stops at our table. He puts his glass down and walks over.

As he stands above us, dripping water on our table, I see he is of slight build and well-groomed, indicating someone of noble upbringing. "I understand you four may be able to help me out," he says in a quiet, quivering voice as he pulls a stool to our table. "I am in need of a group of adventurers."

"Who wants to know?" I ask, while Thorek lays his dwarven battle axe on the table with his eyes trained on the traveller. I can see Nataliya shift ever so slightly and figure she is pulling out one of her elven daggers in readiness.

"I'm an emissary from the Stone Able Council. There is a scroll that has gone missing—the Scroll of Narsist. It is very important to the Council and we need to get it back."

"Then why don't you go get it?" I ask.

"We have tried, but it is hidden deep in the mines of Desporya and many of our men have died in vain trying to get it," the traveller responds.

"The mines of Desporya? Those have been overrun with orcs and ko-bolds ever since they collapsed. It would be unwise to go there," Thorek says in his deep, gruff voice.

"I have heard you are experts in this kind of thing, and the Council will pay you handsomely," the traveller says.

Nataliya strokes her dagger on the table. "How handsomely?" she asks while pointing it at the traveller.

The traveller leans away. "Ten thousand gold nuggets upon return of the scroll," he replies.

I look around at the group, who nod their heads. "Two thousand now and ten thousand when you get the scroll," I said.

The traveller agrees and tells us to go to the treasury in the morning to get our gold nuggets.

The next morning we load up our horses with new supplies and make our way east out of the town.

A few miles down the road we see a merchant with a horse-drawn cart stuck in the mud. As we get closer he waves furiously. We stop some distance away and size him up before deciding to help. Thorek and I dismount, while Brayden and Nataliya stay on their horses to keep watch.

He approaches us. "Thank you, kind sirs. I was ambushed in the forest coming from Gillunton, and as I tried to escape, I lost control and fell into the mud," he says.

"No problem. We'll have you pushed out and on the road in no time," I say as Thorek and I move to the back of the cart and give it a good push while the merchant pulls the reins of the horse. With not much effort, we set the cart back on the road. "There you are, all set."

"Thank you again. Do you plan to pass through the forest?" he asks.

"Yes, we're on our way to Gillunton," Thorek replies.

"Oh … There is a darkness that has come over the forest that wasn't there before. Bandits and foul creatures are all about. I barely escaped with my life," he tells us.

"What sort of darkness?" Braytoo asks.

"One that is not of this world. Before you go, let me give you this." He turns and digs into his cart. Nataliya and Thorek instinctively grab hold of their weapons. Out of his cart he presents me with a small vial filled with a thick blue liquid with a slight glow in the centre. "For your kind gesture, I give you the spirit of light. When it comes across unearthly darkness, it will glow and light the way for you."

"Thank you," I say as I put the vial in my sack and watch the merchant make his way toward Stone Able.

Around midday we reach the forest. It stands before us, a wall of trees reaching high into the sky with trunks as wide as a horse's length. The road seems to disappear into the thicket.

"So this is the forest the merchant mentioned," Braytoo says as he settles his snorting horse.

"Ah, you're not going to believe that silly tale, are you?" Thorek says. He is always the one who thirsts for adventure and runs headlong into things, leaving the rest of us to chase after him.

"We should just be careful and on our guard," I say. "Even if it isn't haunted, the forest is a perfect spot for bandits. I'll go first, then Nataliya, followed by Baytoo, and Thorek will take up the rear." I spur my horse forward and we enter the forest in a line. There is silence, apart from the footfalls of our horses and the creaking of the trees, as if groaning from old age. I feel my horse slow beneath me, urging caution.

As soon as we enter, we are wrapped in a cloak of darkness. My elven eyes adjust, yet I am only able to see twenty feet in front of me. I look up through the canopy to see very little light coming through despite the sun being high in the sky. I look behind at the road disappearing in the darkness. The air is still and has a stagnant smell, as if the oxygen has been long used up.

"Well, this ain't so bad," Thorek yells from the rear.

Nataliya turns to him. "It might be wise to keep your dwarf voice down."

"Oh, pollywash," Thorek says.

"Shh. Hear that?" Nataliya says as we stop our horses. I soon hear a distant sound of wind howling through the trees. I look around but the trees are still. By their expressions, Thorek and Braytoo can't hear anything either.

"Form up," I say and pull out the vial the merchant gave us. It glows brightly, illuminating the knotted and twisted forest around us. "Something strange is coming."

We move our horses facing outwards so our backs are to each other. I notch an arrow while Thorek readies his battle axe, Baytoo closes his eyes to conjure up a spell, and Nataliya brandishes her throwing daggers.

The sound intensifies, becoming a high-pitched wail, but I still can't see anything.

"Banshees!" Nataliya yells as we look up to see five elven women descending upon us from the sky.

I let loose an arrow and see it fly right through one of the creatures. "These aren't real women, more like wispy images," I say.

"Cover your ears. Our weapons are no good here." She conjures up a spell that makes us all deaf to avoid hearing the wailing of the banshees.

Baytoo sends a burst of light almost as bright as the sun shooting out from our location. Through my squinted eyes I see it burn the three closest banshees while the other two move off.

My hearing comes back and I turn to the others. "Are we all good?"

Nataliya and Baytoo nod.

"Thorek, are you okay?" I ask and look back to see his empty horse behind me. "Thorek! Thorek!" The darkness makes it hard to see very far. I dismount and kneel down by his horse. "He's been taken. There are four separate tracks of steps and over here it looks like someone's been dragged."

Nataliya walks over. "Here's his battleaxe. It—"

"Okay it's 4:30, time to wrap up. Please leave the tables and chairs how you found them," Mr. Jacobs says.

Walking home I try my usual attempts to ply Stephen for information about what the adventure holds for us, but he isn't budging. "Come on, just tell me what's down the road or what will happen to Tommy's character."

"Okay, okay. Tommy's character is forced to drink a potion by the Gladiator of Ny, which doubles his strength and his intelligence. As a result, he no longer wants to hang out with you and finds better company in the Rodent Man."

I give Stephen a quick shove and say, "Does not!"

"Well, I told you I wasn't going to tell you," he says.

Patrick Lucas

Everything You Know Is Wrong

AN EXCERPT

I'm racing my motorcycle down the narrow dirt paths of the still sleeping village. Everything is shrouded in a fog, the air heavy, wet, and stinking of burnt mud gone rotten from too much moisture. The path is slick and slippery; my back tire slides and fishtails violently. My vision is limited to just a few feet, but I keep pushing faster, praying I won't hit some stray animal or person. I weave between small thatched-roof and bamboo huts that appear out of the mist, raised up off the ground on stilts, rough-cut log pillars exposed like the bony, crooked legs of old women snatching up the hems of their dresses as I fly past.

I can hear the words my best friend Khamped said to me the last night I saw him. Slurring drunkenly over the lip of his bottle of BeerLao, in broken, stunted, English-as-a-second-language slang, "You know that, Falang Joon? You know you learn (hic) when you know (hic) ..." He pauses for a long time, his inebriated brain searching for the meaning he's attempting to distill. "Everything you think you know is wrong."

My motorcycle rides like the mutant hybrid offspring of a washing machine crossbred with a lawn mower, chortling and rattling loudly. I drop another gear, praying the motor won't backfire like a cannon shot and wake everyone in the village. I cut through yards and back alleyways, taking the route that has the best chance of getting me to where I need to go without running into anyone. I've only got a few minutes before all the women, the engine of village life, start coming out and getting on with their days.

I reach the perimeter of the village and sail through a narrow opening in a bamboo fence onto a raised pathway between two rice paddies. The paddies are flooded, brimming with water. At this speed, riding off the path and into the muddy water on either side would end with a trip to the hospital, the last place you want to visit in Laos.

The weight of the girl on the back of the bike isn't making this any easier. One small arm is wrapped around my waist; her hand tightly grasps my rain jacket. Her body jerks from side to side, threatening to throw me off balance and down into the rows of stubby rice stalks. I can hear the girl's muffled voice as she screams from inside her helmet. I ignore the noise and focus on keeping us upright and moving forward. I have to get her back to the brothel. I can't let anyone see us.

It could destroy everything.

⌒

I woke up with a pounding headache. Rolled over to find the girl lying next to me in bed, a distinctly pungent and sour scent in the air. I got the girl up and we quickly and quietly left the house as I pushed a massive wad of cash into her hands. The currency is so devalued it takes a garbage bag to carry enough to represent any real value. The girl had nowhere to put the money, so she cradled it with the bottom half of her shirt like a kid carrying a trove of marbles. I tried to recall our conversation from the night before. I'm positive she told me she was eighteen.

I took the girl by the arm and pulled her outside to my motorcycle, parked in the front yard. I grabbed my helmet off the handlebars and put it over her head. It was three sizes too big. She looked up and grinned at me through the visor. Definitely not eighteen. I grabbed a faded, dirty yellow rain poncho strapped to the back of my motorcycle, unfurled it, and pulled it down over the girl's head. Now you couldn't tell what she was. Perfect. "Bai bai bai!" I hissed. *Let's go!*

I didn't start the motorcycle to begin with; instead I pushed it out onto the road before jumping on and pulling the girl on behind me. Her ability to run was inhibited by the traditional *sin* dress she wore, a tube-like, ankle-length garment of heavy cloth worn by most women in Laos, even working girls, apparently. The poncho billowed out around her as she clambered onto the bike in a precarious side-saddle position. We coasted down the hill as far as possible before I popped the bike into gear to jump start the motor and drove away at top speed.

We didn't get very far. At the bottom of the small hill, just down from my house, a torrent of water had washed out the road, a thick, fast stream flowing from one rice field into another. I skidded into a sharp turn and raced down a narrow path between the houses.

We reach the end of the raised pathway and the far side of the rice pad-dies. I gun the bike up an embankment and onto a road. Turning a little too tightly, I have to plant my foot down and force us back upright so we don't wipe out. The poncho on the girl whips violently. I'm afraid it might catch the wind and send her flying up over the fields. She's sur-prisingly strong, her grip firm about my waist, her other hand still cra-dling the money against her stomach.

Free from the confines of the village I can afford to open the throttle. "Thu vai!" I yell back at her. *Hold on!* I twist the accelerator and I feel her body jerk backwards, struggling against the weight of the helmet.

We arrive outside the brothel, a row of dilapidated wood and bamboo shacks perched on the side of a steep hill overlooking the Ou River. I come skidding to a stop and we both clamber off, the girl stumbling and nearly falling, trapped and entangled in the poncho. I grab the helmet and pull the poncho off. She stands at the side of the road, slightly dazed and blinking.

I can hear the river down below us. Normally a peaceful, meandering creek, it has turned into a gushing, roaring torrent. Looking over the

109

edge of the ravine, past the brothel, the waters have turned dark, muddy, and dangerous, rumbling and boiling angrily. I can see large logs and tree branches pitching about in its wake.

There must have been a rainstorm overnight, unusual for this time of year, the monsoon season still months away. I have a vague memory of it starting to rain when I was driving the girl back to my house, the raindrops sparkling in my headlight, obscuring my vision. I remember something darting out into the road in front of us. I think we hit it with my bike. A small animal, perhaps? I strain to recall what happened, but my memory is blacked out from a night of binge-drinking.

I shake my head to clear the vision and turn back to the girl. I feel awkward, not sure what to say, anxious to leave and get back home. "Well, khop jai lai lai—thank you very much. Sok dii der—good luck!" I stuff the poncho back under the bungee cords strapped to the back of the cycle, place my helmet on, leg over the bike, kick start and peel off, spraying the girl with mud.

Driving away I look back through my side-view mirror and see that she's lost control of the money I paid her. She dances about at the side of the road, jumping up and down, clutching and grabbing at the vortex of papers swirling around her.

Khamped was wrong. I haven't learned shit.

Christy Dunsmore

Rose to the Occasion

AN EXCERPT

Sam rubbed his temples as he studied his friends, every head bowed over that carved wooden carcass of a coffee shop table. They should have been happy The Rose was back. It reminded him of Ellie's so-called Celebration of Life, which was supposed to have been so much better than a funeral. The guys had looked just like this, with their chins tucked into their Adam's apples. Surely his small lie had not caused all of this.

Niko looked up to the open rafters, the dappled light hitting his profile as if he were in a photo shoot. "It's been twenty-five fucking years. Are any of us the same starry-eyed idealists we were in college? Caspar, Mr. Marriage-is-Forever, has three wives under his belt. Alfredo, brilliant cardiologist, is on the verge of having heart failure as he juggles his wife and concubine. I, artist to the snobs, am still trying to find someone who doesn't bore me to death. And then there's Sam. At least you have the fucking decency to be a widower and you're good with money."

"You shouldn't joke about that," Caspar hissed. "Ellie was a wonderful woman." He patted Sam's shoulder. "And you really are good with money."

"It's called growing up. With any luck, The Rose has grown up, too." Niko said it all so quietly, so firmly, with such agonizing conviction.

"People with terminal illnesses often contact old friends out of the blue," Alfredo mumbled. "Bet he's come back to say goodbye. Christ."

"Probably something to do with a woman." Sam recognized the

slightly higher timbre of Caspar's voice when he was trying to sound optimistic. "It always does. Usually."

Suddenly, Niko pounded the table with both fists, making their coffee mugs jump. "He's just a goddamn fucking man. You should've got over him years ago. I did."

"Asshole," Caspar sighed, playing with the frayed chin strap on his helmet.

Alfredo resorted to his professional doctor's voice, barely audible. "Would you keep in touch if you'd been disfigured? One minute you're this confident, good-looking athlete and the next you're a miserable, disfigured shell of a man." Alfredo pressed his fingers together, giving each of them a thoughtful glance. "Well, would you?"

"You're a miserable, disfigured shell of a man, and we still hang out with you," Niko growled.

The words hung over them for several seconds before Sam saw it: that tiny twitch of Niko's lip, the little glimmer in his dark eyes. Niko laughed first, and then they all did. Sam realized his lungs were working again and the sweat down his spine began to dry.

"Well, gotta get the girls." Sam pushed himself away from the table.

As he headed to his car, he could hear his friends behind him in the parking lot. Alfredo's leather clogs shuffled across the concrete, so light for a big man. Sam knew Alfredo hated those clogs, but they worked with his orthotics and kept his bunions at a manageable level of agony. Caspar's running shoes were almost silent except for a little click from some pebble stuck in the sole. Niko's always-shiny Gucci loafers clicked purposefully over the hard surface, matching his pretentiously slow swagger. Sam knew that Niko had every pair stretched to accommodate his hammer toe, the big toe on his left foot, broken so many years ago on the pitch. Broken by Sam.

"Maybe The Rose is bringing somebody with him," Caspar said, slinging a leg over his dilapidated bike. "That can make a guy nervous."

He pedalled off with a wave, the bike wobbling precariously under his weight.

Niko leaned against his shiny red Corvette. "Think it's smart for a cardiologist to ride around in a car that looks like a fucking hearse?"

Alfredo wedged his body into the massive black Mercedes. He rolled down the tinted window and blew Niko a kiss with his middle finger. "Some of us still have need of a back seat." Then, with a soft roar, he drove off, leaving Sam and Niko alone in the lot.

Sam jiggled open his trunk and pretended to sort the junk that was in there. Jumper cables that didn't work. The emergency kit already pilfered of anything useful. A worn, plaid blanket they used to use for picnics, still matted with bits of grass. He would never throw that blanket away. Sam pretended to find what he was looking for and closed the trunk. "Back to your garret?"

"Think I'll see if that nubile young waitress has any aspirations to be a model."

Sam smiled, he hoped convincingly. "She asked if you had a son."

Niko adjusted his sunglasses, wiping at his eyes as if they hurt. "So she calls me Dad. I've been called worse."

Sam laughed and got into his car.

Niko leaned toward Sam, his elbows on the window, peering over the edge of his shades. "The Rose is okay, right?" There was something in the way Niko hesitated, something in those inky, soulful eyes that worried Sam.

"The Rose is The Rose," Sam said, and part of him believed his statement. "It doesn't matter how many years have gone by, whatever challenges he's faced, The Rose will always be The Rose."

Niko nodded, pursing his perfect lips. "No wonder he liked you best." He punched Sam's shoulder. "Loved you best, probably."

"Better go find that waitress before your steamed milk dissipates."

As Sam drove off, he looked in the rear-view mirror, expecting to see

Niko sauntering back into the coffee shop. But Niko was walking slowly down the street, head down, hands in pockets, without a trace of the arrogance or confidence that made him who he was.

☞

When Sam returned to the house, all he wanted was a bath. He longed to stretch out in the warm tub, even though the porcelain relic was too short for him. It had even been too short for Ellie, but she had loved the Victorian tub with its elegantly sculpted claw feet. When it became too difficult to lift her into it, Sam suggested they remodel and create a huge walk-in shower area. But Ellie refused to let the old-fashioned tub go, wearily acknowledging that while it made perfect sense, she just couldn't give up another damn thing. They had a fight about it, and Sam accused her of being selfish. Why didn't she see that he couldn't bear to lift her even one more time into that wretched white coffin? As soon as he finished his tirade, he grabbed her tightly, enfolding her trembling body into his arms, and tried to kiss each hair on her head, mumbling "Sorry, sorry, sorry," into the lilac-scented curls.

Now Sam didn't want to give up yet another damn thing, so that old tub was still there. It no longer seemed like a looming open casket. Progress of sorts. But the tub had also morphed into something of a safe refuge, a vault where memories were kept secure and could be recalled with the simple turning of the squeaky tap. Being in that tub allowed him to remember the rituals he had shared with Ellie, while the faucet dripped with elongated tears.

Using the tub required practised contortions of hand, foot, and knee. He would slide down, bending his knees so his butt almost touched his feet, until his long torso could disappear under the steamy surface. He'd let the water flow over and around him, a liquid shroud for his bones and skin. Although there was never enough hot water for a deep bath, it was always deep enough to feel the buoyancy. As he gently bobbed in his private ocean, he would fill his lungs with air and watch his chest hairs and nipples peek above the surface like bristly little islands. When he let his head relax, sinking his ears beneath the surface, he could hear his breathing, in and out, in and out. Each breath would become so clear. Initially they were ragged and disparate. Then, with concentration, he could make each intake very soft and quiet, followed by out-breaths as smooth and powerfully even as notes from his old clarinet.

Leslie West

The Year of Other Men

I bought Greg a cat as a surprise for Valentine's Day when we'd only been dating for two months. She was still an eight-week-old kitten when I drove to that run-down house in the slums of Burnaby to choose her from a litter of nine. Really, I got her by default; all the others had been spoken for before I arrived.

A disheveled man who smelled of old sweat and stale cigarettes showed me into the corner of the kitchen that had been penned off for the kittens. He stood by, chain-smoking as I cooed over them, but asked me not to pick any of the kittens up.

"The momma might reject them if you get your scent on them," he told me. "That's the one." He pointed with a nicotine-stained finger, as they wriggled about like worms and I sat down on the floor for a closer look at the orange fluff-ball. She wasn't the runt and she wasn't the biggest. She had no special markings, and nothing about her stuck out in that smelly cardboard box, a squirming mess of calico, mewing, and kitten shit.

This was back in the day when love's first flush infected everything with warmth and magic, and screwed with our perceptions so we made stupid decisions. Or no decisions at all. Since the day we'd first got together, I had been thinking of Greg's touch every waking moment of every day; even sitting on that stranger's greasy floor I was still caught up in this rose-tinted delirium.

I thought my kitten was the cutest of them all. As if figuring this out, she immediately came to me, making an awkward, stumbling kitten bee-line to my lap. I looked up at the man standing above me who was intently staring down my cleavage. He shifted his eyes to meet mine and shrugged as if the cat choosing me was some kind of arbitrary animal behaviour.

116

That was the first and last time the cat came to me of her own accord.

⌒

Two weeks later I drove out to the same house, paid the remaining fifty dollars, and was handed the cat in a shoebox. I was on my way to my Valentine's date with Greg and dressed up in a new pink and red dress that cost more than the cat. I was nervous because my friends had hinted that giving a man a pet so soon into our romance might be seen as moving a bit too fast. The cat got sick in the car and I cleaned her up with some napkins I found in the glove compartment. She still smelled slightly of vomit when I presented her to him on the outdoor patio of Milestones.

Greg was not surprised by my present; he was stunned. There was a moment when my heart stopped as he stared and stared at her, his expression not yet readable. It occurred to me I would know what he was thinking if we'd been together longer, and my friends were right, I was acting prematurely. The little cat started wriggling madly until Greg relieved me of my tiny burden.

"You got me a kitten," he breathed, eyes fixed only on her. I swore I could see tears forming as he held her aloft a long moment before nestling her to his face. People talk about pivotal moments of just knowing stuff, and this was definitely one of mine. There—amongst the other diners at the restaurant that afternoon, looking at her brown, gold, and white fur in the glinting sunlight, and seeing how tenderly Greg's fingers stroked her little face—was the moment I knew he was the man I was going to marry.

"Excuse me, no pets on the veranda." Our waitress interrupted my revelation.

We didn't care, we ordered our food to go and passionately made love as soon as we got back to his apartment, the cat meowing away in her little box next to the bed. It was then, in our post-coital cuddling, that Greg announced he was going to name her Passion. It was this kind of genuine cheesiness in his character that made me love him.

Passion immediately fell in love with Greg the same way I had fallen for him. Maybe it was for the same reasons, but really, who knows what went on in her feline mind? She seemed to know her purpose right away: to please him, take care of him, and be petted. She sought out his lap whenever he sat down, she rushed to the door like a dog whenever he came home, and rubbed herself against his legs in that self-gratifying, masturbation-like way that cats have about them. She took to bringing Greg gifts, half-dead rodents that would stumble as she dropped them at his feet when he got home, wounded birds that flapped around the house for hours as we tried to catch them. All the same, after that first welcome home we ended up banning her from the bedroom for our lovemaking sessions. If we didn't lock her out she would find an uncomfortable vantage point and stare directly into my eyes as Greg made love to me. I think she knew that her banishment from the bedroom was my idea, and held it against me.

Greg and I were engaged later that spring, and I moved into his apartment where I had been spending most of my time anyway. Even so, the cat inspected every box I brought in as if she preceded me.

Our love was like a tornado that swept us along, but unlike tornadoes which leave chaos and destruction in their path, everything fell perfectly into place in the wake of our courtship. We were soon married in a somewhat lavish summer ceremony which did not include the cat. I had just graduated from university and started working later that fall. Greg was promoted and we bought and moved into a new apartment, a ground-floor corner unit with a little yard that looked out to the forest. We started a new life together, decorating the apartment, going on vacation, marking each occasion over the passing years.

It's hard to say where our little story breaks down. Sometimes I sit and try to sift through the more-than-a-decade of memories we shared together and I still draw a blank. My therapist tells me that when I'm ready, I won't have such a hard time looking back; this is a normal part of grieving.

Neither Greg nor I were young anymore, and things that once happened easily became forced somewhere along the way. Nowadays, I would never run out and buy anyone a cat on a whim, and I can no longer remember why my twenty-four-year-old self thought it was such a good idea. I have been trying to decide which car to buy for the last year, a time frame which saw Greg and I meet, get engaged, and then married. Life slowed down somewhere and exciting things just didn't happen that often anymore.

All the same, I felt I was happy enough, so when Greg told me he had met someone and they were expecting a baby together it felt like a slap in the face. I wasn't only jealous of her, but jealous of him too. It was as if he'd rediscovered that element of youth which allowed one to make snap decisions and then jump in with both feet.

⌒

"There's plenty of food in the cupboard for the cat," he told me the day he moved out. I was hovering around our apartment, not sure if I should go out or stay and watch him pack up. I was still reeling from the idea this was actually happening. We were actually getting divorced.

I opened the cupboard and so it was: endless stacks of Fancy Feast, lined up by flavour and colour, in twelve varieties, about a caseload each. Enough to last forever.

"You should take the cat," I told him. But I knew what he'd say, we'd already been through it a few times.

"I can't take her. Joanna's allergic," he explained as he packed. As if I should give a shit his new girlfriend would break out in hives. Or go into anaphylaxis. Or develop a severe case of respiratory distress and suffocate on the spot. I remembered having a runny nose the first few weeks we got the cat, and a doctor telling me that virtually all people are, by varying degrees, allergic to cats. It's a normal immune response and that by repeated exposure you just build up a tolerance to them.

"She'd get used to her," I told him, but he shook his head in that gentle, tired way he had of ending an argument simply by not to arguing at all. I hated that about him. I wanted to argue; wanted to fight, to throw things like couples in movies. I wanted things to get out of control, to have a moment when our worked up tempers would push us into a kind of animal frenzy that would cut past the mundane details of what was happening right now. I wanted things to get physical, to throw myself at him and have that wrestling dissolve into an embrace, then a collapse onto the floor, and one last session of carnal communion before he left. Instead, Greg was packing up his moving boxes, precisely taping them shut, and stacking them up in perfect pyramids in the entryway.

Sensing something was up, Passion sat attentively by the front door, as if ready to bolt. *That's fine bitch, go*, I thought, willing her to make a run for it.

Greg made several trips down to the parking garage with his boxes but no furniture because, in addition to the cat, he was leaving me virtually everything.

I've now stopped sleeping in the bedroom altogether. These days I sleep in a nest of blankets on the sofa. I use the king-sized bed only as a place to fold laundry.

Passion took over the bedroom immediately.

Megan Abele
Art and Story

"The industry has obviously morphed," he said, "but people still crave a good story. I like to think of an editor as a specialist in transmutation." He grinned, his charcoal shirt bringing out the light splatters of gray in his hair. Just as attractive as his profile picture, which was not usually the case. She wondered if her yellow dress and bright purple scarf were too loud, but she'd decided long ago to exhibit as much of herself as was comfortable. As she approached her mid-forties, her desire to please and conform was plummeting at a shocking rate.

They were sitting at a bar in the East Village, one of those dark basement types with a three-piece house band playing standards in front of crimson backlighting. Nora wished she could order a Gin Rickey and say things like, "Ain't this place the bee's knees, sweetheart?" while sucking on a Virginia Slim. Instead, she smiled and nodded, adhering to the first-date convention of restraint. They were at the interview stage. After two years on the dating circuit, she accepted that a question and answer period inevitably led the opening scene.

"I've always imagined that it would be women who would edit upmarket women's fiction. Gross assumption, I guess." Nora smiled encouragingly but noticed that his fingers drummed absentmindedly on his beer bottle and he kept crossing and recrossing his legs.

"I get that a lot," he said. She waited for him to say more, but he went back to watching the band. Six months ago, Nora would have filled the awkward spaces to keep the conversation going. She liked to think of herself now as more comfortable in her own skin, although maybe she was just more comfortable being uncomfortable. Besides, what the hell did occupation have to do with chemistry between two people? She yearned to skip past the banality of getting-to-know-you talk and fast-forward to something more real. What drove him? What dreams of his were unfulfilled? Questions you can't ask on a first date. They screamed loose cannon and desperate.

Nora sipped her martini while doing a quick calculation of her exit strategy. With half of her drink left, and while her date upheld an awkward half-silence of not speaking and fidgeting with the buttons of his shirt, she shifted her attention to surveying the bar's artwork. Large wooden frames covered an entire brick wall. Each frame held a crescent moon-shaped piece of pine stuck to a dark canvas backdrop, acrylic rays radiating out from the inner portion of the arc. Deep purples, burnt-oranges, periwinkle. As if the sun and the moon had merged, and cast out multiple colored beams in the night sky. Nora guessed it was a four-inch brush, possibly three and a half. It reminded her of her earlier work, days spent with carving tools, glue guns, drills, and needle and thread.

"Enough about me," he said. "Your profile said 'artist,' which had me intrigued." He was clearly straining to stay focused. The exact opposite of her last long-term relationship, Paul, who she stayed with for two years after their expiration date. She had met him while working with cellophane. Paint on plastic is tricky; you can never quite get a handle on it, and sometimes when you do, it clings to the skin and has to be carefully unpeeled.

"I've done a lot of larger installations," Nora said. "Entrance galleys, showpieces. I've always been fascinated with taking up space, pushing the edges of what we can do with materials, experimenting with the so-called impossible. I used to get a high from monumental reactions." The language of her world used to be so intoxicating, mental gymnastics flipping her mind, days and nights spent on abstract concepts. Was it possible to just have simple, straightforward?

"So, what do you think of this guy's stuff?" His eyes were back on her, the light catching flecks of pale blue. She liked his soft gaze, the way his eyes held hers.

Nora looked back up at the wall, examined the multiple frames with their symmetrical arcs and bold strokes. Her last relationship had been a whirlwind six months that was so intense it had felt like years. Julio, another artist. Always a bad choice. They had collaborated on a collection that involved photographing different stages of violence toward fruit. Smashed watermelons, slashed tomatoes. After the initial rush, her insides had churned like tectonic plates, early tremors before the eruption.

"I guess I'd say that at one point I would have preferred the tighter arcs with the deep shades," she said. "I would have loved the boldness of the hue, the intensity of the layering of paint; I would have wondered what shades were underneath." Nora's fingers moved in the air as she spoke. She sat upright, her body alight, as if there were a canvas in front of her, waiting to come alive. "Now, though, I appreciate the larger arcs. That one with the light cream shade catches my eye." Her voice softened and slowed. "I bet it would look fantastic, translucent even, under the right lighting."

He smiled at her, and his eyes danced. "What are you working on now?" he said. He leaned forward in his chair and she had a desire to shift back, but stopped herself.

"I'm sending messages in bottles. I've gotten permission to send three hundred of them down the East River over a period of a year. I was hoping to do it all at once, get a sort of mass reading and response going, but the city didn't want to give the impression that throwing bottles in the river was something everyone should do." Nora laughed.

"So, what's in the bottles? Secret messages?" His fingers had stopped their rhythmic dance, his legs were still. The bass player moved into a slow solo, setting a steady, calming pulse.

"Questions mostly, or short vignettes that evoke a response. I put my website in them, and I invite the people who find the bottles to email me. I ask things like 'What's the best thing that has ever happened to you?' or 'Do you mind telling me about the worst day of your life?' I've gotten back one hundred and fifty-eight responses so far. Well, I guess I should call them stories. Beautiful, touching stories for the most part."

Nora wondered if she was talking too much, and stopped. The saxophonist attempted a difficult Charlie Parker tune. She disliked the high-pitched, random sounds strung together, found it confusing and incohesive. "So, do you live in this neighbourhood?" She cringed inwardly as soon as she said it. She had gone and introduced a new narrative in her nervousness, but it was too late to turn back. The words hit the air, threatened to take the conversation in a new direction. Surprisingly, his eyes stayed glued on hers.

"I live upstairs. I lived in the Upper West Side for twenty years, and then needed a radical change," he said, his gaze flickering down for a few seconds. "My wife died a few years ago, and I thought that moving away from our neighbourhood would be helpful." He looked directly at her, nodding a bit. "It turns out your heart can break wherever you live."

Nora nodded slowly. Most of her dates had been like her. A series of beginnings and middles with not enough longevity for a full tale.

"She's the one that told me to start dating," he said.

Nora's spine straightened involuntarily. Was her instinct misleading her? She had done her due diligence—a social media search, conversational emails, even asking a friend of hers who worked in publishing if he set off any red alerts.

"Oh no, nothing like that," he said. He reached out and touched her arm. An invisible electric current sprang from his fingertips. "I mean, this was before she died. She told me to wait two years before dating. If I didn't promise to go on a date by the third year, she said she'd divorce me from the hospital bed." His lips curled up a bit. "I guess I'm trying to explain where I'm coming from, why I've been so distracted. Nervous, really. It's been about twenty-three years since I've been on a date."

They both laughed, nervous notes filling the air. The band moved into some Miles Davis and the backlighting changed to emerald and azure. His body had stilled, his attention on her now. She noticed her own discomfort, a desire to look away, adjust the skirt of her dress. Instead, she leaned in, let the weight of the moment settle between them.

He took the last sip of his beer, started fidgeting again. "Seems like the band is really picking up," he said. "Do you want to stay for a second set?"

Chelene Knight

Junie

AN EXCERPT

1980: She didn't die the way she was supposed to die. No one said it out loud, but Junie knew everyone was thinking it. A year shy of her eightieth birthday, Madeline Lancaster was found dead in her home on Prior Street in Vancouver, fully clothed in her best dress—the one with the white lace scoop neckline—and a painting of Vancouver rolled and tied with a frayed, pale-yellow ribbon, clutched in a tightly closed fist.

Maddie had dreams. Junie knew about these dreams. Back in the day, Maddie had what folks described as the "silkiest pipes this side of town." She dreamed of albums, tours, and the radio blasting her voice, but the drink spoke louder. The drink held her tighter. The drink became her everything. Thinking back to all the drunken nights Junie found her mother slumped over somewhere in their small home, thinking back to all of the arguments and the horrid slurs that spewed from her once-so-beautiful mother's mouth, made her heart ache.

Junie left the burial wrapped in numbness. Even the sun hitting the skin of her cheeks and warming the backs of her ears didn't make her *feel* anything.

Later that evening she walked down Union toward Vie's Chicken and Steaks where some of Maddie's friends and close family would be gathering to share old memories, and talk about good times. Junie was sixty. Sixty years old but she still felt like she was twenty-one and standing in the way of her mother's real plans. The main cause of her drinking. Junie looked around. Listened to the cars buzzing and zooming around her. Looked up at the neon-lit signs. *This whole area has changed so much,* Junie thought. *I've been here all my life, I've watched it change, felt it change, but now it feels like I'm a stranger.*

She walked further down Main Street, past the sounds of back and forth yelling over the price of some dried spice outside of a Chinese grocery shop where bins and bins of dried spices, fruit, and other unidentifiable things were piled high. All the buildings were small but packed to the gills with merchandise. Shop windows plastered with signs that read, "Sale," "Half price," and "Last chance to buy," and she wondered where all these places would be in five years. Even the people that passed her on the street were different. No one stopped to say, "Hello, how are you?" No smiles, no nods of recognition, no "Nice day isn't it?" Folks nowadays didn't even offer up a sideways glance and went out of their way to avoid eye contact.

Junie kept walking and the thoughts in her head changed as she passed different businesses. As she strolled by the local coffee chain, she thought about an old friend. *Estelle.* That girl was lost from day one. Doomed and lost on the inside. They first met forty-seven years earlier and became instant friends. Junie could still see her slick smile, her eyes, and the way she'd twist her soft curls around her thin brown finger smiling, saying, "Junie girl you funny." She missed those days. Now, so much was different and, like this city, nothing will ever be the same. *Estelle gone, my city gone, my mama gone. Lord what you doin' to me?* All the places she'd called home—like the barber shop, the cafe where she'd had her first art exhibit—gone.

Junie stopped in front of Vie's. She stood there for a moment before grabbing the knob of the door for what would most likely be the last time since it was scheduled to close for good in a few months. *The last real remnant of Hogan's Alley's existence*—her neighbourhood—*about to be wiped out for good,* she thought. Junie remembered her son, James, and how when he was thirteen he'd come down to Vie's and draw in his yellow-lined notepad, biting on the end of his pencil like he was deep in thought while sipping on a coke with extra ice.

No more were the black-owned barber shops where men exchanged stories of how they "Almost snagged that beauty at the bar," or the chicken houses cooking up everything you could imagine for their hungry and over-worked customers that would pile in after a long day doing whatever they did to earn a dollar, and the speakeasies that lined the alleys, streets, and corners. No more were the jazz clubs with music pulsing through the alleys after dark, enticing the bricklayers and shopkeepers to spend their last few dollars on a whiskey or gin and the promise of a good time. These were replaced with prim and proper coffee shops where no one knew your name, and you were "Next customer please." Everything was slipping away. Junie looked up at Vie's roof, the window frames, the slow peeling paint. *She gone*, Junie thought. Right before she was about to open the door and step inside she felt two strong arms wrap around her waist from behind.

⌒

1933: They met at thirteen, both entering the same dark, overfilled classroom wearing awkward half-smiles while tugging at the hems of their home-made dresses from that fabric that itched. Un-lotioned knees bending awkwardly beneath new brown stockings, both worried the other kids would point out their shortcomings. Junie noticed the one difference between them almost immediately: Estelle was beautiful. Soft, bouncy hair, shapely body for thirteen, and her smile and eyes matched the ones that belonged to those who danced on stages. She had that same lure. On the other hand, Junie saw herself as overly thin, too tall, too dark, and her clothes sat on her body like drapes sat on a curtain rod. After finding two empty desks placed side by side, they sat down, hands still on the hems of their dresses, the coolness of the metal seats so initially shocking it wiped away their nervous smiles and replaced them with uncomfortable smirks.

"Hey, your mama do your hair? It look fancy," Junie said.

Estelle twirled a ringlet around her finger. "Naw girl, I get up early and do this myself. My nanny help sometimes."

"Nanny? Who's that?"

"Oh, you don't have a nanny? It's a woman who watch you while your mama and daddy off somewhere."

"Oh. Look nice."

"Thank you. Yours look nice too. I could help you press yours if you like. I got me a new comb, it got these—"

"Would the two girls in the back please hush! I'll have you both writing lines till the tips of your fingers bleed," the teacher at the front of the room bellowed.

Junie and Estelle looked at each other and covered their mouths leaking warm giggles. Estelle lifted her hand from her mouth and moved her lips and widened her eyes imitating the scolding teacher's threats, without making a sound. Junie lost it and laughed uncontrollably.

☙

1941: "Friends call me Junie. How you?" The young, slim, dark-skinned black woman shot out her hand with such alcohol-enhanced confidence Dex had no choice but to latch on to it.

"Nice to meet you, Miss Junie. I'm Dex. And might I add you lookin' mighty foxy tonight. What brings you down here all by your lonesome? You know, shouldn't no young thang be here without some protection," Dex patted his not-really-there biceps as if to indicate *he* was the one who could protect her.

"Oh really? Protection eh?" Junie said with a slanted smile and half-closed-gin-soaked eyes. "Puh-lease!"

The music was bumping, people were dancing, sliding, and rubbing against one another. In the air, hot and thick and heavy, a wetness hovered. The room was darker than it should be. This was a basement club and it got louder the later it got. If the walls could talk. The Coal Club was the "it" spot in Vancouver's black community and everyone knew it. Barely-there lighting from coloured paper lanterns hung on strings from the ceiling, low smoke, textured walls: the place to be. And the heat. This was what the clubs were like around here. It looked mystical in a way. A place to let your hair down after a long day of floor scrubbing, hair washing, or brick lifting—people needed to let loose. If you looked at the worn down building from the outside you'd never think this was the paradise that existed inside.

The music was another thing. It was like the walls were vibrating and the floorboards were about to fly up, nails and all. The smell of fried chicken lingered from the early evening chicken ladies that'd come to feed the band before the club opened. It was just perfect. No rules, you could be whoever you wanted to be here.

Junie had all eyes on her. Her green sequinned dress whipped in the air as she swooshed around Dex. She never once took her eyes off of his as she swirled around him. At one point, mid-dance move she stroked the top of his left ear. It was right then and there she knew Dex was in love.

Josh Keefer
The Bus Stop Gentlemen

Sandy ran the lint roller over his blazer according to his fastidious new habit—conducted every morning—even on a Sunday such as this. He replaced the blazer on its hanger, returned it to the closet and, still pajamaed, considered its contents thoughtfully. On the right, his blazer and its cousins, just as new. On the left were stacked boxes of old clothes, neatly labelled by his wife. When they leafed through photo albums she would comment on his leather, his boots, his hockey jerseys. "Oh, look how handsome you used to be!" She adored the old, but Sandy knew she honoured the blazers. He picked out a black pinstripe suit and began to dress for his meeting with Ali.

Ali and he had met in high school and became friends, bonding through their shared state of meager living, surrounded as they were by the offspring of the ultra-rich. Once they graduated, Sandy would wait with his stick and skates at the side of the curb by the old thrift shop, and Ali would pull up in a rusted old car he had bought from his uncle for $200. Sandy would brush the beer cans off the passenger seat and clamber in, and they would drive all over the countryside to the training camps of junior teams. In the car, the plan would be discussed beforehand. "Let's fight," Ali would shout over the tinny radio. "So they know we're tough."

They would carry their bags into the ill-lit dressing room of the moldy rec centre rink, and sit on opposite sides of the room, shoulder to shoulder with stocky young flunkies glowering below heavy brows. Each boy was dreaming of the scholarship that came with a place on the team. During the scrimmage, with the coaching staff seated on the bleachers, pens in hand and pads on their laps, Sandy and Ali would square off in the corner and drop their gloves over some imaginary slight. They would jostle and pull before Ali would purposefully drop his left hand and Sandy would catch him on the nose. He would tip and go crashing to the ice and Sandy would follow him down, applauded by the grudging stick taps of their competitors.

⌒

At the wheel, in his black pinstripe suit, Sandy guided his new car past the old thrift shop. The shop's windows were curtained with thick black drapes and a banner, proclaiming in block letters an upcoming Grand Opening, was tacked up over the store sign. Ali had moved back to the old neighbourhood, but it had changed without him in the years he had been gone. When he and Sandy had driven through these streets as kids, they kept the car doors locked. Now, as Sandy went to meet Ali, his windows and sunroof were all open, and crisp, clean air brushed at his temples.

As hockey and its scholarships withered with no fruit, Sandy worked a retail job at a factory outlet store nearby. With the money earned from that Sandy cobbled together enough for a set of new clothes and a realtor's license. Ali had done the same, though he never said where he had gotten his money. Sandy's mother's house was their first listing. It sold quickly and for high above the market price. When they handed the keys over to the buyer, the buyer laughed. The house was torn down a week later and a set of townhouses sprung up.

⌒

Sandy turned off the main drive and drove down a side road, passing glassy buildings. Either new or freshly renovated, the ground-floor windows reflected the flowing lines of his black coupe.

The only flaw on Sandy's record came early in his career. It was a dingy old apartment he rented, far below the normal rate, to the young woman he would go on to marry. "I know my credit is bad," she implored.

Sandy remembered the way her brunette bangs drifted over her cheeks and her large round eyes. "But I graduate next summer and then …"

Sandy and Ali made money hand-over-fist turning the old properties of their friends and families over to the hands of developers. Friends and families who accepted their small cut of the profits, heaped grateful sentiments on their realtors-turned-patrons, and headed north to working towns flung far from the city, never to be seen again. New tenants of strong blood and good means, with whom Ali could not get along with, replaced the faces they had grown up with.

☙

As the money came in, Sandy bought a house on the west side of town for him and his fiancée. Ali spent his money on drugs and habitual drinking. One open house, Sandy can recall spotting a dusting of cocaine on the kitchen's granite countertop. As the steps of prospective buyers grew nearer he looked out to the balcony where Ali stood smoking.

"What's that?" said one woman.

"Oh, nothing. The current owners are eager bakers." Sandy snatched up a dish towel and wiped the counter clean.

"You've lost your mind, Ali!" Sandy later said. "With guests here? This is the final straw!"

"Fine! I'm sick to my stomach anyway, watching you sell our town to the dogs!"

☙

Sandy slowed his car and parked along the curb. Crammed between the windows of a designer boutique and an Italian coffee shop was a scuffed door of peeling white paint. He knocked firmly twice, avoiding the eviction notice tacked square in the centre of the door.

It opened as far as the chain would go. A face, sunken and sullen and ringed with grey stubble, peeked warily through the crack.

"Ali, my friend!"

133

"I told you I never wanted to see you again. You plaster your face on bus stops, and now you're at my door," Ali replied. He snatched up a hockey stick that was leaning by the door and held it aloft, his hands white and shaking, between him and Sandy. "Fuck off, Saeed!"

"I have good news! Bella is pregnant! We would be honoured if you would be the godfather. Please, Ali, it would mean so much to me." Sandy stood there, arms spread wide.

Ali slammed the door and bolted the latch.

Sandy sat at his desk, eyes wandering from the computer screen to the photo of his wife and daughter when his secretary informed him of a call on line two. "It's your wife. I think she's crying." Sandy switched lines and tried to speak, but was interrupted. He listened intently. Then, dropping the phone and grabbing his blazer, dashed out of the office ignoring the startled queries of his secretary.

He raced up the main road and into the hospital's lot, through the double doors and charged past the alarmed receptionist. He found his wife clutching his daughter's hand with both of hers, gently shaking it, now pressing her forehead to the smooth skin. He fell onto the chair beside the bed. She looked so small under the coverlet. There came a commotion from the hall. Dazed, Sandy turned his head and peeked through the open door. A nurse was barring entrance to the room, slashing her arms in a crossing motion.

Behind her was Ali, trying to push past and shouting wildly, "I'm the godfather! Let me in!"

Sharon Miki

Night Shift

AN EXCERPT

You hear about how you're supposed to see your life flash before your eyes right before you die, but I always knew that was bullshit. So what I'm feeling now—with you looming over my done-for body while I'm clutching the Hello Kitty pillow we bought together last summer at the night market—is smug. Self-satisfied.

Because I was right.

I always knew dying wouldn't be all warm flashes of brightness and childhood sugar highs. I knew I wouldn't see my dead grandfather grinning at me from the other side; wouldn't think about laughing and smiling, riding Playland roller coasters like when I was seventeen. Even when you push down on my lips, sealing the gap between the polyester plush and my airway, I don't feel the light. There's certainly no movie montage. I just choke on the dusty pillow fibres, taste lingering remnants of the alfredo sauce you spilled on the couch a few weeks ago. I try to spit, but inhale more cloth.

Of course you've left my eyes uncovered; I can see your face. You're looking up, sideways, any way but back down at me. I think about how my friends all said I'd go and marry you one day. If only they could see your stupid face now, scrunched up like this is hurting *you*.

"Bmruf," I laugh as best I can. You always hated my laugh, didn't you? You finally look down at me—supposedly to see if I'm gone yet—and I stare right back.

Still here, asshole.

"I'm sorry," you whisper, as if that will hurry this along. I roll my eyes.

These are my last moments on earth and I won't be rushed.

I'm thinking, *great, now I'll never know how* Game of Thrones *ends.*

I'm thinking, *did I clear my search history, or will Mom find my porn?*

I'm thinking, *well, at least now everyone will see I was the good one all along.*

The blackness starts to cloud my vision and I force myself to stop fighting you. I make the decision to go limp. My last second will be by my rules, goddamnit. You never understood that about me, did you? I always get the last word. And if these past few months have taught me anything, it's that I need to fight for what I deserve.

Even if what I deserve is this.

⌒

Before they started dating, Kim spent an embarrassing amount of time fantasizing about what it would be like to sleep with Eric.

She wasn't even that interested in the sex part—she hadn't been overly inspired by penetration and its associated fluids since she lost her virginity to Michelle's friend Rob on a lacklustre lawn-chair escapade back in Grade 10. No, what got Kim really excited was dreaming about falling asleep beside him.

At the warehouse, Kim's day revolved around finding excuses to be in Eric's presence, to get a few inches closer to her fantasy. Nothing major; just little things. She'd cut it dangerously close to scan in for her shift so she could walk to the evening meeting beside him, though he was invariably five minutes late. Or she'd take the long route down the laundry aisle so she'd have an excuse to see his forklift drive by as he brought down pallets filled with chocolate-covered nuts and candy to be restocked. He'd only occasionally reward her with a little, "Sup, girl." Sometimes she'd swap breaks with Lori, so she could spend a few minutes sitting across the table from Eric while he ignored her to read the crinkly Metro newspaper.

When Kim daydreamed about being with Eric, she mainly pictured herself just laying beside him while he slept; she thought about what it would be like to have freedom to stare at him without judgement. To count his gangly lashes one by one, or to trace the lines of his shoulder blades with her eyes. To feel the glow of being as close to his heat as she wanted.

It was an entertaining delusion, but no one can live up to someone else's fantasy of them, can they? At least, that's what Kim told herself the first morning after with Eric.

"Want to come over Friday night. Watch a movie?" Eric had said casually, as they clocked out some Thursday.

Kim wasn't a prude, she knew what watching a movie meant.

So on Friday, Kim spent her entire day off preparing herself for the evening. She ate nothing. She shaved everything. She arrived at his apartment glowing, light headed, and smelling like fresh peaches and baby-powder-scented Soft & Dri.

"Oh yeah. Hey. Yo, did you bring anything to drink?" Eric had greeted her at the door.

She hadn't, so Kim smiled heartily and asked him what he wanted. She was a good sport.

Fifteen minutes later, armed with a six-pack of Cariboo, a mickey of rum, and a two-litre of Pepsi, she returned.

"Cool. So, I have these DVDs I'm willing to watch," Eric had said, smiling above the same lime-Slurpee-stained T-shirt and jeans he'd been wearing at work the day before. He waved a hand absentmindedly at a floating shelf hanging slightly askew on the wall.

"Awesome! Hmm, I haven't seen this one. Is it good?" Kim pulled a well-worn copy of *Pulp Fiction* off the shelf.

"Ugh. Dude, I've seen that so many times. Can we maybe watch *South Park*?"

Kim smiled sweetly and nodded, settling onto the couch. She crossed and uncrossed her legs. She smoothed her ponytail. She wasn't going to be deterred by a lack of Vincent and Jules. She was grateful to be where she was.

Eric poured two beers into glasses—an effort that relieved Kim—and put the rest of the beverages on the floor beside the couch.

They watched half of the *South Park* movie before he started idly fondling her under a sunny orange-and-yellow crochet blanket.

Kim was eager and drunk from nervously gulping beers; Eric never left his seat, his long arms splayed across the back of the couch in a lazy cross.

As Kim rode him, fully dressed but for a lacy black thong pushed aside under her skirt, she saw his eyes flick back and forth, past her to the movie and back again.

When he finished, Kim climbed off of Eric, who promptly passed out on the couch. He breathed deep, satisfied, peaceful breaths. Kim couldn't bring herself to look at him, but she also couldn't help smiling when she woke up in the middle of the night and found Eric snuggled in behind her, his right arm draped over her like a seatbelt.

Eric huffed as he rushed up the driveway, the white-sky morning sunlight aggressive against his sleepy eyes. He shifted the bundle of heavy shopping bags in the crooks of his fingers, the plastic handles cut into his skin as they stretched to the point of almost breaking, and turned his fingertips a moody shade of maroon.

He'd spent his whole shift thinking about the situation, and he was sure. He knew he had to end things with Kim. He just wasn't sure how she'd take it. So he was enacting a tried-and-true method from his past: the brunch breakup.

Dumping women was a skill Eric had prided himself in when he was younger. He had a system: start with his famous eggs benedict, topped with homemade hollandaise sauce—a creamy, buttery masterpiece his grandmother had taught him how to make when he was small. Hollandaise was the only thing he remembered about his grandmother, and his was pure sunshine on a spoon.

In Eric's experience, people always took bad news better when their stomachs were full. After the dumpee had eaten her fill, Eric would conjure up a few tears. He'd break down, sputter about how he was overwhelmed, feeling too much, how he was afraid he wasn't giving her enough. He'd tell her he loved her too much—that was always a nice touch. What woman could argue with that? He was too good of a guy. He'd done this countless times when he was younger, and it had always resulted in a guiltless breakup. Well, mostly guiltless. Usually, the girl ended up feeling a bit guilty.

But the important thing was that Eric would be free.

If Eric was really being honest with himself, he'd known he was settling when he decided to move in with Kim. Even then, he knew he could do better. Hadn't he, after all, been the captain of the lacrosse team? He prided himself on still wearing the same jeans he'd bought in Grade 12. He was a catch.

In the beginning, when he'd found himself getting closer to Kim, Eric felt like he was doing her a favour. There were perks to dating down. It was easy. She was easy. But now, Eric deserved more.

Alyssa Hanada
Matched Socks
AN EXCERPT

Becca stood over the couch, folding laundry. During her quiet moments, it was this: laundry times infinity, ironing Aaron's work shirts, picking up toys. Any time she complained to Aaron, he would give her a little eye roll or scoff. "Come on, Beck. We have a house cleaner for fuck's sake. You should go tell your sob story to the people who are on welfare. I mean, how about we trade places? You go to a soul-sucking job and I'll play with the kids and do laundry."

She knew he was right. Except about the job part. He loved closing deals. The rush was like a drug to him. She would trade him, she wanted to say. But the question was, to do what?

Shirts folded in three quarters, just like her mom taught her.

Cora sat and watched Becca while sucking at the ends of her hair. A habit she had developed in the last few months.

"Stop it, that's gross. Do you want me to cut it off?" Becca's face turned at the thick, wet strands.

Cora blew the hair from her mouth. "Do you even like having kids?"

Becca stopped and looked at her daughter's face. She hadn't said it with contempt or anger, just curiosity. "What a silly question," she tried to smile. "Of course. I love you and your brothers."

"It's not the same," Cora said slowly, tracing her fingers along the seam of the couch. "You *have* to love us, right?"

"Being a mom is my job, Cora. It's the most important job in the world." She said the words she had said over and over and over and over, just like she had heard others say.

Over and over because then maybe it would become the truth.

She folded the laundry faster while her eyes burned. Rolled socks into a ball, then another pair. Aaron's thick sport socks, grey and pink polka dots for Cora, Graham's cuffed blue ones. One of Henry's favorite Spiderman pairs was MIA and he would have a fit over it. Becca tried to think of something to say to Cora. How motherhood was the best and worst thing that had ever happened to her. How it tore at her stomach and ripped at her heart. How one moment she stared at their faces in amazement and couldn't believe she had created humans so smart, beautiful, and full of potential. That they were an extension of her, they took everything from her until there was nothing left but a shadow of herself.

She wanted to say all this to her daughter. Instead, she matched socks.

"But how come you don't have a real job? Like Daphne's mom is a lawyer and Jade's mom owns a restaurant. And Lucy's mom is a philanthropist," Cora enunciated each syllable. "That means she raises money for important causes."

Becca's face flushed. "Daycare is really expensive and your dad and I decided that it would be better for me to stay home with you guys. And I volunteer in your classroom and on field trips. I was the class mom last year. Remember how I helped organize the day at the Food Bank for the second graders?"

Cora shrugged. "I thought Molly's mom did that."

"Do you know how much time I spent sending emails and coordinating parent volunteers?" Cora didn't even care. All that time she was trying to be a super mom, no one even noticed.

"Well, I don't want to be a mom," Cora said matter-of-factly.

"Why is that?"

"Because all you do is stuff for everybody else."

Becca found herself laughing and then she couldn't stop. Cora widened her eyes and stared. You get it, Becca wanted to shout. You get it.

She composed herself and took a breath. "It doesn't have to be like that, Cora. You can be a mom and you can have a career if you want, or you can just be a mom and have your own hobbies. The thing is, I always wanted was to be a mom and nothing else stuck."

"But what would you do if you hadn't had kids?"

"I …" Becca stopped and looked down at the socks. She tried to think of an answer.

There was a thud followed by a high-pierced cry. Becca ran to the stairs. Graham lay sideways at the bottom holding the back of his head.

"Baby, are you okay? Mommy is here. Shh, shh." She gathered him in her arms, kissed the top of his head, and rubbed it gently. She looked at his eyes and his pupils were normal. He flailed his arms and legs and she knew he was fine. "You're not supposed to go down the stairs by yourself." Becca took in a breath. "I'm not ready for this Graham. Why do you have to climb out of your crib?" Her voice shook and chest tightened as she fought back tears.

"What happened?" Cora ran to the stairs with big eyes.

"He fell. It's okay, he's all right. That's why we have to keep the baby gate closed."

"I always close it," Cora shouted. "It must have been Henry."

"I didn't do it," Henry cried from the other room.

"Liar," Cora screamed. "You could have killed Graham."

"Cora, that's enough. He's okay," Becca said.

Graham stopped crying and stuck his fingers in his mouth. He seemed to forget about the pain and squirmed out of her arms to run to the playroom. Becca collapsed onto the couch and closed her eyes. She felt cold fingers stroke her arm and blinked to find Cora standing next to her.

"You're a good mom," Cora said.

Becca interlaced her fingers with her daughter's and stared into her ocean-blue eyes. Her straw-coloured hair. A mirror of her younger self. It was almost scary how alike they were.

Reese Kim Carrozzini
The Lady in the Terraced House

*Inspired by a true character: an excerpt from a fictional story set
in the mid-1990s about an assistant editor who discovers she
may be living with a former female SS Nazi guard.*

One morning at work, I found an email from my boss saying she would
be away for the next few days, and to sort through her mail, courier
over the current manuscripts, and cut out all the book reviews from the
broadsheets. As I was going through the stacks of mail and manuscripts,
I stumbled upon one with black and white photos. Curious, I began to
flip through and realized it was about the SS Aufseherinnen: female
guards of Nazi concentration camps during the Holocaust.

As I read the captions below the photos, one caught my eye. It was
a headshot of a woman who could have been my landlady, Chiara Simmons, more than fifty years ago but without the glasses.

It couldn't be—could it? I thought. I scrutinized the photo again. Minus the wrinkles and glasses it could be her. *Impossible. It would be too
much of a coincidence.*

I read the printed pages accompanying the photos.

In northern Germany, this woman known as Simona Harclotte had
been a guard at the infamous brutal women's concentration camp of Ra-
vensbrueck and Auschwitz. She was described as a fanatical Nazi. Sur-
vivors recounted details of a frightfully evil woman who assaulted and
tortured prisoners and terrorized them with her dog.

I had to satiate my curiosity. I left work early and grabbed a couple books, photocopied the photo and information about Simona Har-clotte, tucked them away into my satchel, and hurried home. My mind was humming with ideas—plotting and planning how I was going to get inside Chiara's flat and get proof of who she was.

By the time I had arrived at the house I knew what to do. It was the perfect time to break into her flat as she always took a nap from 2:30 to 4:00 p.m.

Her apartment was located on the main floor of the house. I tried her front door located in the hallway—as I expected, it was locked. I quietly went around the back of the house and tried the kitchen door. Surprisingly, the knob turned. My breath caught in my throat. I hadn't imagined it would be so easy.

I entered the kitchen with caution, praying she was napping. The apartment looked like it hadn't been updated in years. I tiptoed through the kitchen and walked into the sitting room.

I went to the mantel where several silver-framed photos stood, yellowing and cracked. The first one displayed a little girl with a toothy grin waving to the camera. It might have been her as a child. To my right, were two other photos which looked very much like the woman in the manuscript I found at work. One showed a young woman standing in the middle of a field holding a flower, smiling into the distance. Another, larger photo, was of a couple holding hands. The man wore a suit from the forties and the woman wore a dress with large shoulder padding. I took out the photocopied headshot and held it next to the photos. My heart stopped and a small gasp escaped from my lips.

It was her—Chiara Simmons.

The Jump

An excerpt from a dark short story chronicling
a woman's attempts to commit suicide

*"When you spend almost your entire life feeling or being depressed,
it's almost impossible to conceive what 'real' happiness even
begins to feel like or be like." —Unknown*

Now was the perfect moment. I looked down over the ledge and peered into the vastness below. It felt dizzyingly high. I imagined my body plummeting into the deep murky water and being enveloped by darkness. I walked toward the centre of the bridge far enough away from any rocks or crevasses, planning to plunge myself into the inlet. I wanted to avoid tumbling down the rocks and mangling my body, broken and beaten out of shape.

I took a deep breath to steady myself and used the weight of my body to hoist my right leg up and then my left, seizing hold of the large green pole. My feet felt unsteady standing on the ledge. The countless times I had imagined this moment did not include fear. The sound of my heart pumping hard and fast was deafening. I could hear nothing else, not the traffic, nor the seagulls flying overhead. It was pitch-dark and the glare of the headlights from passing cars was blinding at times.

Seconds, then minutes passed. I didn't have a watch. I had given it away with the rest of my things. I cursed and berated myself for being such a chickenshit. I had to do this. Gazing down into the darkness of the water I gently lifted my right foot a few inches off the ledge and slowly moved it forward letting it just hover in the air.

"HEY!" a voice behind me said.

Startled, my right leg wobbled as I lurched forward. OH MY GOD! *I'm gonna fall*, I thought.

As my left arm held on for dear life, the rest of my body swung sideways. Instinctively, I grabbed the pole with my other arm while my leg floundered about, and finally managed to get my right foot back onto the ledge. My heart dropped to the bottom of my stomach.

"HEY!"

I was not imagining a voice. There was someone there. I turned slightly to my right and my eyes fell upon a very dirty and disheveled man who hadn't had a bath in this century. He looked to be Caucasian in his sixties or seventies but his face was unwashed and buried beneath layers of dirt so it was hard to tell his exact age.

"Can ya spare any change?" he barked.

"Are you out of your fucking mind?! Can't you see I'm busy here?! You almost made me fall!" I screeched at the top of my lungs.

"Look, little lady. Not to be facetious but ain't that why you're up there? Lots of people drop from the bridge. Ya ain't no different. I just figure you ain't gonna need no dinero where you're going."

"I don't have any money. Now go away!" I glared at him, willing him to disappear.

"Oh come now. I'm sure ya got something," he said in his crotchety old voice.

I couldn't believe this was happening. Not now of all places. "Believe me, if I could make you disappear with money, I would. But I don't have any! I gave it all away!" I bellowed.

His brows furrowed and he glared at me with opaque blue eyes. "Why don't ya just jump then and get it over with?" He turned and walked away.

I stood there surprised he was leaving. Of course he was leaving. Why would he stay? I was so confused. Did I want him to leave or not? He was getting further and further away. Dismayed, I found myself yelling, "You're actually leaving?"

He stopped dead in his tracks, slowly turned, cocked his head to one side, and started hobbling towards me again. The foul smell emanating from him reached me well before he did. Standing only a foot away from me, he asked, "What ya doing up there anyway?"

I couldn't feel much of my fingers anymore, but I knew they were still wrapped around the pole, as I could feel the palm of my hands touching the cold steel. "What does it look like, old man?"

"No. That's not what I mean. What happened? Did you lose your job?"

"No," I replied.

"Did ya lose someone you love?"

"No."

"Then what the hell are ya doin' up there?" He said with exasperation. "Well, I can't understand you young folk. You have your entire life to fuck up so why call it quits now? Do it later when you make more mistakes. Then you'll have a reason to jump."

I felt like I was in some bizarre devious universe. Anger burned and raged inside of me. I wanted to be hateful. "You of all people should know. Why don't YOU jump? Doesn't look like you have any reason to live." There—I said it. It was cruel and heartless.

Urith Hayley

Crocodiles and Crocuses

AN EXCERPT

Friday at lunch I'm sitting alone on a bench in the garden outside the Vancouver Art Gallery. I'm trying to cut back on weekly expenses by making my own lunch. But the cold chicken sandwich is tasteless and I can barely swallow it. Someone thought it would be funny to put a box of detergent in the fountain last night, and there is white foam bubbling up and over the edges, spreading like a disease.

A year has passed since Scott's arrest and subsequent release on bail. Twice this week I've run into him. Wednesday evening after work, while riding the escalator up to the fourth floor of the Hudson's Bay Department store, I sensed someone behind me. I moved to the right to let them go by, but it was Scott.

"Hi Kara, you're looking good." Scott smiles as if we're long lost friends. I glare back at him. He takes hold of my left arm. "I've got a reservation at the Hyatt. Let's have a civilized talk over supper and a glass of wine. Amanda's video was just an accident. It was always about you." He leans over and whispers in my ear, "We watched the video evidence today of us making love in the jacuzzi. Do you want that played in open court? Everyone agreed you were having a good time and it's not against the law to film yourself for private purposes." His lips caress my neck and his breath, hot in my ears, sends a shiver down my spine. He rubs himself against my hips. I'm confused by my body's arousal even when I tell myself I hate him.

We finally arrive at the fourth floor and I push him away. I open my mouth to speak but it's dry as if stuffed with cotton and no sound comes out. I almost run down the escalators to the main floor and drive home as if pursued by the devil.

⌒

I toss the rest of the sandwich on the ground, pull out my cell phone and call Sean Morgan, my new lawyer. A fight breaks out among the seagulls for the scraps of chicken.

"Sean here." I picture him, a slight man, thinning sandy-coloured hair, binders open on an oversized mahogany desk, shirtsleeves rolled up and tie off.

"Hi Sean, it's Kara. Scott has been stalking me. I see him everywhere I go downtown."

"There is a restraining order against him in the criminal courts. But he does work downtown and you're bound to run into each other at times."

"This is not a coincidence." I worry my constant complaining may be perceived as crying wolf, while Scott is viewed as a highly intelligent executive who couldn't possibly have done what I accuse him of.

"You can file a complaint with the police if you feel threatened. But you don't want to start another civil action. It will only cost you more money," Sean pauses. "On another matter, when am I going to get your psychiatrist's report? I need to review it and send a copy to opposing counsel. The trial is set for next February. According to rule 40A we need to provide copies of all expert evidence three months before the trial, otherwise it will not be admissible in court."

"Don't worry, you'll get it," I lie. "Is there anything else?"

"No. That's all for now."

I make a note in my daily planner of the date, time, length, and reason for the call. At the end of the month, I will compare Sean's invoice to my notes.

Sean gave me a list of recommended psychiatrists six months ago, but there was at least a twelve-month waiting period for an initial interview with anyone on that list. Next I tried the yellow pages. I was down to the O's before a Dr. Owen agreed to see me. I knew nothing about him. Middle-aged, tall, and clean-shaven, he listened attentively to each new development in the criminal and civil proceedings. The last time I visited him was two weeks ago.

"Mrs. Hunter, when we last spoke, you had an appointment to view the tapes at the police station. Did that happen?" Dr. Owen asked.

"Yes, Constable Leblanc wanted to know the names of the other people in the tapes," I replied, sitting across from the psychiatrist in his office.

"Who were these other people?"

"Well, there were a few tapes of neighbourhood girls applying makeup. There was also another tape of a woman who was so drunk or drugged, she was throwing up while Scott tried to have sex with her."

"How do you know he was trying to have sex with her? Could you see that in the tape?"

At the end of the session he asked if there was anything I needed.

"As a matter of fact, my lawyer needs you to write a report detailing my emotional distress as evidence for the civil litigation."

"Mrs. Hunter, you are a strong individual," he stated while rising from his chair. "Even though what your partner did was wrong, I feel you are coping well and able to continue working and functioning in day-to-day activities. I can't give you any such report." My half hour was up and he opened the door to show me out.

Almost blind with rage, I had to slam on the brakes to avoid rear-ending the car in front of me as I left the parking lot. He never once asked me how I was coping, more interested in the salacious details of what was on the tapes. I didn't bother making another appointment to return.

The sun is blocked by a cloud and the temperature drops a couple of degrees. The wind picks up and foam from the fountain becomes air-borne. I rise from my bench and cross the street to do some lunch hour shopping at Eaton's department store. The corner of Howe and Georgia generates intense winds and I fight to stay upright as hair whips my face. Pedestrians run by holding their collars tight. A revolving door sweeps me into the majestic main floor of what was once a Canadian institution. Now bankruptcy rumours pack the store with shoppers scavenging the final closing inventory for bargains. Sales associates spraying perfume or offering to rub cream on my hands force me to run the gauntlet from the front door to my destination. A myriad of scents—lavender, vanilla, jasmine—hang heavy in the air and I long to be back outside again, but I must complete my task: buy an early Christmas present for my daughter, Amanda, at the advertised "Up to 70% off!" bargain prices. I make my way to the ladies watches counter in the middle of the main floor. My selection is a Mickey Mouse Gucci watch and I pay with cash. While the clerk is ringing in the sale I feel a cold sweat. Little black dots crowd my vision until I can't see. I cling to the display case, determined not to faint.

"I need to sit down," I say to no one in particular.

"Are you alright? Get a chair for her." There is some commotion, and someone takes my arm and guides me to a chair. "Bend over. Put your head down." The voice and face clear to reveal Dr. Yasmin Khorasani, one of the female psychiatrists who interviewed Amanda. Her voice is soft and accented. Her hair covered by a pink floral silk hijab.

"Dr. Khorasani? Why are you here?" I'm so used to seeing her at Children's Hospital that here she seems out of place, like a ship in the desert.

"Just doing a bit of shopping before I go on shift. Are you okay? Can I call someone for you?"

"No, I feel much better now." I'm embarrassed by my moment of weakness.

"How far are you going?" Dr. Khorasani asks.

"Just a couple of blocks, I'll be fine."

"I'm going that way. I'll walk with you." Around us, the shopping madness continues, but I'm now immune to it, enveloped by Dr. Khorasani's protective cloak. "How's Amanda doing?"

"She seems to be okay. We don't talk about Scott. She never wants to talk about it." Outside, the cool October air is like a slap on the face and my head clears.

"Children are resilient," the doctor replies.

I hate that phrase. Everyone—police, lawyers, doctors—all say the same thing; as if to reassure me everything will turn out right. Things are forever changed.

"But you are not doing so well? You must take care of yourself. When there's an emergency on an airplane, they tell parents to put the oxygen mask on themselves first, otherwise they will not be able to help their children." Dr. Khorasani takes my hand in both of hers to say goodbye.

"I need your help. I need a doctor's report stating that I have been psychologically impacted by the events that have occurred," I plead.

"I'm not allowed to help you," her eyes widen. "I'm only allowed to treat children."

"Then can you recommend someone? I've tried everywhere, and I can't afford to wait twelve to eighteen months to see a doctor."

"Don't tell anyone that I told you this," Dr. Khorasani lowers her voice. "If I were you, I would present myself to one of the hospital emergency departments and say you're having a nervous breakdown. You will get immediate treatment and referrals." She gently pulls away from me and, reluctantly, I watch her disappear into the crowd.

Gina-Lily D'Attilio

Swagger

AN EXCERPT

CHAPTER I: KAMIKO

The rain is a multiplicity of tiny leather whips slapping my cheeks and the exposed skin of my forearms. I turn onto Burrard Street and head toward the harbour. Faintly visible houses climb up the North Shore. As I cross Robson and the candy-pink Victoria's Secret window display, stinging raindrops flick the crook of my elbow; they remind me of biting during sex. If I wasn't late for work, I'd linger, let the pricking rain take me to orgasm right here on the street.

I sexualize the mundane like an adolescent boy whose penis hardens at anything remotely reminiscent of female anatomy. This week, my womb is fertile and my body, responsive and tingling, is a Venus flytrap triggered by even the tiniest insect vibrations. The most ordinary things turn sexual this week: the rhythm of my knee-high boots in puddles; my steaming Starbucks coffee; the friction of my panties as I walk. Heat rises between my legs. Today's going to be a good day. When I get to work, as I process the day's trades, I'll spread my legs and press my ankles against the chair. I'll imagine Russell Price, my boss, ordering me not to relax a muscle.

This morning I'm channeling Sharon Stone, the sexy and sophisticated man-killer from *Basic Instinct*. In a navy pencil skirt from H&M, I'm like her. Well, sexy and sophisticated obviously, not a man-killer. My bra shows through the silk blouse, a mini-rebellion against the staid dress code of the establishment.

At two minutes to eight in the morning, I enter Walker Three and survey myself in the mirrored walls. I love my untamable mane of dark curls. The elevator arrives; I hurry inside, hoping I make it to the office before Russell. As I wipe a smear of mascara from my eyelid, the spear of an umbrella blocks the closing doors. Russell, in slate-grey Armani, pitches in behind me.

In his casual gear, he reminds me of a blonde wolverine. Occasionally, when I'm working overtime on weekends, I'll see him at the office on his way to the airport for a business trip or holiday. He's usually unshaven, in a vintage v-neck T-shirt and beat up brown leather jacket that I imagine belonged to a fighter-pilot father I'm pretty sure he didn't have. With his chest straining against the cotton, his shoulders seem even broader and the two-day scruff gives his jawline a menacing, yet enticing, squareness. Even though he's my boss and an old guy in his forties, he's hot.

Russell, umbrella still extended, appraises me with moss-green eyes. My top, translucent from the rain, two more buttons undone, exposes my bra and cleavage. I'm proud of my accidental sexiness, but my cheeks still redden. A rich investment banker, Russell gets off on power. He savours my embarrassment. So, with a flushed, flirty smile, I play it up.

"Oh … look at me …" I let the words falter. "I'm all wet."

He bites his lip; I picture him nibbling folds of me.

Then, I roll my shoulders back, refasten my shirt, and press the button for the seventeenth floor. "We're late. You need to review the forecasts for your 8:30."

Russell scrutinizes the laces on his Oxfords, vexed by my switch to business. As if I'd hook up with him in the elevator. My married boss, whose wife, Arianna—his boss—is Managing Director of the firm.

Besides, I've got Calvin.

Actually, since Calvin and I have a pretty open relationship, starting something with Russell isn't totally impossible.

CHAPTER 2: RUSSELL

Kamiko dominates my thoughts. I can't focus. I've re-read the same stats a hundred times. And the file smells like her. I toss the papers on the desk, hopeless. I want to be prepared. Even for Jason. Especially for Jason. He's a buddy but he's also loaded and my bonus is at stake.

Hiring Kamiko was reckless. Young, fun, sexy; she's a billboard for what I'm missing out on and I'm losing it. Women don't usually get inside my head. I need to control myself.

"Russell?" She perches her perky ass on a leather chair showcasing her tiny waist, her tits.

This morning I wanted to grab her, back her against the glass, tear her shirt open, leave marks. Shit. I'm hard again.

"Jason's here. You want a cappuccino?"

"You're a mindreader." My words have a lascivious edge.

Kamiko winks and gives a coquettish shrug, she knows it's not coffee on my mind. She's a temptation; a risk. But I love risk. My business is risk management. God help me, I want the risk.

But my life is calculated now. An automated sequence of repetitive responsibilities; even the bills are programmed. Risks are not permitted. With Arianna, there's never a hair out of place.

Arianna's turning fifty in June. I should throw a surprise party—it's some kind of milestone, isn't it? But how am I supposed to celebrate being married to a torn up fifty-year-old clam I don't even get to fuck anymore? Jesus, I'm an asshole. I should feel guilty for thinking that way about my wife, the woman who had my children, but I don't. Maybe I feel guilty about not feeling guilty.

CHAPTER 3: KAMIKO

Friday. 4:17 p.m. Almost going-out time. Trance DJ, Otto Knows, is at Celebrities Nightclub tonight. I can't wait. I text Dylan. *Who knows?!?*

He replies instantly. *Fuck yeah, Otto Knows.*

Meet @ Thurlow. Bring BLW ;) I've got MOLLY!! My phone autofills BLW and MOLLY. The cocaine and ecstasy party favours are something of a weekend tradition now.

I pop into Russell's office like I always do before leaving at the end of the day.

"Plans this weekend?" He sounds hopeful.

"Dancing. Awesome DJ at Celebrities tonight. You?"

"Poker with the guys. No dancing for me."

I laugh. "Come dancing! Dancing is where you find your soul."

"So you say."

I turn to leave, look back and wink, "I can get you in tonight, if you come to your senses. But only if you're wearing something spicier than a grey suit."

"I'll keep that in mind."

⌒

The heavy door thuds behind me and the chain lock rattles. My best friend, Saphira, isn't home yet. We love our two-bedroom apartment in this ancient brick building from the seventies. It's like stepping into *American Hustle* except not as swank. Our view is worth a couple hundred kilos of cocaine, though.

Tonight's gonna be an adventure. I can't wait for the music to twinkle through me like Swarovski crystals catching the light. I wonder if Russell will come. I've invited him out before but he never does. Maybe our elevator encounter finally woke him up from his middling life.

Nah. He's way too sophisticated to come out with a crazy girl like me. As if Arianna would ever let him anyway.

I wish he would, though. He's sexy. He'd buy rounds of Patron; we'd dance, do coke, make out. I could molest his hot bod.

Oh, yes please.

Carlie Blume

Where the Lions Are

AN EXCERPT

In all the time I had spent planning Noni's thirtieth birthday party and of all the things I had planned for the evening, being pregnant was not one of them. Nearly four months ago I had started the planning process bright-eyed, over-inflated with expectation. And although I wasn't anticipating on having to navigate through endless waves of nausea and crippling bouts of hunger, there were at least a few things I knew for sure.

I knew that in lieu of a traditional cake I was going to serve a variety of handcrafted white chocolate and pistachio petit-fours, modeled after similar ones Noni and I lost our minds over at this little bakery we visited on our trip to Santa Barbara last summer. It took me an entire day of calling around to every bakery I knew in Vancouver to find a place willing to make them.

I also knew it was going to be somewhat of a formal celebration. As her best friend, I felt it was my duty to make a fuss and, in my mind, formal meant more fuss. And considering both her dad and sister lived in Toronto, I entrusted myself with the role of party planner.

Sure, there was Jordan—Noni's soft-spoken and dry-humoured Danish husband of ten years—who could no doubt be counted on to create plates of food that resembled works of art at the multitude of award-winning restaurants he's worked in over the years. But as far as planning a party, this was best left to me.

Initially I wanted it all to be a surprise, but after years of knowing Noni, I knew surprising her was a task next to impossible to pull off. She had a talent for seeking out the intention in people's eyes. I stopped in at her house in Strathcona before a meeting at the gallery. Before I could even enter her front gate a sudden wave of nausea smacked me right between the eyes; I mercilessly heaved the contents of my twisting stomach into her poor bougainvillea planter.

"You okay? Your face is literally green right now," she said with squinted eyes as I stepped through her door.

She scanned my face, while barely giving me a second to respond, interjecting palm outstretched as if she were directing traffic. I probably should have known better. The woman was like a truffle pig with a secret. And I was a bad liar.

Unfortunately, in all my excitement, my dress for the party was the first purchase I made. A sleek, pewter-grey slip from a boutique in Gastown—that cost nearly half of one month's rent—was now rendered useless on account of my rapidly ballooning mid-section.

"Don't be silly, it still looks super cute Marg," Aubrey said last night, arms akimbo as if surveying a crime scene. I sat slumped over on the edge of our bed, catching a glimpse of my wavy outline in the lengthwise mirror, eyeing the hint of rolling hill buried beneath the grey silk.

"I think you still look super-hot," he repeated as if by graduating the word "cute" to "hot" he would suddenly absolve me of any concern.

Despite this new layer that had somehow tucked itself under all corners of my life, I was determined to show my oldest and closest friend how much she meant to, not only me, but an entire house full of her friends. Friends who would soon exit their warm blanket of downtown with the usual trepidations every time they were forced to cross the glistening curve of the Lions Gate Bridge. I thought trying to get our friends to come out here in our early twenties was a challenge; now it seemed next to impossible. But a milestone birthday is a tacit contract among old friends.

Surprisingly, all the last-minute details came together just in time. With over an hour to spare before guests were set to arrive, Aubrey was dressed. This felt like a record for a man who notoriously hopped into the shower ten minutes before it was time to leave for an event or date. He chose the linen suit jacket he wore at our wedding; grey fitted trousers which groped his jogger's calves, suspenders, a slim navy tie, and a waistcoat stuffed with his grandfather's pocket square. He looked almost identical to how he did six years ago, save for the few extra pounds he had acquired.

Voices in my head tangled and collided, listing off all the things that still needed tending to. I dashed about the house dusting lamp shades, lighting scented candles, wiping countertops. All in an attempt to get closer to the vision of party perfection I had shimmering in my mind like fire.

I placed two large rose-coloured vases on either side of the mirror hanging above the mantle. Both were filled with the fresh-cut forsythia that had sprouted up from our garden with such vigor over the last month. The small golden-yellow flowers twinkled amidst the beige and grey tones of the living room, giving it a cheerful, welcoming aura. Fully aware of their lack of fragrance, I nonetheless inhaled each bundle taking in their benign earthiness.

I stared at the reflection in the mirror. I was grateful I had the foresight to get myself ready hours earlier. My dirty blonde hair was pulled back into a bun that hung low and loose, complementing the understated dress. I had been tempted to replace the dress (with one that might do a better job at disguising my first trimester thickness); instead, I chose to add a long duster jacket buttoned midway. This covered just enough to thwart any suspicions or double takes. I couldn't take any chances. I wasn't ready to answer everyone's questions about the direction of our lives right now. *How will you manage a steady income with both of your work so up in the air? Will you just work on your art while staying at home with the baby?*

I thought you guys weren't ready for kids yet?

We were still digesting everything. *I* was still digesting everything.

I secretly detected Aubrey was relieved the day we watched those double-blue lines slowly take form as the morning light poured in through the frosted glass in our bathroom window. I caught him as he tried to hide the instinctual joy in his bliss-washed eyes with his attempt at a false, crinkled brow and sudden drop in tone. Anyone else might have believed it, but I caught it.

"Oh no waaaaay," he exclaimed, holding back a sleepy laugh while scanning my eyes for a similar deep-seated bliss that perhaps I was holding hostage as well.

He was ready to have kids the minute we got married. Mind you, at thirty-six and five years older than me, Aubrey has always been different from the other men I dated. The art school grads, all of which were my age or younger, that despised anything conventional or trite. The boy-men brimming with the residue of past relationships, chain smoking their anxieties into a tar pit where they would stay until the nicotine eventually wore off.

Aubrey loved family. In fact, it was our second or third date in which he declared how excited he was to be a dad one day. It helped that his parents were still together in the same house he grew up in with his four siblings. Anytime we had a chunk of time off together he would suggest we head up to Nan and Kurt Swan's ten-acre ranch in Lillooet to "unwind a little." I now knew this was code for letting his mother pamper the hell out of him with her gloopy caraway-laden stews and nostalgic stories about how he was always such a kind-hearted little boy. Not a visit went by where his mother wasn't regaling us about the time when one Easter, Aubrey went door to door handing out geraniums he picked from his mother's front garden to all the neighbours. Although it was very much the opposite of my upbringing, I relished the technicolor details of my husband's childhood. It filled me with a misty longing that clung to my empty spaces. The nostalgia of memories I hadn't myself experienced were intoxicating. Almost addicting.

All the while they still reminded me of what wasn't.

Poetry and
Lyric Prose

Fatima Amarshi

Virginia's Wolves

Scribbling women
        roam wild

prowl through orchards
and hills
stalking reverie

they descend at night
shaking mane-fulls
of luciferin wings
on dark, leafy floors

All the wild things of the world
          shiver

Beneath a sliver of cold blue moon
    owls collude
        lending quills

feathered *diamons*   quivering   take up the scent

paper spines
        break open

a millennia of longing unleashes

        incantations
                drop
                by
                drop

tip the sea   repositioning the world

uncharted stars appear
strung   between   the brightest constellations

At the edge of the new horizon

all the wise men of the world
                              howl
At dawn

        the scribes bind their shadows to clouds
        and float
        unseen through mountain passes
        citadels   hearths   markets bustling

to children gathering

        the alchemist
        in the kitchen
        is licking
        her calloused finger
        again

mother

my love

                sails
                on apron strings

        plump onions
        garlic
        and soap

my love

                floats
                on history's debris

        ground anguish
        bitters
        peppered hope

my love

                          undulates
                          in silence

         searching
         for you
         in echoes

                         hush child

i will find you

         with the sonar

i built   into your navel

         when *i*

gave you   to the world

Sarah Amormino
Nona

Notes of subtle plum, dark amber, warm mud
infuse into my skin, soak into my bloodstream,
marinate my muscles, thick around my joints,
shield my bones and cushion my heart when I trip
and fall under, into the air of your sick lungs,
still, covered under the umbrella of velvet blue.
Lighting incense, sparking smoke that lit my senses,
my memory of you
wafts up—over our heads
up, toward the moon,
up, away from the gravity that locks us here,
up, where embellished stars are kept secret from us all.
I ground my toes into the Earth's wet, grit
to better feel your hands
tight around my ankles.
You pull me deeper so that I sink
into notes of subtle plum,
dark amber, warm mud.

Salt

the taste of sour lemons cut
salt
into a wound of open flesh
left by a burning shot
swallowed seeds I did not see
turns spark into flame when
it boils in the pit of my
stomach, the ache
feels like a bullet
hush my body calms, turning acid into gas
it's only
tequila

Sicily

Sun drips lava onto the fig trees
Deep purples, soft greens
Weeping families
Warmed and wet with honey
Basil on my plate
Soft vines twist the melody of cascades in the heat
Sweat with shadows cast
Goose bumps on my skin
Vines of grapes are singing chords
Summer's salty winds
Watermelon season
Pouring down my chin
Autumn's breeze is knocking
Begging to come in

Leslie Jenneson

Here's What
You Must Do

I wonder if others wake up as I do
          considering
what will endure and what will not and why
          or maybe
what is real and what is not real or maybe even

what is good and

          what is not good

those bright circles you cannot climb out of
          (why don't others scream when their eyes shut closed to
          the light why don't others scream when their eyes

          shut)

here's what you must do:
          press your flushed cheek to the cold tiled floor
          stay there
          not until your face cools but
until your body makes the earth as warm as you are
until the earth takes from you
          some heat

Today, Soup

today I was making soup:

  mild green in colour   cutting up herbs
  like basil and coriander
                  and also lemongrass and

I found myself hitting (the stalk of the lemongrass) with the heel of my
knife
  for a little too long
    and perhaps a little too hard

(it was a)   cathartic pounding

                  (it was)   not harmless

and of course we know the result:

        sweet aroma fragrance rising

sometimes grief shows up this way

Poem for Sleepless Nights

this is also meditation:

      consider now the feverish scurry of rats in dark alleys
      the raccoons who hide behind dumpsters and scream
      and the woman you saw that day howling naked in the street

every moment is holy

      remember now how it feels to run your hand down the
      belly of a salmon

      remember now how smoke looks in the night sky
      when it hangs cold and suspended

      remember now this humming silence

listen to it

It Is Wonderful to Contemplate that Infinite Variety of Creation

I fold my hands and watch
  the shaggy haired rooster as he
crows morning into existence
  his flesh like gullet shaking in the aftermath
          makes me laugh

the wind
  she needs no accompaniment

there is pig sauntering
  she is pregnant
  has straw hair
  vibrating low-toned snorts

sheep who are studious
     and thick
         earthy
    walking in packs

the chickens come running
      their small eyes myriad shades of glowing oranges,
reds
      like sunset

in the distance someone is cutting through wood

and there is black bull
  standing solitary in a field of snow

Kurt Trzcinski

Five love poems

I.

There was a wind today
pushing rain
so the *plick* and *tuck* came
from one window
then the other

I worked at a screen
words lit from behind
to reach my eye and I wanted
the old page lighted by a yellow lamp

I had to turn
to look at water running
braided streamlets
down the window panes
I was not with the cedar, dark clouds, or mud

But with you
your last smile
the shake of your curls
and what I caught in your eyes
in our goodbye

2.

A grey-blue pain
mixed with orange-red longing
pumped to my fingers, my toes
breath exchanges this colour
with the light green of new buds in spring

And I cannot name it

Bricks carry silence
the union of fungi and algae
grows a wider ring
on marble gravestones

I know I am alive
that coffee has not lost its bitterness
and the lemon is yellow

I know not despair
but some strange love
a foreign taste
a kindness uninhibited
a wondrous comet more golden
than the daffodils to come

3.

When you stand before another
you must share what you deeply hold
what shakes the ground
to hold onto something stable
you fear
you reach
you heed
not to be alone

This suffering creates a third leg
that stops the swing of the land
and the fall of your mind
you behold the face before you
as a hope that you are known
you exist
and are not alone

4.

You are the deer walking to water's edge

You bob your head
lower then higher
your ears search
in front, then behind

The soft forest light
touches your shoulder
     a golden red-brown
     a tenderness of safety

You take another step
closer to river's edge
where the cedar bough reaches over
almost touching

And I ripple past
     always gone
     always present
making the last step muddy and cool
before you drink

5.

How much pain
do you have
can you put it on the table
can you place it there
before me   before us

The risk of letting go
your secret
becoming ours

a trembling leaf
not knowing but—now—

not unknown
to the wind

This gift
drowning together
now forcing, shifting apart
I am now the crack and fissure
splintering your eye
as I reach across the table
for your hand
to put my fingers
into the darkness of your palm
and believe in you

Cara Waterfall

Abidjan Aubade

Roadside,
doleful icons
glisten, listening
in the penumbra
of green
tarpaulins

A Madonna
beseeches,
swaddled in blue,
eight pale replicas
at her feet, bleached
folds of taffeta
flecked
with soot

Men crouch
on a strip
of cracked tarmac,
palms touching mat,
as bats slouch
toward the city
in the close-mouthed
dawn

The cathedral
looms, entreats
the lagoon
with a quaver
of prayers,
its concrete regalia
made radiant
by morning
In silken pews,
women fan faces,
bright as July,
as a crimson ellipsis
of lips assails psalms
an octave below
a siren's wail,
each syllable
swabbing
the stained glass
clean

Waking rituals
array the day
with elaborate intention
            until the unshackled sun
unravels grace   and
            makes a wreck of them
        and they melt
                into the bright unrest
                                of morning

emerge 2017

Fanicos: The Laundrymen of Banco

Abidjan, Côte d'Ivoire

I see
a fleet of men
in frothing water, waist deep;
clothes implacable as weeds
clinging
to the scant banks of Banco Forest:
flotsam of the laundryman
gilds the sky
and eye

Ode to the Peacock

for Esther; Accra, Ghana

Who can resist the wing's satin ripple, the virile fringe of quills? Behold the cobalt crest, the opal cummerbund, the gaudy centerfold of tail. And how you brim with vim! Hubris hatches from your plump body. You prance, as if to say, fawning is expected. (An *ostentation* of peacocks— how appropriate.) But, foppish pheasant, you do have flaws. Fussy and aloof, you rebuff ducks and chickens. You inhale orchid blooms, leaving the roots destitute in their charcoal beds. You badger the cook for rolled oats, burnt toast, papaya shells— scraps incompatible with a bird of your stature. Lesser aviator, you're prone to pratfalls; puny wings labour to achieve lift-off. You schlep from roof to roof, splatter excrement, then split, spindly legs in tow. Some days, you roam the parking lot; others, you stalk the perimeter of our hotel room—feathered gargoyles uncoiling your tinfoil necks each time I unlatch the door. But is there more to your blast and bluff? Does such conceit hide secrets? The owner of this hotel told me a story. There was a woman who lived here for a year, who fed you every day—first on the balcony, then in her room. Three years later, you must remember: voice lush as grass, palms gloved in breadcrumbs. Three years later, bright kingdoms of want still unspool; hope sustained by any rosy constellation behind the pane.

Natasha Sanders-Kay
The Pool

swollen dancer feet walk

to an indoor pool

free of people
full of baby blue

clean chlorine scent
after hours of Ruby Slippers stench
choke of cologne alcoholic air
ten o'clock shift hazed in beer sweat heat

she slips in
enveloped in buttered turquoise
electric aquamarine

blood-rush   endorphin dance

more intoxicating than
brown and green bills
candy martinis
loud pop trance
dancing

scissoring wildly
she spreads   seals   spreads   seals   her legs

froggy swim
flying-bird freedom

emerges seal-slick
envying droplets
fall
from
fingers easy escape

mermaid arc of back
she dips back under
no poles in here
bends in ballet poses

        teasing no one
here the only eyes are her own   wide open
                 chemical sting

wisps of her hair tinged seaweed-green

                                wave

              swirl
warm wet glow

           pink of outstretched fingers in blue

            trail
                star-bubbles

everything
            empty silk

       she slows
             kicks

               floats

near-naked in water's palm

this planet of a pool

by herself

Stephen T. Berg
Lead Boots, Blue Sky

For a sky this blue you need lead boots to keep from flying
up. I learned the hard way: One morning I stepped outside,
looked heavenward, noted the sheer depth of blue and began
to rise. I reached for the leader of the spruce tree by our front
step but wasn't equal to the magnitude of lift and it slipped
through my fingers. I gathered speed. Our house shrunk. The
city became a cerulean map with microdots moving along
fading lines. The air was a vast sea that sought to push me to
its surface. An indigo intensity deepened as the oceans came
into view. The curve of the earth tightened and I was lost in
azure. I shut my eyes, focused on the fawn-browns of
fall—clamorous trains of ultramarine still steamed through my
mind. Approaching the poison shores of ether, I breathed,
released, mused on shades of earth while rapidly repeating a
string of mantras that came, as it were, out of the blue—soil,
summer-fallow, clay, loam, dust, humus—and flew straight
down with such speed I'd have shattered the sidewalk. But I
invoked the gods of green, came mindful of verdant grass
swaying in mesic rangeland; I channelled canola fields in
bright citrine bloom and floated slow as a winged seed,
landing on our front step. Deb was just coming out of the
bathroom and asked if I would make eggs for breakfast,
sunny-side up, which was peculiar, as she always prefers
scrambled. I said I was happy to make eggs, but needed to go
shopping later. At the scuba diving store I asked if they
carried any lead boots.

The sales lady said, "We only have one pair left."

"I'd like to buy them," I said.

"You're the ninth person this week to buy lead boots! What's going on?"

"I don't know but I will need them when my meditation is off."

"God," she said, reaching for her purple scarf.

"I love this town."

Approaching the 45th American Presidency

I leave Planet Earth Poetry at Hillside Coffee
after listening to an enjambment of poets
fervently consider the current state
     of the American presidency,
and on my way home remember I need to prepare
and marinate
the chicken for tomorrow night's dinner,
     that's the chicken
I bought from Drumpf Meats earlier in the day
that I thought (although I didn't ask)
was fresh-fresh, but was in fact alternatively-fresh,
as I found remnant formations of ice crystals
     in the cramped cavity,
and the oblique neck, stuffed within, was polar-stiff,
and the gelid giblets, notably the orange-hued heart,
     was glacial-cold,
meaning this or more: that the bird hadn't come straight
from the abattoir
to its place behind glass, but had spent time in cryogenic rime,
and I remembered too,
     that a chicken
can live without its head for an ungodly duration,
which beyond all reason,
made me approach the fridge
with unimpeachable apprehension.

Geography of Injury

*For Connie Howard (1956-2016), whose fight with cancer forced her
to withdraw from TWSO; whose own writing, courage, and
plain-spoken honesty continues to inspire.*

She looks east
    across swells
    of plain
    broken bodies
    of grassland
    fold into
    valleys dark
    with wolf
    willow and
    buckbrush

Her landscape hidden
    lesions gape
    beneath lime
    and clay
    where rivers
    of rain
    vanish into
    fathomless
    caverns

Her body knows
        abyssal sea
        of injury
        hardpan
        horizon
        of pain
        that prayer
        cannot
        penetrate

Viola Prinz

Pedestrian

Eyes to earth   two   three steps per
square of concrete   careful
not to step on lines   break
my spine on give way signs

It comes in matte black   fire red
an exhaust of silent dreams
I wait   three four
a city in single file
creeping in increments   skip
over the crack   don't look back
no time for pause   I'm obsolete

I offer my plea to traffic gods   samaritans
skylarks   crickets   wish myself   away
with pollen   become something new
like spindrift in a desert

I feel it pass through me   lift
heel   from   sole   no more
counting   squares minutes in circles
while   there   my shoes
a pair   alone   still wait where
paths and forks and lives
converge

Pelicans

look up from the traffic haze
of morning monotony.

forget what blindness
you woke with.

the sweeping curve
of a black-tipped wing
tilts left over the river road
and the clumsy release
of feet, webbed and wobbly,
lands, a fleck of orange
on a narrow perch,
where the cream sliver
of a waxing gibbous moon
fades into pale blue
behind each sinuous neck
as they fold into snaking
letters, tuck ballooning
bills to breast, bellies full
of sun-kissed fish.

see how they sleep,
unperturbed on streetlights—
feathered zeppelins,
bright silhouettes
against the circuitry
of haste.

sunset swim

a girl plays with her dad on a beach
peals of laughter on the sand

a couple dances with the waves
taunting teal swirls of undercurrent

a woman sits alone on a crumbling dune
as if waiting for a friend

a towel strewn across the shore
collects shells with mauve edges

a dripping dog runs ahead
debossing murky trails

a daughter cartwheels into the swell
salt tangled in strawberry curls

a head bobs above the restless surface
mistaken for a buoy

a cloud passes dusty pink
over the sea of half-buried sandals

the sound of a car

that familiar turn of ignition,
a stifled cough in your throat,
that sweep of steering wheel,
your palms skim together,
that soft murmur of engine
like the hum of your voice,
that gearbox in slow crescendo,
the cadence of your laugh,
that crunch of gravel, scratching
stubble against my skin,
that rush of air, its audible speed
a sigh from your lips

I wait for the squeak
of brakes, the rumbling quiet,
of an idle car; a thump
of door, a jingle of keys,
the gate closing with a clang.
I almost recognize the scrape
of your foot, loose shoelaces
click on concrete, the soft tick
of your watch, your ruffling
cotton sleeve, reaching—
coming home

Graham McGarva
The Estrangers–1971

Not with a bang but a whimper, is where the necessary comes—the "Revenge of the Moderate Man." But first, the prelude, a memory from his youth, when it could have all have turned out so different.

The third time I nearly got killed,
was deliberate;
stalked by wounded honour with a switch blade.

In the middle, I fell back to sleep.
My girlfriends didn't,
Jane and her sister tensely awake
the second night in a row,
as a Tunisian schoolteacher
lurched around the park,
flashlight shining in startled faces,
and in his other hand
the forward thrusting glint of a long knife.

We had surrounded ourselves
with six strapping German lads.
but my prudence was exhausted,
I wanted sleep more than anxiety.
So, it was a jolt in the blue-black night
to awake to Fran's hissed whisper
"He's coming round again";
his flashlight ranging indiscriminately

over our couple dozen of the hitchhiking class,
too broke or too late,
for bunks in the Paris youth hostel.

The previous night the three of us,
coddled teens despite the roads we travelled,
had shared wine and bread and cheese
with a swarthy trio from Tunis.
Didn't mean that much to us,
to mean that much to them.
So, night time in the park,
one of the men puts his sleeping bag down
close to my girlfriend's sister,
and puts his hands down even closer.
And then closer,
her protestations only urging him on.

The night before that,
seeking shelter,
no room at the hostel for Jane, me, and her
voluptuous, tempestuous, (better-not-let-Jane-see-me
glancing-sideways-at-her) sixteen-year-old sister;
we had walked off with four Arab guys
down one too many dark roads for comfort.
Let us say I misunderstood their Arabic,
their intention to foster international relations—
but as we ran away,
I felt hung, drawn, and quartered;

As I would two months later on the Beirut waterfront,
when discussion of sharing some red Lebanese hash,
led me away from the suggested rendezvous—

199

the better to protect my by-then ex-girlfriend.

On this night I was being stalked,
"I will kill you"
was the teacher's explicit promise
when I called him an Arab pig,
in the grounds of the Paris youth hostel
at the gathering of dusk.

Amazing how the mild expletive "pig,"
translated into electrifying effect,
uttered in French to an Arab.
He only wanted one of the two girls,
he didn't mind which, the blonde or the brunette,
either would satisfy his wanderlust;
they both had drunk his wine, eaten his bread,
were friendly, laughing and smiling—
with skirts almost higher than their thighs,
(dark bulges of their womanhood beckoning him in.)

Going to fetch our sleeping bags
from the pitch-black store room,
We circled, not wanting our bags slit nor stolen,
heart pounding, eyes burning,
like cats warily stalking a kill.
"Not all Arabs are pigs",
turned out to be my magic password,
as I brought our three backpacks to the park,
where we rounded up our Aryan circle.
Nothing more unifying than us against them.
So, I slept. I hadn't signed on for terminal anxiety.
According to Jane and Fran, he had left by dawn.

(Perhaps his battery ran out, I would have said,
if not embarrassed by a good night's sleep,
surrendering watch to the others.)

Too early for breakfast, I went to the washbasins.
Only one other person at the long steel trough.
Of course it was him, shaving,
white Father Christmas of foam, razor in his right hand.
I couldn't resist and set up right beside him.
He turned, looked, gathered his kit and marched out,
his white ruff resplendent in defeat,
as scared as I of the rising stakes.

Now I felt weary of this treadmill—
stereotypes of otherness,
of worlds imperfectly colliding and misunderstood.

In the cafeteria, I found my adversary's two companions,
apologized for misunderstanding.
They told me he was a schoolteacher,
kind and gentle at home, close to his faith.
He should not have been drinking, could not hold it,
had mistaken friendship for opportunity,
when he found I was neither brother nor husband.
But this was another country, a long way from home.

To get to Beirut,
we hitchhiked through Turkey to Syria.
At the frontier,
having brushed aside the Syrian border guard,
refusing to pay his bribe,
we were instructed by the Captain

to carry a plain clothes policeman to the next city.
Gathering darkness and consternation,
not a word of shared language between us,
we rode into a dark, dark place.

Motioned with authority to wait at the sidewalk,
minutes dragged into ages.
Jane, the French driver and I
considered escape across the desert.

The policeman re-appeared,
led us up three flights of single light-bulb gloom.
I was thinking that by now
I should have learned to read the signals,
only mildly encouraged this wasn't Tunis.

The door opened
to a room with carpets and a low table.
As we sat down to the largest bowl of strawberries,
I could see,
behind the not fully closed door to the bedroom,
the smiles on his two children,
the pride behind the veil of his wife.

The embrace of strangers

takes   many forms

Junie Désil

Broken

A condensed version

Part i

[January 12, 2010.

magnitude 7.0   —aftershocks—52 registers

after.   shock.]

    white church spire   toppled
    askew

    damned accusation   surrounded
    by coloured rubble—colonial pinks

    pastels   white sugar dust
    coated

    bodies, hills
    pile like blankets

    broken wails broken hymns
    shattered lives

broken prayer   like the white
church spire toppled

heavenwards   the hope
these broken bodies

piled like blankets   the land
too broken   too scarred

to cradle
a last embrace

families on knees
send prayers

upwards   the sun   God
hastens the breaking of

skin, tissues, cells, ligaments
overwhelming streets, morgues

mass graves   (un)intended holocaust
damned accusation surrounds

coloured rubble—colonial pinks
pastels and white sugar   dust coated

prayers, broken hymns,
broken bodies held aloft

church spire pointing out the
sins of their parents revisited

Part ii

[the seismic fault line runs through the island of Hispaniola.
the fault lies in the people]

televangelist Pat Robertson:

pact to the devil   those
Haitians … under the heel of the French

you know, Napoleon III and whatever.
And they got together and

swore a pact to the devil

they said

we will serve you if you will

set us free

from the French   true story

and so the devil said

ok it's a deal …

but ever since, they have been cursed
by one thing after the other

true story

Part iii

[From *The New Yorker* May 10, 2010
Queen Latifah, appearing on the *Today* show:
I want to just go and get some of them babies.
If you got the hookup, please get me a couple of Haitian kids.

On the US State Department website someone writes:
I would love to take about twenty or more kids in my home.]

in the aftermath of the magnitude 7.0 earthquake   how to
make *operation babylift**

operational again:

don't worry about lawsuits trauma dna tests (or not) living relatives
too poor to keep their kids   relatives too overwhelmed (and too poor)
to take in their relatives' kids
don't worry that the island's infrastructure can't actively and ethically
support international

                    (crisis) adoption
instead:

take advantage of the chaos—*it's better for everyone* rescue these poor orphaned children empty orphanages within the month   don't ask
 or look for potential relatives
never mind legal documents—proof—of who they are who their parents are

leave children in legal limbo when people change their minds

put them in American (or similar) juvenile centres – because
no one wants to deal with the

        legal   nightmare

what is clear (perhaps) 2000 (approximately) Haitian kids who may or
may not have been orphans   put on chartered flights   with (or without) papers   accompanied (in some instances) by ministers   US gov-
ernors   anyone with money   to burn

        and a private jet

*Between April 3rd and 26th, 1975 more than ten thousand Vietnamese
children were evacuated and adopted around the world at the end of the
war. It was not in the best interest of the children and not all of the children were in fact orphaned.

Mak Berry

Grief

grief that grew
    into river lilies
        despite the tide
            reside strong
           from dusk
               till dawn
                  fly or fall

                        time won't heal
                        wounds that go ignored

                grief knows only
                  the breath
                  you breathe into it

            you must bud from bulb
              to bloom
the presence the pretense the pain
 the beauty the bravery the beginning
    to be feeling the past
        and reeling the future

            beautiful is the becoming of
                river lilies

Wish

wishing you'd told
me
knowing why you
didn't
claiming you
couldn't
seeing you
should've
when cowardice
overtook
when love kept
you shook
you wished away
kept secrets
tamed realities
into tales

still i knew no
different

saved me from the
truth of you
(wish i didn't
miss the old you)

Story

"Once I was a little girl wishing for a grown-up world. Now I sit,
adulthood blessing from my fingertips, in angst and awe,
throwing myself at a past I cannot visit."

Story Facts:
> Lies. Love. Lies.
> Lies to family. Lies to friends.
> Gut over manipulation.
> Thoughts fade. Words brand.
> He won. Still losing.
> Hatred. Regurgitate. Reality.

Accept missing who he told me he was.
Understand deception is the villain/not the world.

Story Arc:
> Habitually healing.
> Refuse the monster.
> Rinse. Relapse. Rage. Revision.
> Repeat till ready.
> Rewrite to how self sees fit.
> Move on with the story.

[once.I.was.a.little.girl.wishing.for.a.[DELETE]]

"I do not belong to the system and the system does not belong to me.
The system is not for me and I am not for the system."

No More

Wouldn't *you know what* love is, you genius of human
emotion, you. To rewind humanity's mistakes ten times over
just to *watch it fall* at your feet again. *Plead* ing, *bleed* ing
just for you only, always. Craving your soft imprinting thumbs
to press *to* temples, *awash* ing *all that was* n't supposed to
bruise but did. *Because* wouldn't you know, as you've always
shouted to know, what love is.

sOrRy hoNeY, i doN't giVe A DAmN no MoRe

Before Us

Beyond Humanity
swathed in sea salt
stones shimmered
under smooth tides
tails swam idle as gills exhaled
bubbles tossed past inhaling reefs
twisting toward an endless blue ceiling
meeting sky and sea as one

doe's hooves sink into shores
bird's whistle after flight
moss held heavy from branches
wooed waves sing

seagulls dip brush strokes
into water
beaks peck birch into flakes
that fall and float
onto spotted backs and antlers

tranquil ease oozes
flower's sharp scent
destruction's absence
natural world mid-motion
in creature's creativity
at peace
Before Us

Paolo Marcazzan

Elemental Analysis

Surely under duress
one can crop the dictionary, decant it
into honed sediment.

This aspect of precipitation
on the way to substance
purification.

Or was it sentiment.

Work in stillness, cold,
trespass saturation.
As near to immobility

and the wan
long time of restraint, slow
evaporation. Then harvest.

Be II

Thin ice you were.
Walking on no surprise.
Then, not that you.
Should think only.
Spring veining to cause.
To slip through some.
Skittish excuse to call.
Life out on its cracks.
You will find several.
Accounts for this, and that.
Is a thing we can explore.
As your wish makes you.
Content not unambiguous.
Depending on stressed.
Syllable the foot shifts.
And colours, not you.
Who has to decide.
What's in it or isn't.
The truth or close to.
A version of it that.
Be it iamb or trochee.
It will be matter.
Of disposition or will.

Christine Leviczky Riek

The Water Moth

*Excerpts from a docu-poetry manuscript about the lives of the
author's ancestors in the Carpathian Mountains of Central Europe*

Conscriptio et Urbarium—1782, 1735

nothing but strange
old reports to shape my
little girl stories

ahol volt
ahol nem volt

the days of sheep and goats
oak and beech forests fattened
pigs and linseed oil

ahol volt
ahol nem volt

the days of dry
meadows steep valleys birch
trees and a small creek
with one mottled water moth
nymphula nymphaeata

Military Reconnaissance—1782

the village is in a valley
surrounded on both
sides by high
places
7)

the road through
high places
is very
steep
6)

the road through the
valley is slightly
better
6)

the road to the next village is not at all busy 6)

if
you
travel
through
the forest stay
on the marked cart
path
4)

STATISTICS AND GEOGRAPHY—1837, 1901

in the mountainous wooded countryside
live catholics and jews   [current status]
[3rd ed.] with not one foreigner among them
a water mill and a beautiful forest
men and women, some with their hair
down, or without women, or together
in a house, wood mostly
stone, brick, or sticks
if they hadn't heard the tale; many
missing   [current status] for the   [3rd ed.]

[evidence]
[manifest of alien immigrant]
:

age   thirty   eight   cannot   read   or   write   crippled
left   side   spinal   curvature   dislocated
limb   smallpox   marks   four   feet   ten   inches
tall   eight   dollars   at   the   port   of   new york
destination   pennsylvania   [1901 ed.]

SEARCHING FOR ANNA—FEBRUARY 1847

Friday, February 5th, Anna	1 year, smallpox
Sunday, February 7th, Anna	3 ½ years, smallpox
Monday, February 8th, Anna	8 years, smallpox
Tuesday, February 16th, Anna	50 years, illegible
Saturday, February 20th, Anna	67 years, starvation

result: unsuccessful

[nyugodjék békében]

A Place—n.d.

where someone will ask
for more money
than I want to give

to tell me so little

        delivered with an unspoken promise

to never tell me more

                    it is too much
                    to talk about

and the words
are gone

Non-fiction

Kimberley Phillips Boehm

Leaping into the Warm Air

AN EXCERPT FROM
"GROWING UP A BLACK ARMY BRAT"

My first memories of life as a black army brat began when we moved to Fort Benning, which was outside of Columbus, Georgia. My two brothers and I were some of the millions of U.S. military brats born during the Vietnam War years. Along with our mothers, the military classified us as our fathers' dependents. Maybe we got named brats after the acronym used by the British military, which called the children of soldiers British Regiment Attached Travelers.

My father was commissioned as a U.S. Army officer in 1958. By the time I was born two years later, he'd already attended Jump School at Fort Benning. From the time he became an officer, through the late 1970s, he was one of the few black officers in the Army.

In 1963, he volunteered to be a paratrooper and became a specialist in high altitude jumping. As one of the elite amongst the paratroopers, he was reassigned to the reactivated 173rd Infantry Brigade based at Fort Benning where he became one of the thousands of Sky Soldiers—fighting soldiers from the sky. People wrote songs and made movies about these men, "fearless men who jump and die." In the early morning, I heard their feet thunder as they ran miles in full combat gear. I didn't know it then, but he helped prepare paratroopers in the 173rd for the largest combat parachute assault into Vietnam. I wasn't quite four years old.

We lived in a three bedroom brick home, one of the hundreds of quarters reserved for officers. On our block, which ended in a cul-de-sac, all the men were captains in either the Airborne or the Armor Brigades. Though the nearby city of Columbus remained stubbornly segregated, the base was fully integrated.

Most of our mothers had college degrees, but they spent their time trying to keep us clean and fed while we moved like locusts from one house to another, slamming screen doors as we left. We went to the same schools. We swam together in the post pools. In the Georgia summer evenings, we played Kick the Can in the street until the mosquitoes chased us inside.

We roamed the nearby streets and pine forests playing war games. We wore castoff Korean War helmets and played with gutted bazookas and grenades. We kept our toys in old World War ii footlockers, their musty smells seeping into my dolls' fake hair and plastic skin. Most of us had German Shepherd puppies, the ones too small to be scout dogs in Vietnam. Our fathers named them after famous generals and the dogs joined us on our adventures. Daddy named our puppy Beauregard, but we called him Beau.

We played with other toys besides bazookas and grenades. We'd lived in Germany before we came to Georgia, so our toys were mostly European. The kids on the block especially loved our metal Matchbox cars, which we kept in an orange bucket outside our back door. We took the cars into the woods, cleared the debris from under the trees and built roads and bridges out of twigs and Lincoln Logs. If we weren't home, our friends took the bucket into the woods and returned it when they finished.

One day, the bucket disappeared. We found it later that day, broken and empty. My father came out with us to look for the cars. Beau sniffed the trees and needles as we searched through the grass and bushes. Then Beau sniffed the bucket and he bolted for the street towards the Medina's quarters. My father followed him and that's how we found out what happened to our cars.

My father told us to stay on the sidewalk and ordered Beau to sit. He knocked on the door and Captain Ernie Medina answered. My 6'2" father, his legs in a wide stance, loomed over him. Beau snarled and growled, but my father didn't tell him to stop. We heard the Captain yell at his kids to go find our trucks. Evidently, the middle kid admitted he'd taken the bucket out into the woods and emptied it, throwing the cars so we couldn't find them.

Before the cars disappeared, Daddy had told us not to play with the Medina kids, but he never said why. Anyway, after the incident with them, Beau growled at them and they stayed away. Soon after, Captain Medina got orders for Vietnam and the family moved. Years later we saw pictures of Captain Medina on the evening news. During what became known as the My Lai Massacre, the military charged him—and others under his command—with numerous charges of murdering civilians.

⁔

Not long after I started kindergarten, one of the kids in my class warned us that if our fathers came home early, it meant he had orders for Vietnam. As more men received orders, the kids and their mothers on our block moved away to live with their families. Soon, I heard my parents discuss the deaths of one man or another in Vietnam.

When I came home from school around noon each day, I began to watch the clock, hoping my father would not come home early. I refused to take a nap and I sat by the front door. Sometimes I sat in the driveway and I'd start to cry when he arrived at his usual time. Another day, and he didn't have his orders—yet.

One Saturday, I woke from my nap weeping and calling for my father. Suddenly, he appeared and picked me up, asking if I wanted to go see a movie. When we got there, the theater was filled with young men watching a black-and- white film of men jumping out of the back of a huge airplane. Their translucent parachutes filled the screen and looked like the jellyfish I'd seen in *National Geographic*. As each man leapt into the air, the men in the theater stomped their feet and yelled "Airborne!" over and over.

After my special trip to the movies, my oldest brother, Tony, demanded to see a real jump. Daddy agreed and after that, Tony and Kenny—an older boy in our neighborhood—started leaping out of the pine trees behind our quarters. The boys used ropes to pull themselves up to the lowest branches and then yelled "airborne" as they fell into the piles of pine needles below.

My brother wouldn't let me jump out of the trees, so I had to resort to my own training regimen. I decided to test out the slide at school. My first jump was more spontaneous than planned and I didn't properly prepare my landing site. After I climbed the steps of the slide, I looked down its gleaming metal surface and glanced to my left, spotting the sandy ground below. I don't recall the leap, but I do recall the small crowd of kindergarteners gathered around me as I sat with sand up my smocked pinafore dress. Eyewitnesses assured the teachers I didn't hit my head. I was embarrassed and proud all at once. I'd managed to survive the jump, but I couldn't remember if I shouted "Airborne!" as I leapt out into the warm air.

That night, when my mother tucked me into bed, I told her about a little girl in my class who fell off the slide.

"Oh, Kimmy, did she get hurt?"

"No, Mommy, it wasn't a long fall and she was brave, like the soldiers."

She kissed me and left the room. But she returned later, this time to tell me my teacher called to see how I was doing. Yes, I admitted, I was the little girl who fell. My mother called my father into my room. Did I need to go to the Emergency Room? What if I had a concussion? Did I feel like I needed to vomit? Neither one asked me why I'd lied or commented about how I made my first practice jump.

Not long after my failed jump, my father came home with his news. Mama's knees buckled and she fainted on the floor. I'd just come home from kindergarten and I still wore my school clothes. Chicken soup simmered on the stove for our lunch. Daddy stood there in his khaki uniform, his arms at his side. He said "I'm sorry" over and over again as he helped her to the couch. Later that night, Daddy took a picture of Tony, Michael—my younger brother—and me, our arms wrapped around each other, our eyes wide.

We watched Daddy roll his fatigues into the dark green duffle bag with the maps of Vietnam encased in thick plastic. He checked his parachutes, field boots, and helmet. Then he packed them with his canteens, ammunition belt, and holster. Daddy sent these bags with the hundreds of soldiers leaving on a train for San Francisco where he'd meet them after he drove us to Los Angeles.

We worried about how my father would get to Vietnam and my mother bought a globe to show us Daddy's route. She took my finger and traced a line from San Francisco across the Pacific and west towards Vietnam.

"It's a long trip," she said.

"How will he go?" Tony asked.

"By ship."

The movers packed everything in a rush, including my favorite doll, Teeny Tiny Thumbelina. I'd left her near the suitcases we'd take in the car. As I grabbed at the door of the moving van, Daddy promised to find her. After he sorted through so many boxes and she was nowhere to be found, Mama told him to stop.

"You'll see her soon," she said to me. "Besides, Daddy needs to drive us to Los Angeles, buy a house, and get you enrolled in new schools."

Daniela Cohen

These Walls

AN EXCERPT FROM A MEMOIR

On the first day of Grade 10, I couldn't wait to get to school. It was 1993 in Johannesburg and the public schools across South Africa had just opened their doors to students of other races. Until then, my school had been all white. Greenside High was located in a leafy suburb down the street from one of the largest golf courses in the city. The school was enclosed by high walls and a big black gate that opened to let us in at the start of the day, and out at the end.

I was one of a handful of Jewish kids. During religious education classes, we sat in a separate room with booklets on the noteworthy aspects of Judaism to complete.

At recess, Lesley and Judy tried to convince me of Jesus's status as God's son and the existence of Hell for sinners. I told them there was no such thing in the Jewish religion, but they wouldn't listen.

I had latched onto Lesley and Judy as familiar primary school faces after my best friends went to different high schools. But I knew I was not like them; I wanted to get to know people who were different from me, not convert them.

My great grandparents fled to South Africa from Russia to escape religious persecution. My grandfather arrived in Johannesburg as a teenager. His mother battled to feed nine children and he never forgot how it felt to struggle to survive. He became a doctor and worked in Soweto, Johannesburg's largest township. He used to walk 27 km through the suburbs—filled with large houses and spacious gardens hidden behind electric fences—to the rows of tin shacks that lined the streets of

Soweto. Every day he walked from one world to the other. He was one of few white doctors who ventured into the townships at that time and people lined up outside the makeshift clinic to see him. They called him Doctor Number One. He was my role model.

So far, high school life had not been everything I hoped for. I still craved interesting friends who would value our differences. Most of all, I longed for an African peer. I was tired of living in a country where the majority of people were black, while the only black person I knew was our maid, Hilda. Today I was determined to cross the divide and make friends with a black person.

I stood in the quad dressed in my summer uniform. Sweat from both heat and anticipation dampened my white blouse and green pleated skirt. Teachers called out names and we lined up behind them. I stood with Judy and watched to see who else would be in our class. I craned my neck over the crowd, searching for the new black students. I waited to see where they would go. Two black girls walked up to our line, Nandi and Zobhule.

The bell rang as we entered the first class, English. Nandi sat in the desk behind me. My heart raced. My moment to make a black friend had arrived. I turned around.

"I'm Daniela."

Neat, short curls framed Nandi's light brown face. Alert brown eyes examined me from behind her glasses.

"Hi."

The bell rang and Judy bolted to our next class. I walked with Nandi down the long, grey corridor.

"Where do you live?" I asked.

"Orlando West."

The name meant nothing to me.

"In Soweto," she added, at my blank expression.

I had imagined the township as one big area. I had no idea it had different parts. She described a neighbourhood that sounded relatively well-off, like the Sandton, Johannesburg's fanciest suburb of Soweto.

This didn't fit into my TV-constructed schema where all shacks were created equal.

"How do you get to school?"

"I take the bus. There's a bus that brought us here this morning and will take us back again in the afternoon."

"Oh ... How long does it take?"

"It's an hour each way."

"An hour!"

"Yes."

My mother drove me to school. I did bus back—to a friend's house—where I waited until my mother finished work. But that bus ride was only twenty minutes.

The next day, I waited for Nandi between classes and Nandi waited for Zobhule, who moved at her own leisurely pace. Zobhule's stylishly combed, straightened hair framed her wide, dark-skinned face. We walked side by side to our next class—Zobhule, me, and Nandi in-between. Nandi switched from Zulu to English to converse with both of us. Sometimes I nodded when they spoke Zulu, pretending I understood.

Near the end of the first term, I turned on the TV to news about Chris Hani. Hani was the head of the South African Communist Party and an icon for young blacks in the townships. He had been shot by a far-right extremist outside his front door. Four days after Hani's death, thousands of black workers went on strike. Police and protesters clashed. Over five hundred people were injured. Seventeen people died. Images of flames, blood, and broken glass flashed on the screen night after night. The country hovered on the verge of a civil war. In a national broadcast, Nelson Mandela urged people of all races to stand together against violence and move toward the only feasible solution—the democratic government the people had long been waiting for. His plea prevented the country from falling over the edge.

During this time, Nandi and Zobhule didn't come to school. I wondered if Nandi was okay. I had no phone number, no way of getting in touch. As days went by, I had nightmares about her caught in the crossfire in Soweto. I missed her laugh.

When they returned, I didn't know what to say. So much had happened.

"Are you okay?"

Nandi paused, then looked at me with tired eyes. "I'm okay."

I waited for more, but it didn't come. I never mentioned it again. What had I expected? We lived on different sides of the country's reality, and this was a conversation neither of us was prepared to have.

The next day, I walked with Nandi and Zobhule between classes. This time, Zobhule walked in the middle. She spoke to Nandi in Zulu. Nandi didn't look at me. I walked silently beside them. I didn't understand what had changed.

A few days later, Zobhule didn't show up for school.

"Can I sit?" Nandi asked during our break. She joined me on the wall in the sun.

"Sorry for the other day. It's hard ..." I raised my eyes to meet hers. "They call me a coconut."

"What do you mean?"

"You know, the way I talk, my pop music ... Zobhule and the others say I'm black on the outside, but white on the inside. They won't stop teasing me. The more you and I talk, the worse it gets."

I was silent for a moment. "Nandi, I didn't know—that is so stupid!"

Nandi shrugged and moved a pebble along the ground with the toe of her shoe. The bell rang and we moved silently to our next class.

At the beginning of the April break, the girls in my class made plans to visit each other during the holidays. I said goodbye to Nandi at the school gate. We got on our separate busses—mine to Blairgowrie, hers to Soweto. I never asked Nandi to my house and she never asked me to hers.

Thinking back, I don't know how I would have felt if she had visited me at home. How could she have sat at the kitchen table and had lunch served by our maid? And, although I was curious to see where she lived, how comfortable would I have felt as a young white girl in an all-black area where violence often flared up without warning?

I wonder if she ever thought about seeing me outside of school. She never mentioned it. I don't know what her parents would have thought of the idea. I know my mother would never have driven me into Soweto.

I wonder what her house looked like, if going there or her coming to my house would have revealed many more differences I was not aware of. If this would have put a dent in our friendship. Or if it could have brought us closer. I will never know.

In my Grade 10 year, I became friends with a black girl from Soweto. We attended the same school, and our friendship was bound by its walls.

Rebecca Fleck

A Shift in India

AN EXCERPT FROM A MEMOIR

On my nineteenth day volunteering with the Missionaries of Charity in Kolkata, my mental tectonic plates began to shift and I began to crack. It wasn't just one thing. Yes, it was too hot, but I was in India in May, the hottest month of the year. Yes, I was volunteering with mentally ill women in the morning and sick and dying women in the afternoon, but I could handle anything I put my mind to. India could shake me but I would never crumble.

"You know, Rebecca, most volunteers work in the morning or the afternoon, but not usually both," Cecilia, my kind landlady, said to me one day. Maybe she had seen the haunted look in my eyes or the dark circles beneath them. "You look like you're losing weight."

I was beginning to realize that forcing myself to volunteer with the mentally ill women at Shanti Dan was not doing me, or them, any good. It was simply not a good fit for me. But I loved working with the sick and dying women at Kalighat. They were not just a group of terminal, silent patients. There were many lively, funny women there with distinct personalities. Some had cancer, some had tuberculosis, some had unknown afflictions. One woman had had hot oil thrown in her face by her husband. I felt instantly at home at Kalighat. The longer I stuck around, the more I felt trusted and accepted by the women.

Day nineteen began poorly. I got up after yet another night of little sleep thanks to the man next door, who blasted his music all night long. Sometime during my morning commute I lost my sunglasses and found myself squinting in the glaring sun. During my morning shift at Shanti

Dan, I was surrounded by screaming people and felt pushed and pulled and yelled at from all directions. I was kept late at Shanti Dan and only had time to for a short nap before I had to catch a bus to Kalighat for my afternoon shift. On my way to Kalighat, a pack of men groped me in the street for the nineteenth day in a row; I needed India to cut me some slack.

At Kalighat I performed my usual tasks. I served water, handed out medication, and washed dishes. The bossy Indian Sister made the volunteers walk the sick women up and down the aisle between the beds.

"You!" she bellowed out to me. "You! Walk her! Up and down! Three times."

Then the Sister made me give Aadita her pill. Aadita clearly did not have much time left in this world. Her tiny body wasted away more and more each day. Her fine flesh just covered her small bones. The pill got caught inside of Aadita's mouth and I had to pick it off her hard palate with my fingernail. I could barely get my finger inside her tiny, wasted mouth. She was hooked up to a urine bag, had bedsores, and needed to be turned periodically. Her high pitched cries pierced through the air when I tried to move her and her face crumpled in agony.

"I'm so sorry, I'm so sorry," I whispered to her. "This will only take a minute. I need turn you over to your other side."

Aadita's cry was like a faint siren and I was horrified by the knowledge that I was causing so much distress to a frail, helpless soul. I couldn't even finish turning her before my eyes filled with tears. I gently finished the job and then ran into a storage room. I don't like to cry in public and put my vulnerability on display.

Someone must have seen me run away and hide because the Head Sister came into the storage room with some tissues. "It's okay to cry," she told me. "What happened?"

I blurted out vague sentences like, "Aadita. We're hurting her. I don't want to hurt her." I was so embarrassed for making a scene and for not being able to control my emotions. I hid my face in my hands.

233

"This is part of life," she said. "These women are lucky to be here and to be cared for; they could be dying in the street." She patted my arm and said, "Stay here until you feel better. Take your time."

I washed my hands and splashed my face with cold water. I went to the kitchen and washed dishes for a while to keep my mind off of Aadita. I served dinner, cleared dishes, and wiped down beds.

When we had completed all the chores I told my friend, Aimee, that I was just going to head back home instead of having tea with the other volunteers on the rooftop deck.

"I've had a bit of a rough day," I said, involuntarily tearing up again.

She got her things and walked with me to the metro. She loaned me her sunglasses so I could hide my puffy red eyes while I told her what had happened and how everything had been building up over the last three weeks. India was so intense and volunteering just added another level of severity.

"Have you ever broken down before?" I asked her.

"Yes. Once, after I saw one of the Sisters pulling maggots out of the head wound of one of the ladies. And one other time after I was attacked in Gujurat."

People sometimes ask me why I wanted to volunteer. I think I was on a quest to figure out how to fill the emptiness inside of me. I cannot remember a time when I wasn't asking why. Why am I here? How can I find meaning and purpose in the short time I am here? I was starting to understand that service would be one aspect of my fulfillment.

But I often wondered if I was truly helping anyone other than myself. I wasn't curing anyone and I wasn't fixing anything. But maybe I was providing a tiny bit of comfort. Maybe one person's day was made slightly more comfortable by my sincere efforts.

On my way home from the metro, I passed two volunteers from Shanti Dan and they invited me to join them for dinner. We stayed out late, drank beer, and ate spicy noodles at a rooftop restaurant near New Market. At midnight, I walked home alone. No one was on the street except for me and the sleeping homeless people. Kolkata was a different city at that time of night, a much calmer one.

When I got home, I discovered that the front gate was locked. When I first moved in, Cecilia and her husband, Richard, told me they locked the gate at 9:00 p.m. and showed me where the doorbell was, but I hadn't paid attention. "I will never come home late," I told them confidently.

I ran out to AJC Bose Road to look for a phone stall so I could call Richard's cell phone, but nothing was open at that time of night. I looked around desperately and saw two men sitting on a low wall. I approached them tentatively. One man wore a shirt and pants. The other man wore nothing but a very short white dhoti, a small piece of cloth wrapped and tucked around his pelvis and knotted at the waist.

"Excuse me, but could I borrow a cell phone?" I asked, trying to direct my request mainly at the man wearing pants. "I can pay you, of course."

The man in the dhoti immediately pulled a phone out of Brahma-knows-where and said, "This is an emergency, no?"

"Yes!" I said, "I'm locked out of my house."

He asked me for Richard's number, dialed it, and then passed me his phone. Richard answered and said he would be right down.

I thanked the man profusely and offered to pay him again. He bobbled his head at me and said, "What do you mean? This was an emergency, no?" Then he smiled and held the phone out to me and said, "Would you like to make another call?"

"Maybe tomorrow," I said and put my palms together in grateful appreciation. I scuttled off to my India home, where Richard was waiting.

As I fell asleep to the din of my neighbour's music, I knew I needed to formulate an India survival plan: I needed to find a calm, cool place where I could seek refuge from the chaos. I needed to reach out to my friends back home. And I needed to allow the boundaries of my heart to shift so I could ask for assistance from my new friends in India and, perhaps, even strange but kind men in dhotis.

Crystal Dalman

Crossroads

AN EXCERPT FROM A MEMOIR

September 6th, 2012 is a day I will never forget. A day the realization dawned that one chapter of my life had died and a new, unknown chapter was about to start. I was in Venice, Italy for the first time, without a map or itinerary, no clue of my surroundings, where I was going, or what lay ahead. My once colourful life, now erased, spread before me—a large white canvas without a single drop of paint.

Two days prior, I had made a last-minute decision to cancel my ticket back to Vancouver, Canada from New York and booked a one-way ticket to Venice using my Air Miles. Europe had been on my bucket list for years, though imagined quite differently.

Normally, I would be excited to explore the Old World; instead, I carried the weight of emotional exhaustion from a string of losses and pain: the end of an abusive relationship, repeat miscarriages, invasive surgeries, harsh fertility and hormone treatments. I did not recognize my body any longer; it felt like something had taken my soul and placed it into a foreign object.

⌒

I stand outside the Venice airport full of uncertainties and heartache, with one bag full of summer clothes (for what was to be a two-week trip to New York) my journal, and my camera. Imagine Linus from Charlie Brown, dragging his blanket behind him. I watch couples, families, and friends walk past me, all going somewhere with a purpose. I love to travel but this time is different. I am terrified. I think of my once vibrant life, full of dreams, passions, and goals. My amazing childhood, my fulfilling years in Whistler, my mountain-biking days, and my career as a professional stuntwoman; the community I cherished and beautiful homes I purchased to share life with friends and family. With a broken heart and a pit of sickness in my stomach, I begin to process all the losses. The ache triggers my tears and they roll freely down my face.

I follow people on a path as they exit the airport and they lead me to the boats that transport people to the islands. I board one headed to the island of Venice and sit by a window, mesmerized by the bright, greenish-coloured sea which splashes wildly. The sky is a vibrant blue; the sun warm on my skin. I drift between present and past. The boat crashes into the dock with a thud and everyone sways with the force of the hit. I stand and step onto the solid ground of one of the most romantic places in the world.

Curiosity pulls me down a narrow path that leads into a maze of walkways. I find a boutique hotel nestled between two small canals— Hotel Varadero. On a whim, I book a single room for four nights. After I've freshened up, I head out to explore my new surroundings.

I stumble through the narrow cobbled streets with my camera and journal in hand. I snap photos of the detailed Venetian architecture, old bridges, and gondolas paddling in the canals. There is so much to take in: impressive statues of Roman gods at every turn and colourful people that litter the plazas and streets. Wonderful aromas fill the air as I pass the cafes and pizzerias nestled between designers stores stacked with Italian boots and fashions. Murano glass glitters in shop windows, and street artists display their wares. I enter each church I pass, each time lighting a candle and whispering a prayer for guidance.

On my first night, I find a nice little restaurant, the Florida, next to the Grand Canal and the Rialto Bridge. A waiter greets me, "Buonasera Signora!" and escorts me to a lovely table dressed with a white linen cloth. A glass vase with a single flower adorns the table. The well-dressed patrons of the restaurant chat together and the hum of their conversation is comforting. The tourists in the restaurant stand out, so casually dressed as to be unmissable. Music wafts from the nearby canal.

I order a dish of pasta and a glass of white wine—my first drink in years. I'd kept away from alcohol voluntarily, due to anxiety around my ex's drinking. With thousands of miles between us, I feel safe to enjoy a glass of wine with my first genuine Italian meal in Italy. All the lovely aromas have awakened the first genuine hunger I've felt in over a year.

"Buon Appetito, Signora."

I inhale deeply as the waiter places the dish in front of me. With a smile, I reply with my only Italian word, "Grazie," and place my napkin on my lap. I twirl the thin noodles and take my first bite. My taste buds soak up the delicious flavours from the sauce—salsa di pomodoro—and my mouth is in heaven. I think of my late grandfather, who loved Italian food and made an amazing homemade spaghetti sauce. I tried to get his secret recipe, but it went with him August 5th, 2002, when he held my hand and took his last breath. He'd served in World War II in Italy, and I can still hear his voice, "The best thing about Italy was the women, wine, and food!" Suddenly, I do not feel alone.

"Grandad, if you can hear me, I finally made it to Italy, though my life is a mess, and I am completely lost. Please, if you can hear, help guide me."

I wipe the tears from my face with the napkin. I must find the places Grandad spent his time during the war.

During my second day, I visit the Doge's Palace and St Mark's Basilica in the Piazza San Marco. I'm awed by the Venetian Gothic style with its grand arches, decorative marble details, and ornate carvings around every doorway. The four horses of St. Mark stand proudly above the entrance to the basilica, watching over the whole piazza. Here, in this stunning historical landmark of Venice, I sit with an Italian coffee, and I people-watch. I'm drifting in and out of thought, and pull out my journal to write.

That night, I walk the now familiar streets and piazzas after dinner.

Ahead of me, three people pause. One holds a map and points in one direction. His companion points a different way. The one with the map approaches me.

"Hello. Do you speak English?"

"Yes, I speak English."

He points to a spot on the map. "Great! Can you help us get here?"

I begin to explain the route to their destination.

"What are you doing right now?" he asks.

"Walking."

"Would you like to join us? We will never find this place ourselves and you seem to know where you're going." "Yes, please join us," his friends echo the invitation, smiling. I consider briefly, then decide. "Why not!"

We continue to introduce ourselves as we walk. Two are a couple from the eastern United States, and the third was a DJ from Boston, whom they'd met only earlier that day. Within minutes, we are chatting like old friends. Our destination is a club. We dance and laugh the night away and for a few hours I'm free from the heaviness I carry. I don't remember the last time I felt this open and unburdened. Leaving the bar for Mr. DJ's hotel, we pick up pizza on the way. We eat and chat until dawn.

I help the couple find their hotel, and we arrange to meet for dinner that evening. The normally crowded streets are bare and I enjoy the sounds of the birds chirping as I make my way back to my room.

A few hours later, I catch a boat to the Island of Murano, where the famous glass is made. The day passes in a jumble of emotions—fascination and wonder tinged with moments of loneliness.

At dinner, I meet up with the couple from the day before. We talk about the adventures of our day. Mr. DJ has invited us to join him at another club that night, but we're all exhausted. We hug goodbye and go our separate ways. The couple will leave early in the morning for the Amalfi Coast. Me? I have no idea.

In the morning, I ask if another room is available in the hotel. There is nothing. A search for availability in other hotels yields nothing. I pack my things, catch a boat to the train station, and take the next train, departing for Milano.

After an hour on the train, I feel led to get off at the next stop—Verona, the lovely setting for Romeo and Juliet.

I begin to explore its cobbled streets, and attend my first Italian opera—Notre Dame De Paris—in the open Roman Theatre. The next day, I meet two couples who had just finished a cycling tour in the Dolomite Mountains. It sounds delightful. Maybe another time. In a quick Skype call with two girlfriends, just before I need to check out of my hotel, I learn about an Italian cycling hotel on the coast and decide to take a leap of faith and call them. A friendly, soft voice answers.

"Hello, Hotel Belvedere. How can I help you?"

"Hello. Do you have availability?"

"What are your dates?"

"ASAP, I am in Italy."

The girl laughs and then replies, "We book a year in advance."

I'm crushed. Then I hear someone speaking in the background.

"Wait! Apparently we just had a cancellation an hour ago for next week."

Without a pause I say, "I will take it!"

Amanda Deitz

His Eyes. Her Eyes.

AN EXCERPT

1980. The news. *I am not ready* are the only words in my head so obviously they were the only words out of my mouth when she told me she was pregnant. How can this be happening to me? My dad is going to want me to marry her and I don't want to be married. I love her but I have too much life to live to be tied down. SHIT ... SHIT ... SHIT.

1981. The Birth. I missed it. *The whole thing.* The baby was five hours old by the time I got to the hospital. As soon as I saw her, I knew she was mine and I loved her instantly. She was perfect with her mountain of dark hair and glowing blue eyes—*my* blue eyes. I would die for this person. How can that be? I can hardly remember the last nine months of wishing her away. I will give her the whole world. Anything she wants. I am her daddy and nothing will ever change that.

1983. The Break-up. It's no surprise to anyone we're calling it quits. We've been been fighting for months. Money is tight, work has been slow, and she's been supporting us on her wage and tips from the bar. The baby is a lot of work. There is so much to do *all* of the time. It's too hard. I never said I was cut out for the *dad* thing or the *husband* thing. I suppose that is why she is asking me to go. I hope the baby doesn't forget me. In a perfect world, I would be the father she deserves. But I know there is something in life I need to find in order to be happy. I don't know what it is yet but when I find it, it'll make leaving her worth it.

1986. Where is he? Nothing seemed off until I started school. I am learning lots of new things. The biggest thing is that *all* of the other kids in my class live with their mommy *and* daddy. I am too embarrassed to

241

tell my friends the truth. How can I be the *only* kid who is different? I have a daddy; I just don't see him very much. Mommy promises that he loves me but if that's true, how come he isn't with me? Where is he? I am learning a lot of really important things in kindergarten. The most important thing is that I need a daddy.

1989. She is growing so big. This visit with her is different somehow. She seems more mature. Which is crazy because she is eight. I mean, she is still a child. But she asks me all sorts of questions I don't know the answers to and it makes me wonder if my child is smarter than I am. When I listen to her talk, it is hard for me to believe she is mine. If it wasn't for her face—those big blue eyes that I see everyday in the mirror and that smile that belongs to her mother—I would swear she was adopted.

1990. He's not like other dads. He showed up at grandma's house today. It's been so long since I've seen him that nothing about him felt familiar. Until I heard his cowboy boots sweep across the wood floor. That sound is ingrained in my mind. He sat with Grandma for a few minutes before asking me to go for a drive. Truth be told, I don't really care for drives but I don't like to hurt his feelings and he promised me a swim at the lake. When we arrived, I was so wrapped up in my own excitement that I didn't see him disappear. By the time I noticed, I was furious. I made my way out of the water to find him and that's when I saw him at the far end of the beach, under the trees, watching me play. That's when I knew he wasn't like other dads. He likes to be close but still needs to be far enough away that he never feels trapped.

1992. I just can't. This whole dad thing is too much. I had her alone for the first time this whole summer. Maybe things would be easier if she were a boy. At least then I would know what to do with her or say to her. When I look into her big blue eyes—the ones I gave her—I can see that she expects something from me; something I cannot guess. She hasn't realized yet that I am unable to give it to her. One day she will clue in. And I won't know what to say except that part of me always knew being a father was out of my league.

1995. Whose family is this? He is getting married tomorrow. I am not sure how I feel about it. He cannot even take a weekend to visit me now, how is it going to change once *they* get married? Will he go have a family without me? I feel like I don't belong anywhere. Everyone here is acting like I don't exist or like he is finally happy. I am his family. I was here first! Now I just don't count because he is going to have a wife. That hardly seems fair.

1997. Driving ... sheesh. She arrived today with a smile on her face and a learner's permit in her hand. Her mother warned me she wasn't very good and asked me to work with her. I know I don't see her often but she seemed so much younger the last time I saw her. Now, the jeans are lower, the top is higher, and the government gave her permission to drive a car. I am realizing all that I have missed. She has no idea yet. I wonder how she is going to react when her thoughts catch up to mine. It never really occurred to me that she would grow up—at least not this fast.

1998. Does he even love me? It's weird sometimes—being with him and his family—his wife and their kids. I watch them go about everyday life as though I never happened. My cousin asked me if I were jealous. The word *jealous* made me feel petty and insecure and after all the promises he has broken to me over the years, that is the last way I want to feel. But it is hard to visit my dad and watch him raise his new kids the way he never wanted to raise me. I mean, as a kid, I shouldn't have to wonder if my dad loves me. And, I do. *All* the time.

1999. Is that a boyfriend? I watched my daughter graduate high school. I am a proud dad today. She has already accomplished so much in her 17 years of life and she did it all without my help. I am full of pride—I suppose because I did not get all the way through high school. But my joy was blindsided by the appearance of her boyfriend and before his bony hand tried to grip mine, he gave her a kiss, *on the lips*. My heart stopped. The way she looked at him, with her big blue eyes—the ones I gave her—made me realize that time has moved forward without my permission. And though he won't be the only boy she falls in love with, he is a definite symbol of the changes to come.

2002. Does she even love me? She has been grown for a while. And she no longer pretends she needs me. We are in a strange place right now. She has made it clear to me that I may be her dad but I am not her parent. I don't feel the same way. I *am* her father. I have been since the day she was born. That title does not get taken away because she decides it. Her detachment from me is unnerving and I don't understand it. How can she be so willing to forget me? I have always loved her, and now I am forced to wonder if she even loves me.

2007. So, this is the guy. I have often wondered what he would be like. *The guy.* The one that was going to walk into my house, shake my hand, and steal my daughter. They say girls always marry their fathers, but knowing her the way I do, I was always willing to bet she would steer clear of any guy like me. And I was right. He is educated, well spoken and extremely polite, but *most importantly*, I can tell by watching them that she trusts him. Which must mean he is stable and reliable, the two things I have never been for her.

2011. Was she even mine to give away? I have known for sure, for about a year, that this day was coming, but nothing could prepare me for seeing her in that dress. My baby is a bride today. The second I saw her, every single moment I have ever had with her flashed in my mind. She is a stunning woman. When did that happen? I feel undeserving of the role I must play—*father* of the bride. But when she looked at me with her big blue eyes—the ones I gave her—I knew it was right. As I placed her hand in his, I asked him to promise to do right by her. I know she is not mine to give away, but I needed to hear him promise.

2025. It is time to say goodbye. He is sick. The end is near. I know it and I am quite certain he does too. I have loved this man my entire life. How am I supposed to accept this permanent goodbye? I felt no need to ask for an explanation, but out of the blue he gave one to me. He said he was just a boy when he found out about me. He said he always loved me.

He said he could have tried harder and he could have been there more. He confessed that his absence was largely unexplained and definitely inexcusable. He said he was always so proud of me and that my accomplishments surpassed any imagination he had for his own life. He said he was happy I was stronger, proud that I was smarter, and ready to go because he knew I was going to be okay. He looked at me desperately, with his big blue eyes—the ones he gave me—and said he was sorry. And that was all it took. That word washed every question, confusion, piece of anger, and hurt away. It was just us again. Me, his daughter and him, my father.

Jo Dworschak
Mitch and the Kid
BASED ON A TRUE STORY

Mitch starts the morning with twenty pushups and a protein shake. It's his first day as a single dad and he has planned a grand adventure. He's watched *Daddy Day Care*, he's ready. The diaper bag is packed with wet wipes, Band-Aids, and Bactine. Mitch and the kid are dressed in matching red polo shirts and blue jeans. They look so much alike, except the hair. The kid has a full head of golden curly locks. Mitch is bald, all he has is a *Magnum, P.I.* moustache, which he grew for his interview with the police department. He's still waiting for the call.

Despite his better judgement, Mitch has offered to take the ex-wife's dog, Shepherd, for the day. He hates that dog. It was the last straw when he said, "It's me or the dog," after Shep stole the groceries while Mitch was putting them away. Now he lives up the block in a one bedroom apartment. The only reason he offered to watch the dog today is to impress his crush, Christa. They met last week at the local church. She's exactly what he imagines Christ would be like, if he were a twenty-two-year-old female.

They don't have much in common. She's an unemployed actress, watching the pastor's children for the summer and paying off her student loans. Mitch has never been one to enjoy theatre but can relate to the issue of gainful employment and student debt. Mainly, he's impressed by how good she is with children, and she has golden curly hair, just like his son. The three of them would match nicely. He remembers that she's from a small town and misses her family dog, a German shepherd. He's sure she'll be glad to see he's brought a dog. Even though Shepherd isn't a real German shepherd. He's too thin, his coat too smooth, and his tail curls up when he's excited, like a husky's. Shepherd's proud like a shepherd. So proud that Mitch had to promise his ex-wife he wouldn't call him a mutt.

Today's the day Mitch and the kid go on their first trip to the park together. He packs an impressive lunch. Two thousand calories, which Mitch needs to consume before the kid's nap time. He packs everything. Two cups of blueberries, Greek yogurt, Goldfish crackers, carrot sticks, and two links of kielbasa from the Polish deli. Shep and the kid love kielbasa. All that food is too much to carry; luckily there's space in the undercarriage of the baby buggy. You can fit a basset hound down there.

That buggy is Mitch's prized possession. It's Italian. It's sleek yet tough. It has eight-inch inflatable tires and a first-class all-wheel suspension system. Mitch had dreams of taking it off-roading before he realized it's too big, even when folded, to fit in the trunk of his Toyota Tercel. The kid's old enough to walk to the park, but Mitch insists on taking the buggy on this adventure.

Mitch has the whole trip planned. The kid will play independently, while he gets some quality time with Christa as they play fetch with Shep. Mitch can hurl the ball two metres farther than the overpriced Chuckit! launcher they sell at the pet store. He rolls up his sleeve so his triceps and tribal tattoo pop out when his arm extends.

They are ready. Mitch straps the kid in the buggy, loops Shep's leash three times around his wrist, swings the diaper bag across his chest, and sets off for their epic journey across Commercial Drive. Just two blocks east to McSpadden Park. Mitch walks tall and proud. His arm flexes effortlessly as Shepherd pulls at the leash. The kid can't wait to play. Shepherd can't wait to show how fast he can catch the ball. Mitch can't wait to flirt again, after years out of the game.

They arrive at the park fluttering with excitement. The kid squirms in the stroller and pulls at his seat belt, eager to be freed. Mitch pulls out his flip phone. "First, smile for the camera," he says as he takes a shot of them to post on Facebook. Mitch kneels in front of him and in a calm yet assertive voice says, "I'm gonna let you play all by yourself. Okay?" The kid leans forward and mutters, "O-tay," without hesitation. Mitch sets him free and he runs triumphantly toward the playground.

Shep tries to run too and catches Mitch by surprise, almost pulling him over. Luckily no one noticed. Before Mitch unclips the leash he sees a sign, "No Dogs Allowed Within 15 Metres." They're both disappointed. He counts his steps to precisely the distance of 15 metres from the playground's perimeter. Mitch ties Shep to the buggy and is sure to put on the brakes. Then Mitch kneels in front of him and in a calm yet assertive voice says, "Now stay." He really hopes this time Shep listens.

Christa stands in the shade of the horse chestnut tree, angelic in her floral summer dress and vegan Birkenstocks. When their eyes meet, they both light up. Mitch's right, she loves the dog. He assures her Shepherd's great with kids. She agrees it's a shame he isn't allowed on the playground. They decide to go to the field and play fetch with him once the children finish playing. Everything is going so well.

Mitch's pleased to see the kid's also doing well. It seems the kid has decided to try the slide, all by himself for the first time. Mitch is so proud to see his son pushing himself. That's how his passion for being in peak physical condition was born. He offers the kid some crucial words of encouragement: "That's my boy. You can do it." It's just what the kid needs to hear. He's ready. Mitch's ready too. This is the day the kid will conquer the slide without adult supervision.

Shep's not ready. Furthermore, Shep's insulted no one has consulted him. His tail curls up. Shep knows the dangers. Shep can smell every drop of blood and tears at the base of that slide and he groans with disapproval. If only he weren't tied to the buggy, then he could help the kid without interfering with Mitch's pursuit of a new mate. Shep's certain by now he's broken the world's record for longest stay by a German shepherd while tied to a stroller. Not to mention bonus points for ignoring the kielbasa in the undercarriage.

The kid climbs up the ladder, barely two feet off the ground, but it's two feet too far. Shep cries an achy bellow of disapproval. The kid reaches the top of the slide and Shep's greatest fear comes true. No one's there to catch him. So when Shep sees the kid stand and wave at him he's certain it's a call for help. Shep tries to pull the buggy. The brakes are on. It won't roll, but it does move. First it slides a few inches, then it flops on its side. He pulls it behind him as he runs across the playground. The buggy bounces four times and then whirls behind him like a dreidel. Shep narrowly misses a young girl playing in the sand. All the food flies out of the undercarriage: two cups of blueberries, Greek yogurt, and kielbasa. The the Goldfish crackers hit one of the parents in the face.

The kid goes down the slide. Shep runs faster. It's the first time Shep's ignored food that has fallen on the ground. The kid is almost at the end of the slide. Shep runs the last five metres in one second. Christa breaks from Mitch's gaze and sees what's happening. Her hazel eyes flash open as she screams, "Dog attack!" Mitch screams, "Jesus Christ!" Christa whips her head back at him, eyes red with anger. Mitch doesn't have time to apologize. He runs and herds the children from the line of fire, then races to the slide.

By the time Mitch makes it to the slide it's too late. Shep's already caught the kid. His mouth is clenched onto the collar of the kid's red polo shirt. It looks like the kid's being eaten alive, but he's laughing hysterically, the kind of laugh that can easily be confused with a murderous cry. Christa's certain he's being mauled. Mitch grabs Shep by the scruff of his neck and lifts him in the air. "You stupid mutt." His triceps flex as he's about to choke him. Now the kid cries. Shep doesn't understand.

Christa asks if she should call 911. Mitch stops himself. He sets the dog down. "No! Don't. He's okay." He unclips the leash from the buggy and Shepherd runs. He's about to run all the way home when he sees the two links of kielbasa.

Shepherd grabs it. One link of kielbasa in his mouth, the other smacking him in the face as he runs laps around the playground. Mitch chases after him, tackles him, and grabs the kielbasa. "Let go!" he yells. The links break apart and Shep devours that kielbasa like it's his last meal. If Mitch had his way, it would be.

Mitch grabs Shep, clips on his leash, and loops it three times around his wrist. He checks over the buggy, not a scratch. He clips the kid in and without a goodbye to Christa sets off for what he prays is a less epic journey back home.

That's the last time Mitch offered to help with the dog. It's also the last time the dog offered to help with Mitch.

Lynn Harrison

Meet the Abrasive Leader

AN EXCERPT FROM
"COACHING THE ABRASIVE LEADER"

"Really? That is what they are saying about me? After all I have done for this organization?"

My client slumped back in her chair, frustrated, angry, and bitterly disappointed by her co-workers' comments in her performance review.

"People said they hate me. *Hate me!* And here I thought I was doing God's work. I have worked day and night to get this organization to a better place."

As a coach I, too, was baffled by the litany of complaints about Carmen's leadership. In our interactions, she was charming, witty, and clever. She was not the temperamental ogre described by her co-workers, known for her outbursts, controlling behaviour, condescension, and threats. It was as if Carmen was both Jekyll and Hyde, and I was just seeing the good Dr. Jekyll.

I was curious about what led to her co-workers' experiences. It was evident that Carmen was not aware of the kind of impact she was having or what needed to change. I wondered how things had gotten to this point and whether they could be turned around.

By all accounts, Carmen, the executive director of a large medical research facility, was smart, hardworking, and committed to her organization's success. Although her career to date had mainly been in the field of law and she had never led a management team, Carmen believed she could use her corporate experience to turn around an organization that was badly in need of reform. When she took on her role, she was determined to make a difference in her country's healthcare system.

The medical research facility was in much more difficulty than Carmen had anticipated. Not only had it been bleeding financially, with debts mounting in the millions, it had been without a leader for some time; talented people were leaving and several key business processes were broken. Carmen realized that she had taken on an enormous challenge.

Her boss instructed her to do whatever was necessary to improve the numbers, stating, "You've got to right your ship. You've got to make your target margins, and we don't care how you do it. Just get it done."

Carmen responded to these orders by closely overseeing the team around her. Unsure of her staff's abilities, she made all the key financial decisions. As she put it, "I kept a tight leash on everyone." She spent most of her time in her office, which she referred to as her bunker, working fourteen hour days, poring over spreadsheets, trying to find ways to get costs back on track. As she saw it, there was a battle to be waged; the ship would only be righted if she could accurately analyse what was currently occurring and make some tough decisions. Eventually, by significantly changing the organizational structure, reducing headcount, and streamlining processes, she was able to bring about some improvements to the perilous financial situation.

Under this immense pressure, however, Carmen admittedly became tense and sometimes impatient with co-workers. People who did not grasp ideas quickly or who wanted to engage in casual conversation were wasting her time and she was quick to let them know. She said, "I had no time for all that yakety-yak."

At one point, two female managers accused Carmen of bullying behaviour. The women privately took their complaints to the Human Resources department, alleging that their boss was rude, abrupt, condescending, and ill-tempered. To Carmen, this was an anathema. When the organization was downsizing, she had saved these two individuals from the chopping block. They were single parents and she had given them a break. And now they had the nerve to charge her with abusive behaviour.

The bullying complaint was a close call for Carmen. After a lengthy investigation, she was exonerated. In fact, when the accusations came in, her boss backed her, stating, "Those managers don't know the kind of pressure she is under." Carmen felt vindicated and somewhat relieved. After all, she had the organization's best interests in mind. She had been the saviour, in her view, not the villain. The two managers subsequently left the organization.

With that crisis averted, Carmen continued her pattern of aggressive leadership. She focused on getting results, and had little patience for anyone who impeded her progress. The reign of terror finally ended when a lower level co-worker calmly told Carmen that she was not prepared to talk to her if she was going to be disrespectful. This employee did something no one else had done: she took a stand with the executive director in the heat of the moment. Left dumbfounded by this act of assertiveness from a junior employee, Carmen realized that she needed help. She turned to the Human Resources Director, who recommended executive coaching. That was when I entered the picture.

As a coach who has worked with many executives, I soon realized that Carmen fit the profile of an abrasive leader: she was excellent at getting results, but lacked interpersonal skills and emotional capability. Psychologist Harry Levinson used the term "abrasive personality" to describe such executives and it seems apt. Like the proverbial porcupine, the abrasive leader often jabs people in a hurtful way and over time, wears others down. Unlike a bully, however, such bosses do not typically target certain individuals or set out to do others harm. In their ardent quest to attain goals, deliver quality work, and exceed their own high expectations, inflicting pain is collateral damage. In most cases, the offending leader has little comprehension of the extent to which he or she has created distress for others.

In addition to these dispositional qualities in Carmen, I also recognized the signs of a dysfunctional organizational system, which had allowed this unhealthy leadership pattern to occur. When the allegations of bullying surfaced, the institution's leaders were willing to turn a blind eye, protecting the executive who was achieving desired financial results. Carmen lacked the skills needed for the director position in the first place; she had no experience in leading a team and was not given the feedback, training, and support to carry out that role. Like many organizations, her institution failed to recognize the importance of effective leadership and its impact on the system as a whole.

Despite all of this, Carmen's story had a positive ending. Although at first her reactions to the negative feedback ranged from disbelief to anger to remorse and to shame, she was eventually able to bring the self-discipline and fortitude she possessed to a new goal: being a more approachable leader. It was not an easy road, as she had to overcome mistrust in others and her own self-limiting patterns and beliefs. However, after a few months of hard work, determination, and coaching, things began to change. Spending more time talking with employees, Carmen was surprised to discover that not only did they have some great ideas about how the organization could improve, she actually enjoyed the interactions. Moreover, in letting others share the load, she was able to enjoy a more balanced life, with time for reflection, relaxation, and pleasurable pursuits outside of work. Her perspective on the role of a leader took a dramatic shift, as she began to see that it was not just about getting results, but creating an environment in which people could flourish and feel valued for their contributions. Indeed, Carmen went from being abrasive to being impressive, a positive transformation that not only improved life for those around her, but for herself as well.

⁓

This book aims to expand understanding about abrasive leadership, its impact, and why it occurs in our workplaces. Through stories gathered from my doctoral research with formerly abrasive leaders and many years of executive coaching, we will examine the origins of this behaviour as well as practical steps that can be taken to help abrasive leaders to change. Better yet, we explore ways to keep this harmful pattern from occurring in the first place.

People spend much of their lives at work and a toxic environment, caused by poor leadership behaviour, takes a profound toll not only on individuals, but on society as a whole. The stressed-out worker brings that distress home, impacting family, friends, and the community. Over the past few decades much has been done to attend to the physical safety of workers; however, more effort is needed to ensure workplaces are psychologically healthy.

The good news is that it appears that the most successful companies are finally getting the message that talented employees will not stay in jobs that do not recognize this corporate responsibility. This book is intended to support such changes.

Alissa Messner

The Spinster Cat Lady: An Anthropological Approach

ABSTRACT: Our subject was observed over the course of a week. Social, physical, and psychological factors affecting behaviour were recorded. We discovered a number of patterns emerging, providing insight into a deeper understanding of subjects of her kind. Comparisons to other studies of this nature pointed to our subject being an unusual example of what is generally considered to be the normal circumstance for others of her age and life phase.[1]

CONTEXT: The typical Canadian female in her forties has been established, based on generally accepted research and confirmed analysis, to present as attached, having produced offspring, and settled in to a confirmed life path. Research also shows that when there is deviation from this general norm, a multitude of impacts ripple through the subject's life and that of those around her.

This study was undertaken with the intent to contribute to the body of existing research in attempting to understand the effects of operating in life as an exception. Using a subject with such outstanding and marked differentials from others in her cohort provided an opportunity to shed light on the factors and implications such differentials impart on the subject and her environment. Using an anthropological approach

---

1 Not that she cares.

allowed us to record a vast array of behaviours, emotions, and physical tendencies of the subject as she negotiated life in her natural habitat.

METHODOLOGY: The subject was observed for seven days. Additional interviews and ongoing questioning were undertaken to provide insight into the psychological and emotional elements. All information was recorded from the perspective of detached, objective observers. The authors were careful to not disturb the natural activities of the subject or her environment. The subject was not harmed during the course of this study.

Table 1: Confirmed Diagnoses/Conditions/Afflictions/Pains-in-the-Arse

AFFLICTION	PHARMACEUTICAL INTERVENTION?
Major depressive disorder	Good God, yes
Dysthymia	Ibid
Prediabetes	No—managing with diet (not cheese puffs)
Heartburn	Yes, but it doesn't really help, dammit
"Something neurological" creating visual disturbances	Nope
Heart murmur	No, thank goodness
Gilbert's Disease	Not required
Migraines	Oh yeah
Panic disorder	OMG what's happening??? Aaaaaaaggghghgh
Dermatitis	Don't ask where
Tinnitus	No treatment available
Polycystic ovary syndrome	Yes, but doesn't negate chin hair appearances

RESULTS: The subject is suffering from a number of physical ailments, annoyances, issues, and diagnoses. As noted in Table 1, the specific nature of her conditions presents considerable breadth. Professional members of the medical community working on her plethora of complaints are too many to list here. The amount of time required to devote to such treatment and care takes up a significant portion of our subject's existence, at least 4,430% more than the average.[2]

We noted that the subject's physical issues prevented her from being mobile. Time spent inert on the sofa was calculated at 64% of the waking observational period, double the norm. During these times, frequent swearing and whining was noted. As well, nutrition habits seemed to fail, as we noted a frightening volume of cheesy poofs eaten. The subject also ingested many pharmaceutical interventions for symptom and discomfort management. We noted a wide variety of drugs in her possession, all in the "extra strength" and "value pak" form. When questioned about the quantity of pills taken, the subject replied, "Drugs are your friend" and "no need to be a hero."

Our subject's sleep was severely impaired. Routinely she was up in the night and could only sleep about two hours at a time. Dark circles under the eyes were evident, as were yawning and even more swearing.

Psychological elements comprised the largest amount of data recorded.[3] Frequent bouts of crying were seen, as were lengthy and involved discussions with her cats. The psychological intensity of her relationship with her cats was one of the most striking features noted by the authors.

The subject's daily routine averaged thus: work, TV-watching, emotional eating, and not sleeping. Throughout these activities, we observed her to fluctuate through a variety of emotional states, from gentle sobbing whilst in the fetal position to raucous laughter while watching cat videos. The most common emotional display was a general morose demeanour, with the companion behaviour of cat-cuddling. When asked

---

2 It really is quite ridiculous.
3 It is clear our subject is completely whacked out.

to expound on her emotional state, the subject said she thought she was "going uphill," but always seemed to encounter "roadblocks." Snorfling and weeping ensued, demonstrating psychological dissonance with the present and ideal life-state.

SOCIAL: Our subject exhibited a strong and unnatural lack of intended social contact. It was recorded that, over the course of the entire observation period, she only spoke on the phone to her mom and neglected basic tenets of making oneself attractive (for example, wearing ill-fitting pants that exacerbated stomach rolls). Saturday nights were spent reading and watching *Hockey Night in Canada*. The subject does, however, have a small but significant social network. She reported she enjoys spending time with her best friend on the weekends, when they go out to eat fattening breakfasts with lots of bacon and then retire to one of their houses to play with the cats.[4]

When asked if she would ever want to find a partner or reproduce, the subject indicated, "Why have human kids when you have the best cats in the world? Who would ever want to be with a forty-two-year-old cat lady who plucks the occasional peri-menopausal chin hair?"[5]

DISCUSSION/CONCLUSION: Our results indicate our subject to be, essentially, a nerd shut-in with no hope of ever getting a life. We are obligated, as objective researchers, to point out that our subject is doing nothing to deflect stereotypical labels of "spinster" and "weird lady with chin hair who isn't married at her age." Defying social norms can sometimes be revolutionary, but we believe the subject is doing nothing to help her state in life.[6] Ingesting the amount of cheese puffs and painkillers observed is not helping, and we encourage the subject to recover a

---

4 It should be noted that this friend is also unattached and has three cats. Good grief.
5 We don't know.
6 Like, really. Come on, already.

sense of physical purpose through regaining an active lifestyle.[7]

The authors believe our subject would benefit from ongoing study in an effort to improve her outlook on life and positively influence her choices going forward. A considerable amount of resources would be required and we would encourage research institutes to consider devoting a longitudinal study with a cross-disciplinary team of global experts. We thank our subject for allowing us to achieve insight into the phenomenon of lifestyles of the human single female in her forties.[8]

---

7 We noted a high volume of workout wear in her armoire with the tags still on.

8 Step away from the cheese puffs.

Becky Block

Looking for Love in All the Wrong Places

AN EXCERPT FROM A MEMOIR

Like a store-bought birthday cake, online dating starts out looking great, but once you've swallowed a few bites you realize the aftertaste isn't worth it. As my foray into online shopping for love progressed, the routine began to look, well, routine. The bacheslor of the hour and I would spend a few late nights exchanging get-to-know-you details, desperate to locate areas where our lives might intersect.

"You grew up loving *Three's Company* too? Who was your favourite, Chrissy or Janet?" (They all say Chrissy.) "I loved Chrissy too!" (Not true. I was definitely a Janet girl. I even considered flower-arranging school.)

I convinced myself that everyone in this online pool must be just like me—a lonely workaholic with no time to date. Eventually the prospect and I would feel comfortable enough with each other's small chat that we'd decide to meet in person to see if we were what the site claimed, a Match.

I was such a natural that I slept with the first guy I met, on the second date. The first date was "lunch" at a motel bar where the special was a Reuben with lemon rice soup and the bartender/waiter wore a grease-stained white shirt to match his sweat-laden scalp.

I arrived on time, but he let me know he'd just finished.

"Sorry about that, I was really hungry."

"Oh no problem." I smiled. "I don't usually eat lunch anyways." (Lie. I always eat lunch, ya inconsiderate prick, and if I'm being honest, I'm usually snacking both before and after.)

I ordered a Singapore sling because it seemed like a good balance of flirty with the maraschino cherry, but with enough booze to be taken seriously, like a confident woman who knows what she wants (I was applying my go-to public relations strategy of fake it till you make it).

He was classic handsome: dark hair and eyes, muscles popping out of a basic black tee. He looked like a construction manager, which is what his profile claimed he was. Judging from his poor manners, however, I deduced that he wasn't really looking to date me over the long-term.

What happened to the good old days when men were subtler at disguising their ultimate goal of getting in your pants? I hadn't dated in about ten years; didn't the three-date rule still apply? You know, where you were wooed with flowers or a night out at the ballpark or a ride on a Ferris wheel? Nope. I got happy hour and a grope.

He must have sensed I wasn't fully convinced to take my clothes off quite yet (I'd barely reached the Singapore in my sling when he announced he had to get going), so to close the deal, he pinned me against the payphone in the lobby as we walked out and kissed me, intensely, like a dog eating peanut butter out of a jar. I kissed him back. I won't lie, his direct approach was a turn on. Have I mentioned I hadn't had sex in a year?

He asked me to meet him a few days later, citing he couldn't stop thinking about me (and other x-rated expletives I'll leave out to protect my sweet mom's ears). I responded like any modern (ahem, horny) woman would: I would absolutely be interested to meet him at his office, after hours, to "look around."

When the day came, I left work early so I had ample time to shave my everywheres and dunk myself in all things desirable: lotions, potions, and lip gloss. I arrived, attempting to act like I hadn't been thinking about this moment all day, like I hadn't just spent the last ninety minutes primping and plucking and tucking and then driving across town in rush hour traffic to meet a stranger in his office.

As it turns out, my backstage tour didn't take me beyond the reception area with its faded blue carpet and the full-length leather sofa where I was encouraged to sit down and relax. The next ninety minutes were an irresponsible haze of red wine, cigarettes, and some serious hibbity-jibbity.

It felt good to be wanted, to assure myself I was attractive and still in the game. In hindsight I wondered if this guy, who I never did see again, was actually the office janitor and not the owner he claimed he was, but you only live once, right? Sigh.

Once the afterglow of the afternoon delight wore off, I mustered the enthusiasm to give online dating another try. Chin up, as they say.

This fellow was shorter than I'd like but worked in IT and seemed intellectually stable. By that I mean he could complete a sentence without errors, which put him well ahead of the curve.

He had no car, so I had to pick him up. Strike one against the sexy factor. I don't wanna be that girl who puts on airs about money and expectations, but if I gotta pick you up on date one, it doesn't make me think of you as The Man. He then "took me" to Chili's. Fucking Chili's. Automatic strike two. You can see where this is going. Strike three hit home like a bull in a china shop. Apparently my blooming onion appetizer came with a side of morality and abortion. He seemed to think these paired well together, and over the next hour, lectured me about how indecent women are in their pursuit of pro-choice. Cheque, please.

After a few more of these fantastic fuck-ups, my confidence started to wane. My gal pals assured me I'd just had a few bad apples and that I'd be alone forever if I didn't get back on the horse and put myself out there. I'd seen *The Golden Girls*. Giddy-up.

My next hopeful date was a father with a decent sense of humour. He had warm eyes and deep smile lines around his mouth. He described himself as a soft-hearted romantic who enjoyed writing poetry.

For the love of sarcasm with a side of foreshadowing, let's call him Mr. Wonderful.

We met at a local Greek restaurant. He'd enticed me with a promise of the best cheesecake in town, which prompted me to put on a dress. None of my dates so far had lasted long enough to include dessert. This felt promising!

While I poked my way through my meal of what was probably chicken fingers and fries, Mr. Wonderful entertained me with small talk and loads of smiles across the dimly lit booth. He was highly complimentary, which included a few lingering glances at my chest. I'd put on my good bra that night, hoping the emphasis on my top half would disguise the roundness of my bottom half. Thankfully the '80s Muzak masked the sound of my bare upper thighs making fart noises on the vinyl bench as I shifted about in the summer heat. Things were going well, by online dating standards.

I was daydreaming about their cheesecake menu when we moved to the topic of exes and kids. I had neither, at least in an official government-defined capacity. He explained that he had two children and that they lived with their mother. No big deal. I didn't mind children and was open to dating a parent. At one point, though, he mentioned that his wife lived in his house. This piqued my curiosity.

"Wife? So where do you live?" I asked.

"With my mom. That bitch won't leave my house."

"Oh." I paused.

"She thinks just because she has the kids she can keep the house," he added.

"So you're still married?"

"Technically, but I refuse to divorce her because then I'd have to pay child support."

"So she wants to separate?" I asked, my fork probing around my plate in search of anything to stir this conversation away from where it currently was.

"Oh yeah, of course she does. But then I'd have to pay," he said.

"Sure, but it really prevents you from moving forward, doesn't it? I mean, it's nice that your mom is helping you out, but I'm sure you don't want to stay there forever."

"Well, it works for right now, since I don't have a job. And if I get a job, then I would be court-ordered to pay."

I brought my napkin from my lap to the table and swallowed any hope I'd felt earlier about having a decent date with a handsome, albeit slightly older man.

"I'm sorry, maybe I'm misunderstanding you. So you're unemployed by choice and live with your mom so your wife won't ask for child support?"

"Well, just for now."

Fuck me. This wasn't happening. I went to the restroom and called a friend to stage the classic breakaway move of the emergency "I gotta go" call. I chain-smoked my way to her house, where we commiserated the evening away between spoonfuls of Chunky Monkey.

Later that evening, he sent a text like nothing was out of the ordinary at all. "You sure you don't want to come back for cheesecake, sweetheart?" Let it be known that this may have been the only time in my life I turned down cheesecake.

Jennifer Heron

Hey, Bug Lady!

AN EXCERPT

"Hey, Bug Lady," Kate said with a smile and a wave as she passed, "I'll come and find you in a minute." I was at a social event where I barely knew anyone and making small-talk with a few folks I had just met at the snack table. We were bonding nicely over our love of cheese and fresh bread. After Kate's greeting they both had confused looks on their faces. "Bug Lady?" one repeated and the other followed with, "That was insulting." We had covered two of the three typical small-talk topics, kids and pets, but hadn't yet got around to our respective professions. I laughed and replied that I was an entomologist, a scientist who studies insects. I loved being called Bug Lady and most female entomologists I knew proudly embraced this title. Two blank faces stared back at me. One responded with a look of mild curiosity, "Oh interesting." The second was unable to hide a look somewhere between confusion and mild disgust. This person's eyebrows went upwards and their nostrils flared just a little. After swallowing their cheese they replied, "Yes, how interesting," while simultaneously and involuntarily taking a step backwards.

It was not the first time I had someone exhibit this response after I told them what I did for a living. I find this reaction intriguing rather than offensive, and amongst other entomologist friends, we frequently exchange stories about people's reactions to our chosen profession. Reactions such as, "My daughter has diabetes too!" Well, I suppose they may have heard endocrinologist, so that's an honest response. Or "So do you pick bugs out of dead bodies all day?" Well, I'll give you that one too; many crime shows include a component of forensic entomology. One of my favourites is "You don't look like an entomologist?" Or even better "You don't look like a bug?" While I find these responses humorous, I've not quite figured out how best to answer those questions.

After the initial response to my chosen career, the follow-up question is some variation of why I became an entomologist. The short answer is, I have always loved bugs! But the longer answer is a fondness for nature that started, and was encouraged, from a young age. My childhood home had a dilapidated garden shed in the backyard. The white paint had chipped away with rot in places and had lost all the window panes. The shed leaned to one side when the wind blew too hard and on occasion my parents would express mild concern about it falling over.

My sister and I had so much fun in that garden shed. We would create snail farms and worm houses, keep wood bugs in pots, moths in cups, and catch beetles in jars. We'd encourage spiders to weave webs in the broken window panes and carefully place grass on their silk, hoping we could trick one to mummify the blade. We'd leave the bug houses situated between our dolls, Barbies, blankets, and teddy bears. Our pet cats, Snowball and Daisy, liked to hang out in there too because they always had something to chase. My love of nature continued when we spent time at our grandparent's summer cabin which backed onto a large, bushy ravine. I spent hours rummaging around in that jungle.

One Christmas Nana and Papa gave us the encyclopedic *New Book of Knowledge*, a whole alphabet of books through which I spent hours scouring each page for nature facts. Later that same week I not so subtly hinted to my other grandma that we had received this gift. She immediately took the bait and bought me a subscription to *Owl* and gave me full rein to take all the reference books from her musty basement. Somewhere between those pages I formed my love of insects.

When I arrived at university I had grand plans for law school. These plans were quickly replaced when I found out the school had a collection of dead bugs, all identified and labeled neatly in drawers, on the fourth floor of the zoology building. Along with this room of bugs there was an extensive entomology library, with microscopes, a computer, and dot-matrix printer. Here I could blissfully hang out, volunteer, and talk bugs with other people who liked insects too. There was no turning back.

Once people know you are an entomologist you are frequently called upon to identify various critters. To be specific, entomology is the study of insects, which have six legs, and although bugs are a specific order of insects the word is also used as a general term for insect, spider, or terrestrial arthropod. I'm fairly liberal in my definition of bug and tend not to chastise those who include snails, worms, pill bugs, or other terrestrial arthropods. To my astonishment though, frogs, snakes, salamanders, lizards, bacteria, fungus, plant seeds, and spores are often included in that definition. C'mon people.

During my thirties I had a small business running a museum of live bugs that was open to the public. We had a gift shop and offered birthday parties and educational programs to school groups. On occasion, we'd get a phone call from the random public with a request to identify insects collected in their home. There are an estimated 60,000 arthropods in British Columbia and arthropod identification is no trivial task. However, there are approximately 50–75 species that could be considered the most frequently encountered, and most of the time can be identified.

Surprisingly, we could identify most of the public's identification requests based on a brief description over the phone, a photo, a quick internet search and a few follow-up emails. Some people could not be convinced to send a photo, they wanted to bring the bug in themselves. These were the identification requests we knew to be suspect.

In general, we'd get a phone call from an extremely polite and articulate person with concern they may have insect pests in their home, and they have strange bite marks, rashes or itching caused by these bugs. This is a legitimate question and valid concern. Pets get fleas, carpet beetles and clothing moths munch on fabric, flour moths and fruit flies abound, scabies is common and bed bugs can thrive in even the cleanest home. A recent study by the University of Guelph recorded 112 arthropod species within an urban Canadian home.[1] Many people want to know if a spider is venomous (they all are) and more specifically if it's lethal to humans. We would explain that we are not medical doctors, and cannot diagnose skin reactions or bites, but that we are more than happy to take a crack at identifying the bug.

When the person arrives, they are holding a jam jar, margarine or yogurt container, sometimes sealed with tape or covered in plastic wrap with the lid over top. As entomologists, we are slightly cautious (if the contents are alive you don't want it getting away) but intensely curious and raptly excited (what could it be?). Some people don't want to needlessly kill insects, which I respect, and on occasion we received live spiders and bed bugs—critters you don't want escaping.

When opened, the container most often holds specimens carefully folded within pieces of tissue and paper. After initial inspection, however, and in my experience, I only find fluff and hair, clipped nails, and other bits I'll leave to your imagination. Most of these requests came from those we suspected with the mental illness called delusional parasitosis, "a mistaken belief that one is being infested by parasites such as mites, lice, fleas, spiders, worms, bacteria, or other organisms."[2] We'd gently explain we could not find any arthropods and encourage them to seek a medical professional.

The bug museum was a kitschy collection of live and dead insects, books, and bug paraphernalia assembled to enable children to learn about bugs. The best part about having the business was teaching children about insects, arachnids, and other invertebrates. When a child is first shown a giant stick insect, they have the initial look of awe as they observe the animal's long, spindly legs slowly and carefully walking along. When asked if they'd like to hold the bug, there is sometimes a

1 "Human Skin Parasites | Delusional Parasitosis." 2017. delusion.ucdavis.edu/delusional.html
2 Mortillaro, Nicole. 2017. "Our homes are ecosystems for bugs—and we don't even know it." CBC News. www.cbc.ca/news/technology/bugs-in-our-homes-nature-of-things-1.3971033.3

slight hesitation but more often a look of glee and a big smile would form; the bug would tickle while crawling across their palm. Almost daily, a parent or other adult family member would choose a quiet moment to express to staff that they themselves suffered an irrational fear of bugs, even now as an adult. They didn't want their children to be fearful, and this was why they were visiting the museum.

Years ago I attended a lecture by a preeminent entomologist. Interspersed within his talk were random factoids about the profession. He listed entomologists as some of the longest-lived, following composers and constitutional monarchs of Europe. I'm not sure how true that statement is, but if longevity comes from satisfaction with your profession, then entomology is working for me.

Diana Carter

Lights in the Rain

Winter in Vancouver. The rain had fallen for eons, bringing with it the tramped in mud and household mess engendered by prolonged periods indoors. The children were irritable and fighting. The air smelled of cooking and cat pee. We were late for a dinner engagement with my husband's colleagues: a couple, both physicians, whom I barely knew. My head ached and I just wanted to go to bed and sleep.

Driving in Vancouver at night in the rain is a crazy game of chance. You never know when the next pedestrian, so rain sodden that they have lost concern for their personal safety and hiding under a black umbrella, will leap in front of your car. The windscreen misted and the wipers struggled to keep up with the rain as I peered over the dashboard, trying to see hazardous objects past the reflected glare of oncoming car lights.

Feeling miserable and irritable I had precipitated a bitter argument with my husband and my yelling increased the window fog.

"You say that you *knew* Leslie had cancer, why didn't you *do* something?"

Leslie was a close friend who had been sick for some time; I had just learned her diagnosis was cancer.

"What could I do, nobody asked me. Mind that truck!"

"I asked you to at least find her a specialist who could give her an accurate diagnosis. I did ask you! *Stop* bloody back seat driving!"

"It's not that easy, especially if I don't have the details."

"You never do anything I ask you. Never, never, never!"

"That's not true. For Christ's sake, change into fourth."

"Can you fucking stop back seat driving! You don't do what I ask you! Remember when I asked you last week to be home in time to look after the children so I could go to my meeting? I told you how important it was and you didn't come home until it was way too late. I'm so upset about Leslie; she's one of my best friends and you're not helping. I can never rely on you. Sometimes I think I'd be better off on my own!"

I jammed on the brakes at the last minute to avoid running a light. My husband grabbed the dashboard with both hands. The car skidded and stopped, jutting into the pedestrian walkway. A crowd was crossing the road and a couple of people thumped angrily on the hood. I resisted the urge to give them the finger.

Then came the final straw: the Canucks were playing at home and the couple we were visiting lived very close to BC Place in a building without parking. We were so late that the only recourse was to drop my husband off first—no doubt he was relieved—while I parked the car. After circling many city blocks, I found a space downtown, at least a twenty minute walk away from my destination. The nightly parking rate had temporarily quadrupled because of the game. Thank the almighty, at least I had my umbrella with me.

I launched myself out into the night, feeling like the weather: overcast and dull. I fought back tears that would destroy the thin veneer of normalcy created by my makeup. My shoes soaked up the rain making my feet cold and damp and my umbrella was buffeted by gusts of wind. Walking away from downtown towards Chinatown, I started descending some poorly lit steps leading down near the viaduct. I walked fast, both because of the surroundings and because I was now offensively late for dinner. At least, I thought, the rain will keep the panhandlers away.

Out of the darkness and into the watery twilight of a street light loomed a stooped figure, blocking my path and holding an empty disposable coffee cup. My own despair and venom focused itself on this person in front of me. I could see from her shape that she was a bedraggled woman, a well-worn toque on her head, her long, thin hair poking out from under it, dripping, a blanket round her shoulders, the rest of her lost in darkness.

"Can you help me with some spare change?" she asked, eyes downcast and cringing as though she expected to be hit, which paradoxically increased my anger.

"No," I answered. Tears of self pity and frustration were close to the surface. I just wanted her to go away, "I have nothing to spare, I need help myself."

She reached towards me. The thought flashed through my mind that she was going to hit me and, as I recoiled, she put her hand on my arm.

"Are you alright?"

"Yes, yes, thank you." I pulled back.

She released her grip but looked at me intently with a look of concern. She hesitated as though wondering whether to reach out and give me a hug. She wanted to help; she was no stranger to distress. I imagined hers were shoulders that had been there for others to lean on, and no doubt she, too, had leaned on other shoulders.

I walked on, leaving her in the darkness. I knew I had rejected her; I knew from the moment she had approached me because I didn't want to see the reality of the different world that she showed me. I didn't want to have to reframe my imagined, dark world for the privileged one that it actually was. I was late; I was in a hurry. I had no time or space for her in my hard heart and I didn't want to be reminded of my meanness. But she had interrupted my chain of destruction, forcing me to focus on her act of kindness and generosity. When she reached out to me she had touched something much deeper than my arm. As humility crept in, I acknowledged the moral superiority of this woman and in some corner of myself her action softened the skin covering the boil of my self-pity. I started to think about her rather than myself. I wondered where she slept, if she had friends, if she was addicted, how did she survive, and was she safe. Women regularly disappeared from the streets of Vancouver.

My preoccupation with my own trivial troubles burst open like an abscess and the pus of anger and selfishness leaked out causing self-disgust. Compassion overwhelms anger; kindness is stronger than selfishness. I had needed her compassion more than she had needed my loonie and, though I had left her nothing, she had handed me a great gift. The further I left her behind, the more these thoughts absorbed me. By the time I arrived at our host's apartment building, even the rain seemed gentler.

I rang the doorbell and the wife came down to let me in.

"Good to see you. What took you so long?" she asked.

I hesitated for a second.

"Nothing really, just hard to park."

Tara McGuire

It's Between Him and Me

They told me his body lay on a mattress in a room that wasn't so bad. They told me he was covered and peaceful. They told me he spoke of love that night, that he laughed. They told me he made plans for tomorrow before he closed his eyes.

Next morning, in the warm heart of summer, his body lay cool and slack, the scaffolding that held up his being for twenty-one years, now absent. When his soul flew, the tent poles collapsed. Only a quiet skin covered with markings remained.

And a story.

Confusion isn't new, he wakes up in weird places all the time. Holden is an accomplished couch surfer because he isn't picky. The first question he asks himself most Saturday mornings is, where am I? The second, who is beside me?

He's at Kara's place, a studio apartment in the Metropole Hotel in Gastown. He stays here sometimes when he is too tired to make it home, or too faded. Today something is different though and Holden is trying to figure out exactly what that difference is. He is on his back with a red pillow under his head. A colourful Indian tapestry drapes across his middle. Bare chest and feet, tattooed arms splayed by his sides, his mouth yawns, his eyes are closed.

Once, a professor at art school asked him to walk around a nude model until he found a perspective that interested or challenged him. Today's view is like that. Off kilter. He sees the room from a peculiar angle, and so, he knows a different truth. He isn't awake. He is aware.

The grey mist has cleared off and a pared-down crispness has taken its place. Rather than looking out at the world, he can see into it.

A feeling settles in, something rare that he hasn't experienced in years, not without artificial enhancements anyway. He is, although the word is not quite right, buoyant. This lightness takes him some time to identify. It seems to be more of a non-feeling, a lack of sensation, and this nothing yells so loudly at him it commands his attention.

Holden makes a sort of mental checklist starting with the physical differences; no headache, no urge to vomit, no parched dryness in his mouth. He is not agitated, aching or weighted with fatigue; which comes as a relief.

The inner alterations are more perplexing; there is not a trace of guilt, self hatred, or shame. There is no worry about being too little or too much. Dread has walked away for good. No discomfort of any kind is left in him and it is the vacuum, created in the wake of their departures, that makes him realize something enormous has rolled away. He has been wiped clean.

His leather steel-toed boots, caked in dirt, lie tipped over beside his body, laces snaking on the bare floor, harbouring no ambitions. They too have laboured their last.

He has made his last mistake.

What the fuck? I was just trying to have a good time. I was just trying to feel better. This was not supposed to happen.

Over by the brick wall, Kara sleeps, snoring softly, unaware. Her ivory face is smooth and young, unburdened by what she is yet to know. Kara is not his girlfriend any more but there is a spot in her heart reserved for him. Her chest rises and falls with effortless rhythm. Holden notes the stillness of his own ribcage, the silence enveloping his frame. His thoughts hover as the realization of what has happened begins to crystallize. A blurry downloaded picture sharpens into focus.

Last night they met up at the bar downstairs. They played some pool with a few other friends and drank a few beers. He popped out to meet somebody and was back in ten minutes. Around midnight Holden started nodding off at the table. He needed a bed.

Can I stay with you tonight K? I feel like shit.

Of course you can, just don't barf, okay? Or you're cleaning it up.

I promise not to hurl, I just wanna sleep. He slurred.

They rode the elevator up to her room above the bar. Holden draped his arm around Kara's neck.

Even though we're both with different people at the moment, I will always love you. Can we just hang out all the time and drink gin?

Sure, we can build a house with gin on tap and raise ferrets.

I mean it K, one day I'll get my shit together and we can try again okay? I'll be whole-den. See what I did there? His heavy eyelids drooped. He leaned into her and rested his sweaty forehead against her neck, his rough reddish beard prickled her bare shoulder. She stretched one thin arm around his low back to hold him up. They both looked across at their joined reflection in the elevator's mirrored wall. Her pink hair loose and long. His head shaved close. She pulled the sunglasses down off her head, set them on her nose and smiled at him.

We are BFF's all day, every day Holden. You're just fine. What you need is a big glass of water and a good night's sleep.

Inside the apartment Kara yanked the top mattress off the single bed and let it fall to the floor while Holden slumped onto the only chair, fumbling with his phone. He nearly toppled forward but Kara put a hand on his shoulder to brace him just in time. She kneeled to help him pull off his boots, then his shirt. He collapsed onto the mattress and let out a long sigh. She propped up his head, slid a pillow under it, then she covered him.

Thanks K-bomb, Holden said into the pillow. You're one of the good ones. Can you make sure I'm up for work?

He was asleep instantly. She bent down low and kissed his cheek.

Good night you big mess. See you in the morning.

⤳

A seagull screams outside the window, the ocean is close. A square of morning light glows from behind the blackout curtain. The fridge hums. Down in the street a man shouts. A truck hits its brakes then accelerates with force.

Just last week Holden pulled a drowning man from the ocean at Wreck Beach. The man was drunk and went swimming wearing jeans. When the weight became too much the man had struggled and called for help. Holden didn't hesitate. He ran across the hot sand, dove into the sea, swam out, hooked the stranger under the arms and dragged him coughing through the green salt water back to shore.

So much for all those years of life guard training.

He remembers the fabric of his own t-shirt and cargo shorts curling around him like vines that day, strange and cumbersome against the skin of his chest and legs. Laundry swishing in a washing machine, pulling him down.

This morning the weight, the pulling and the awkwardness are gone. He swims naked, released from the resistance of gravity and fear. He is painless. He is free.

⌒

Children are not bound by earthly constraints. The lost ones disregard the limitations of oxygen and blood. A mother's child is a mother's child always.

I hold my son now, as I did for his breathing years, and I wonder how such a beautiful song could be so abruptly halted. From full throated choir to … echoes. He was fully and completely alive just a moment ago. It is impossible.

Though he is gone, he is going nowhere. Nothing I do can erase the ending, which creates a difficult problem. All the why's are never answered. Sometimes, the ones we love most remain swirling smoke. No amount of sleuthing, guesswork, or naive maternal assumption will make sense of this, but I have too much love left unspent to let him be.

So, I follow the breadcrumbs through the forest.

I dig to understand more of how his path led to the room above the bar with the brick wall and the colourful tapestry. Though I have uncovered some of the facts, truth is a slippery fish. My view is tilted too, making this an imagined story, and a reluctant one. It is a love song to my son, who grew too old too young.

They told me his body lay on a mattress in a room that wasn't so bad. There can be nothing good about the room housing the body of your child. They told me he wouldn't have known what was happening. That he slept through it. Someone said small mercy. It may have been me.

Stephanie Candiago

Bonded by Smoke

AN EXCERPT

There's nothing better than a cigarette. I always knew I would be a smoker. I couldn't wait to smoke. Growing up, I had watched my father and grandfather sit at the kitchen table for hours drinking coffee and smoking Rothmans Blues while discussing the old country, the world, the neighbourhood, and the Canucks. My mom would come home and lament how the whole kitchen was a cloud of smoke and how unhealthy it was. I desperately wanted to be part of the unhealthiness. I wanted to be part of the smoker's social circle.

I had my first cigarette at thirteen. I slid my thumb down the blue Bic lighter, heard the click, inhaled, and coughed. Even with the head rush, I was in love from the first puff. The first drag is always the best. The first pull, as the smoke fills your lungs and exits in a burst of dragon's breath, is almost orgasmic.

A cigarette is the perfect accessory. It pairs best with coffee or a cocktail, but also goes well after a meal or sex. It can spark a conversation or give you an excuse to end one. It relieves stress and anxiety and kills time when time needs to be killed. The downside, of course, is that it can also kill you.

I shared my first smoke with my dad when I was seventeen. I had just returned from a six week trip in Europe and I fancied myself a grown up. I had been to the top of the Eiffel Tower, taken a picture with the guards at Buckingham Palace, and danced all night in the clubs in Milan. Surely my dad saw me as an adult now and we could share a cigarette together. Sitting at the kitchen table, I reached for his pack of Rothmans and he didn't protest. Just like that, I became part of the smoker's circle.

We smoked half a pack between us as we sat there. He asked questions and I answered them because being part of the circle meant opening doors that had been previously sealed shut. I remember quickly butting out my smoke when my mom came home, not wanting her to know about my new bond. The smoker's circle was intimate; you had to be a member to be privy to the conversations. Up until that point, my dad and I had not shared much in the way of conversation. Once we had discussed Mario Lemieux's latest goal or how A.C. Milan beat Juventus, we had nothing left to talk about it. Being a self-obsessed, hormone-charged teenage girl did not leave much time for dad, so he was happy to have something to share with me again. When I was a young girl, he was the center of my attention. We never really recovered from me becoming a teenager. The day my attention shifted from dad to boys was the day we split.

I remember the afternoon it happened. I was fourteen and my brother's friend came over to show off his shiny new black Camaro. Always a fan of fast things, I asked him for a ride. We sped around the block and I walked into the house with a big smile.

"If I ever see you get into that car again, I will break your legs."

I went to my room and shut the door. I emerged hours later a full-blown angry teenager, who wanted nothing to do with her father. Years later smoking brought us back together.

I would go downstairs into his workshop or the garage where he would be designing, building, or fixing something and we would share a smoke. Of course I knew he did not like the fact that I was smoking, but he allowed it so he could spend time with me.

I remember when he bought me my first pack. I wouldn't recommend starting with Rothmans Blues. They are very strong and harsh on young lungs. I switched to Matinee Extra Milds pretty early on. All my friends smoked Du Maurier, but I refused to. I thought they were too common. So, on the early morning of my brother's wedding, my dad dropped me off at my future sister-in law's home to get ready for the big day. He knew I was less than enthusiastic about spending the day getting my hair and makeup done in the company of twenty women. As I was getting out of the car, he handed me a pack of Matinees.

"I figured you could use these."

"Thanks Dad." I smiled and hugged him.

We shared countless cigarettes over the years. Some of our best conversations happened over smokes. We talked about how he came to Canada with twenty dollars and a suitcase. We talked about him growing up in Ethiopia and how his family fled back to Italy when the revolution began. We talked about how he ended up in Vancouver, the jobs he had, and how he eventually started his own company. We talked about where I was going with my schooling, how I hated my part time jobs, and of course, we talked about how disappointing the Canucks were. We talked about how angry he was with the poor choices my oldest brother was making. We talked about "the more" that he wanted for his kids. He talked about what he dreamed of doing, but he never spoke of why he didn't do it—that would come later. With each cigarette, I learned a little more about my dad, and he about me.

Then he decided to quit and that split us up once again. I never wanted to quit; I enjoyed it so much. Sometimes he would quit for weeks and, other times, for months. During those times, our relationship was strained. Without our common ground—our secret habit—my dad and I had no conversation starter and, by my early twenties, I had formed my own smoker's circle. But he always went back to smoking. I know he felt he failed, but he knew I wouldn't judge him. He knew I was happy to have my smoking partner back. And together we shared guilty cigarettes, picking up where we had left off.

When his granddaughter was born, he quit for good. Then he was always on me to quit. He would go on about how much better he felt, now that he had quit. He had more energy, he was breathing better, foods tasted better; all the crap the pamphlets say. Despite what he said, I knew he missed sharing a smoke with me. But I was happy for him because he was proud of himself for finally doing it. I know he wanted nothing more than for me to quit too so we could be non-smoking buddies, but I had moved past smoking with dad. I had my own life and I was still very much in love with my cigarettes. I was not willing to give them up for any reason. That is, until a reason presented itself a few years later.

In those early days of my father's palliative care, when I did not know what to do, cigarettes were no longer my friends. It was a beautiful early October day; it was crisp and cold, but the sun was out. I used to love smoking on those days. I was sitting outside the hospital on a bench; the leaves formed a copper blanket at my feet. I lit a smoke and inhaled, but the thrill was gone. I didn't enjoy it and it didn't help relieve the stress and anxiety of knowing he was lying upstairs in one of the beds. I butted it out on the bench and threw out the rest of my pack.

"That's it, no more smokes," I told him.

His face lit up. The dazed film—caused by the heavy-duty narcotic cocktail—disappeared from his eyes while what I said registered. Then it became our thing to count the days I was smoke free and it would make him so happy. I was counting so many things back then, making so many bargains with God or the Devil, whichever one would save my father first. Desperation reduced me to magical thinking. I believed if I never lit a smoke again I could save him.

One day, I took him out in the wheelchair to get some fresh air. There was a guy smoking and we both agreed it was disgusting and the guy must be a degenerate.

"How many days today?"

"Three, four, seven, ten, seventeen …"

"I'm so proud of you. I knew you could do it."

And then the counting stopped.

There's nothing worse than a cigarette.

Barry Truter

Underground
All the Way

It's a sultry Vancouver day and I'm running late for a meeting. Ducking into the cool of the Langara SkyTrain station, I jump on the next train heading downtown and stand with others in the aisle. The train lurches forward for the fifteen-minute ride to its Waterfront terminus, underground all the way.

A drift of deodorant hangs in the air, mingling with the sweaty presence of others less groomed. Bodies sway. Puffballs of conversation float by like fluorescent fragments dangling in subway dust.

"I waited three days for him to call …"

"… obscene profits the banks are making …"

"… this green top … what a bargain …"

Passengers ear-budded to their devices studiously avoid eye contact, immersed in their private worlds, oblivious to the intriguing soundscape.

It's a long stretch between Oakridge and King Edward stations with a couple of significant bends. The train screeches on the track as it veers first right, then left. I clutch a backrest handle. My glance rests on a young man of medium height and narrow build with neatly trimmed dark hair. He wears slim jeans, canvas shoes, a blue-grey t-shirt. A leather satchel is slung over one shoulder and across his chest. He balances while working a smartphone with both thumbs. His face is in profile, intent on the screen.

The train pulls up at the station platform, disgorges a load, accepts replacements, and moves on. My eyes wander around the carriage and are triggered back to the smartphone user; his demeanour has changed.

It's obvious he's received a disturbing message. His hand reaches to his face in a gesture of shock. Reading from the phone, he shakes his head in disbelief. I watch as his face crumbles, knees fold, and he drops squatting to the floor. Now his right hand shades his eyes while his left still holds the phone. He looks at it in dismay, then buries his face in the crook of his arm.

The synthetic voice of the automated assistant announces: *"This train is bound for Waterfront. The next station is Broadway—City Hall."*

I'm alarmed. What's happening here? Evidently a troubling text, but what could it be? A family crisis? Relationship breakup? Job termination? A couple of other riders notice the young man's misery but turn their heads away. My impulse is to offer assistance, to let him know I'm concerned. Yet I hesitate, unsure whether the intrusion would be welcome. I could ask him if anything's wrong but that seems innately foolish. Clearly something's wrong, though I have a sense he may not want to draw attention to himself and I wouldn't want to embarrass him in this most public of spaces.

Meanwhile, he rises to his feet, brushes tears away, and looks again at the phone. He glances around. I can see he's partially aware of his surroundings through the curtain of his distress. Dropping to a squat again, he shakes his head and covers his eyes, once more seeming to seek anonymity.

The train comes to a halt at Olympic Village Station. We are minutes away from my destination. People exit, leaving empty seats. I'm on the verge of saying something when the young man rises and takes a seat. He rests his head against the window, body slumped sideways, revealing the depth of his unhappiness. I have the urge to reach out and put a reassuring hand on his shoulder, to let him know he's not alone. Instead, I find myself shipwrecked on an island of indecision, in a sea of urban indifference, torn between offering comfort and respecting his privacy.

Yaletown Station approaches; it's my stop. I have little time left to act. His eyes are closed, his shoulders drooped in an attitude of resignation.

My heart cries out but he has asked for no help. Perhaps he wishes none, only to be left alone.

Yaletown is here and I must leave. I exit the carriage with one last backward glance. I'm shaken by the experience, feeling uncertain, confused, on edge, with my stomach in knots. The image of his hunched body haunts my mind. Am I overreacting? His physical safety is not in question. Had he fallen to the floor clutching his chest, I would have responded immediately. But his heart failure has nothing to do with heart attack. It's about heartbreak, and my first aid training doesn't cover this. Even so, I feel deeply impacted by his emotional state, connected in a disjointed way, sharing something of his sorrow, bearing something of his pain.

Ahead of me on the escalator is a young woman. Her cropped hair is tinted with blue streaks. She wears green and gold patterned leggings and flat shoes, and carries a bouquet of red roses. She stands to the right to let me pass. I feel a visceral need to engage in conversation with a fellow human being.

"Lovely bouquet," I offer hesitantly.

She smiles back. "Yes."

"Gift?" I ask.

"It's my birthday," she beams.

"Congratulations."

"Thanks," says Birthday Girl as, together with our fellow travelers, we emerge into the Yaletown street scene. It's a sultry day.

Thi Tran
Of Mom and Men

Not long after I turned fifteen, Mom denounced all romantic relationships with men. She was forty-four. In a way that is both epically tragic
and confusingly powerful, she kept her word. She hasn't been intimately
involved with a man since 1997 when Beanie Babies were all the rage,
Mmmbop entered the pop culture vernacular, and *Titanic* shelled out
impressive box office numbers.

Mom made the announcement after her second marriage had ended.
After he lunged for her throat in front of our dinner guests like a drunk
tarantula. After he grabbed the car's steering wheel as she drove, veering
the car into a roadside ditch. After it was discovered he did not in fact
own an auto mechanic business and the fancy American Express card he
brandished like a lasso was deep into collections.

After he left, Mom came into the room I shared with my sister and in
the same cadence she would use to tell me dinner's ready, she said, "It's
over. No more. I'm done with men. All they do is give me a headache."
She pointed her finger in the air. "I'll be happier alone. Finally at peace."
It was as if the gesture sealed her fate.

I wondered if it was surrender, acceptance of her failed attempts at
love, or if it was righteousness, claiming ultimate solitary freedom. Or
both. To me, someone who's copped to being boy crazy since the first
grade, it was hard to understand her decision, the finality of it, the loneliness. There was a prickle of fear that I, too, would be doomed to repeat
the family history, that I would inherit this flawed part of the maternal
legacy. As she closed the door behind her, I remember thinking, *Poor
Mom. I never want to be like you.*

It was around this time that I met Vu. I never had a serious boyfriend before him. He was my first. Vu had a gnarly set of chompers, his two front teeth were grossly bucked, blackened at the edges, but apart from that, he was beautiful. The edges of his face, his high cheekbones and elegant jawline were perfectly symmetrical. He wore a blue silk bomber jacket and drove a Beamer with leather seats that felt like butter against my skin. When I think of him today, he is wearing the same jacket in every memory.

A friend of mine had introduced us, saying to me, "You're totally his type." I felt flattered I could even be that. I had just started the ninth grade. He was older. Already out of school, he spent his days frequenting cafes on Kingsway and Chinatown karaoke bars at night. When driving, he preferred listening to electronic trance beats with no vocals but instead let me play Mariah Carey's melodic, ballad-heavy *Butterfly* album in an endless loop. His patience—the thing that made him gentle—shone as I stumbled in my inexperience: at the introduction to sushi and raw oysters on the half-shell, when he showed me how to safely ride on the back of his motorcycle, the time he took me to a revolving restaurant high up above the city skyline where all I could think of was how my socks didn't match.

That December, Vu drove me out to Spanish Banks where he parked in front of the sandy beaches overlooking the Strait of Georgia and the North Shore mountains, only I couldn't see any of it because it was pitch dark. He flicked off the headlights, leaving us cocooned by the night sky, only the lights of the dashboard illuminating our faces. It wasn't long before he took my hand, interlocked his fingers with mine, and kissed the back of my hand. He stared into me so hard I thought I would crumble. Then he whispered, "I love you." I. Love. You. I had never heard those words before. It felt impossibly romantic. Outside it was probably near freezing, but I warmed so much that I could feel a sweat mustache forming on my upper lip and was thankful for our darkened enclosure. My heart lifted with pride, a sense of winning, because he had said the magic words *to me*. It was then that I was sure I had broken the spell and certain I wouldn't end up like Mom.

☙

When I was a small child, my father removed the glass Seiko clock from the wall and smashed it into Mom's face. As blood gushed from the gash above her eye, she tore through a handful of money, throwing them at my father in a shower of rainbow coloured bills. After he left, I found Mom crouched on the floor, piecing together the money with Scotch tape. My sister and I helped by creating a puzzle game, matching up the shreds of coloured paper, proud when we found a corner of a five-dollar bill, or the corresponding half of a two-dollar bill.

☙

My knee-jerk response was to say nothing. I didn't say, "I love you, too" because the enormity of it precluded me. And because I had never said it before. It got caught in that place behind my vocal chords, as if God had forgotten to program the words in me. "Do you love me?" he asked. "Yeah. Okay." Was all I could come up with.

☙

Mom is a dragon. I was born in 1982, which makes me a dog. According to the Chinese zodiac, the two signs sit on opposite ends of the disposition spectrum, describing dragons as self-possessed lone rangers and dogs as emotionally insecure pack animals. Imagine for a moment, a powerful, majestic and mythical creature with golden scales, breathing fire and flying across the land. Now picture a cocker spaniel. Puppy-dog eyes looking up at you, searching your face for signs of affection.

Mom has never said "I love you" to me. Not ever. *Words of Affirmation* is not the *Love Language* in our household. It's not that we don't believe it to be true, we just don't throw around the expression the way it's done on primetime TV. The sentiment weasels into our conversations and translates more or less into, "You're too skinny. Are you eating enough?" or "You should become a teacher. It's stable income and you'll get three months' vacation." She also has a morbid habit of reminding me she took out a life insurance policy on herself, often mentioning it casually in the middle of dinner. "Don't worry, I'll take care of you when I'm dead."

⌒

Later that night, I wrote in my diary: *December 11, 1997: Vu said the "L" word to me! Yup, that's right. He said I love you. I don't know if it's for real because he said it before we were gonna do it. But if it is for real, I guess that's really sweet! P.S. We've been going out for two months.*

I hadn't seen it coming. And even if I did, I didn't stand a chance. February 4, 1998 my diary entry reads: *It's almost our four-month anniversary, but everything is so different. I found out he was cheating on me with some chick with an MR2.* A betrayal that felt like my fault because he dumped me for a girl with a flashy Toyota. She was likely more experienced than I was, probably had salon-grade highlights and wore expensive jeans and here I was with my BC Transit Concession Pass and mismatched socks—why wouldn't he upgrade? Each time I called, the line went dead. Each time the line went dead, I spiraled deeper into hurt. Hurt turned into desperation. I phoned his friends to ask about him and got half-assed, pitying replies. I left messages pleading for him to call back. I waited listlessly by the phone, bargained with God, panicked by the thought that no matter what, I'd end up like Mom. He never called back.

First heartbreaks suck. They exist as a kind of existential hazing; everyone gets inducted.

For a teenager, six months is like forever. That's how long it took to recalibrate my senses, to feel like a version of myself. During that period, I wallowed in self-pity and blinding disillusionment. I discovered the many "stages" of heartbreak, some of which include anger, guilt, hurt, and desperation. Through the cracks, the moments when I was exhausted thinking exclusively about myself and Vu, I thought about

Mom and her relationships. About all her misadventures with men. Her hard life. How I must've inherited some residual misfortune of hers. As Mom remembers it, she left my father with precisely eleven dollars in her pocket, me attached to her hip, my sister waddling behind. All before her skin had a chance to acclimatize to the dampness of the Pacific Northwest. Mom left my father or my father left us. It's still unclear. But moving through the emotions of my first heartbreak, there emerged a pain that I could try to parallel, at least to some degree, to the kind Mom had experienced at the end of her second marriage. A pain that, when repeated in its brokenness over time, could have driven her to make the final call, on her own terms. Acceptance being the last stage.

⁓

In the summer of 2015, I attended a banquet hosted by a friend celebrating the sale of his company. I sat alongside friends, my plate piled with prime rib and crustaceans, sipping my third or fifth glass of Sauvignon Blanc. Just beyond the rim, I saw Vu. He looked exactly as he did when I was fifteen, only he was wearing a crisp black suit. The wine must've taken hold because I thought it was totally within the realm of possibility that he could be a vampire. It took a moment to register that he was floating towards me.

"Is that you, Thi?" I'm sure he was surprised to see me as much as I him. He smiled wide.

"Vu … your teeth. They look great!" I raised my glass to him, "Cheers."

Contributors

FOREWORD

Gurjinder Basran's debut novel, *Everything Was Good-bye*, was the winner of the Great BC Novel Contest in 2010 and the Ethel Wilson Fiction Prize in 2011. Gurjinder's much anticipated second novel, *Someone You Love Is Gone*, is being released by Penguin Random House in August 2017.

AUTHORS

Megan Abele is a writer of both short and novel-length fiction. Many of her story ideas originate from her twenty years spent working as a counsellor, parent educator, and child advocate with high-risk families in Vancouver. Her current novel, "This Is My Normal," tells the story of Lauren, a seventeen-year-old girl who is raised by a mother who is bi-polar. It explores themes of parentification, the blurring of boundaries between parents and children, and the challenge of healthy separation. Megan lives in Vancouver with her husband and two teenage daughters.

A child of diaspora, **Fatima Amarshi** comes from a multi-generational family of immigrants who travelled from India to Tanzania, and eventually to Canada. As a queer woman raised in a strong and resilient community of faith (Islam), navigating these multiple identities was, and continues to be, a complicated affair that informs her work. Currently living in Vancouver, Fatima is working on her first book of poetry and learning to play the ukulele.

Sarah Amormino is a poet/fiction writer with a background in journalism. Originally from Toronto, she moved to Vancouver in 2016, leaving behind her co-founded venture, *Broke Magazine*—a project for emerging artists in the city. Her creative writing challenges ideas of isolation, discovery, and spirituality.

T. M. Baldwin was born and raised in Penticton, British Columbia, where she fed her early imagination the steady diet of science fiction and fantasy that continues to influence her work in the speculative fiction genre. She moved to Vancouver in 2013 after spending eight years in Shanghai, China, where she worked as a magazine editor and in marketing communications. Through the sometimes futuristic, sometimes fantastical, sometimes overt, and sometimes subtle speculative lens, her writing aims to capture the difficult truths and beautiful contradictions of the human condition. She is currently working on her first novel.

Samantha Balliet has an overwhelming life experience of twenty-one years. Born in Hope and raised in Mission, she studied sciences at the University of British Columbia (UBC) for two years before she gave in to her desire to write—one of her many guilty pleasures. Beyond writing, she also enjoys eating, watching dogs from afar (while praying for hand-to-paw interaction), and singing loudly in the shower. Few appreciate her refined assortment of hobbies. If she could one day become a full-time writer, she would be the happiest of all campers.

Stephen T. Berg—disappointed hippy, approximate monk, writer, poet—lives in Victoria, B.C. Earlier, he spent twenty-five years in Edmonton, Alberta, working for an agency caring for homeless people. A frequent contributor to the *Edmonton Journal*'s religion page, he wrote articles on social care and justice. His prose and poetry have been employed in staged performances and have appeared in such publications as *Orion, Earthshine, Geez, Prairie Messenger, oratorealis,* and Vancouver's *Westender.* His first chapbook, *There Are No Small Moments,* was published by The Rasp and The Wine (2014). For more of Stephen's work, visit growmercy.org.

Mak Berry is a manic/wordy writer whom you can often find among the mountains, accompanied by bike and books. Caught between poetry and lyric prose, she has been scribbling down fleeting ideas, or staring off into space trying to catch up with said fleeting ideas, since 2012. Mak grew up in Kamloops, B.C., with her twin sister, Gabrielle, and moved to Vancouver in 2013 for the ocean and the experiences, hoping one day to spin her thrill for alliteration into a career.

Becky Block will tell you that if you don't count the pitiful diary entries or teen angst stories with dramatic arcs that rival *The Real Housewives* series, her career began writing stories for a Canadian military newspaper in a post-9/11 environment. In her current work as a corporate communicator, she spends too much time overthinking her use of commas and not enough time creating buzzwords to compete with the young and ambitious. This is her first memoir, which spans across the prairies and into palliative care as a witty, poignant look at intimacy.

Carlie Blume is an emerging writer of short fiction, poetry, and creative non-fiction. She is currently working on her debut novel, "Where the Lions Are." Her writing centres on women's issues, motherhood, one's sense of personal belonging, and sexual politics within relationships and marriage. She is constantly inspired by the complex framework that makes a person who they are. Her work has been featured in *Pulp Mag*. She was born in North Vancouver and currently lives in White Rock with her husband and two children.

Kimberley Phillips Boehm is the author of books and articles about U.S. history. As a child, she moved twenty times before she turned twenty-two years old. She is now working on a memoir about growing up in an army family during the years of the Vietnam War and Civil Rights Movement.

Tanya Boteju is an English teacher and aspiring novelist. She is a native British Columbian. Tanya's writing life has mostly consisted of teaching writing at York House School in Vancouver, where she has learned as much from her high-school-aged students as she hopes they have learned from her over the past fifteen years. Tanya is currently working on a young adult novel, and she has been grateful during the process for her patient wife, supportive family and friends, and hot mugs of tea. She hopes to contribute to the ever-growing collection of young adult literature representing diverse characters and experiences.

Maureen Butler grew up in Toronto and worked in the Yukon for six years before moving to B.C. Her play *Tom Tom at Jake's Crossing*, co-written with Larry Saidman, won the Nakai Players 24 Hour Playwriting Contest and had a successful run in Whitehorse. She wrote a series of poems for a photo exhibit called *Alone, Together* in Langley, B.C. After years of teaching literacy and high school and college English, she is writing her first novel. To avoid writing, she plans trips to Arizona and cleans her toaster.

Stephanie Candiago, a Vancouver native, has always wanted to write, but did everything else instead. The eternal student, she holds a bachelor of arts in English literature and certificates in editing, business, and logistics. Currently she manages the distribution of most of the concrete used to build the Lower Mainland. After losing her father suddenly, her life shifted to the left. "If not now, when?" she asked herself, and applied to the Writer's Studio. Now she hopes to string some words together that will create a new landscape for her life. "This is the part where you find out who you are."

Lorna Carley is an emerging fiction writer whose work has been published in *Grain Magazine*, the *Globe and Mail*, and online. She is at work on her first short story collection. Lorna and her family divide their time between Calgary and Canmore, Alberta.

Reese Kim Carrozzini is an EFL educator and artist from Vancouver. After a long period living and travelling abroad, she is back to her roots—pursuing her passion, writing fiction and creative non-fiction. Her imagination, observations, experiences, and great curiosity about people and cultures take the reader on a journey into the minds of her flawed characters to discover a little piece of her in the stories she writes. As an emerging writer, she strives to write with compassion, wit, and self-deprecation as she explores the dark, emotional topics of personal relationships and their fractious nature.

Diana Carter is a retired psychiatrist who lives in West Vancouver. She has published in medical journals but has only recently taken up creative writing. She is grateful for the gifts of mountains, forest, and ocean. She also enjoys re-exploring stones, sticks, shells, bugs, and other small things with her grandchildren.

Elecia Chrunik is a prairie-born, Vancouver-based writer. She has written, edited, and taught many things in many forms over many years. This list includes magazine articles, an award-winning zombie movie script, ghostwritten novel-length autobiographies, and poems. She is currently writing long-form fiction, which is a new landscape for her. Her story is set in a time before time, and is a both a creation story and a story about family, healing, and the journey to return home.

Daniela Cohen emigrated from South Africa to Canada in 1994. In 2008, she returned to South Africa to volunteer with Amazwi, a media arts non-profit organization working to empower rural African women to share their stories. She documented her experiences through a monthly column, "Homeward Bound," published in the *Canadian Immigrant* online. In 2009, she was featured as a monthly contributor on the *African Blog*. Daniela's stories focus on themes of division and connection, displacement and belonging. She hopes to give a window into worlds that may otherwise remain unseen, and bring people together beyond barriers that may separate them.

Crystal Dalman was born on Vancouver Island and grew up in the lovely community of Mesachie Lake. At an early age, her love for adventure, sports, and creativity was evident, and eventually led to her successful career as a professional stuntwoman. Crystal travelled the world, finding joy and inspiration through writing stories and letters to document her experiences. She takes delight in sharing these stories with others. Currently a student in the Writer's Studio at Simon Fraser University (SFU), Crystal is excited to see her memoir excerpt published in *emerge 17*.

Gina-Lily D'Attilio, from the wilds of Salt Spring Island, is a traveller in the world and in life. A screenwriter, apprentice novelist, and writer of many songs you haven't heard, her work has been praised for its originality and its blend of creativity and analysis. Gina-Lily is an alumna of the Writer's Studio at SFU, and she is enrolled in SFU's Southbank Writers' Program. She is pitching a romantic-comedy screenplay, "Four's a Crowd," and finishing a first novel, "Swagger," about the descent of an investment banker who begins a drug-fueled affair with a partygirl, and the freedom she represents.

Junie Désil is a Haitian-Canadian poet originally from Montréal, raised in Winnipeg, now living on unceded Coast Salish Territories. She has performed at various literary events and festivals, and her work has appeared in a variety of print media. She is currently on break from the non-profit and academic world, trying her hand at writing.

Robyn Drage is an illustrator, writer, and visual artist with a BA in creative writing (UBC). She recently snuck into animation as a background painter on TV shows for Disney and DreamWorks. No one has caught on (yet) that she might not belong. This is good, because she can keep wearing T-shirts adorned with terrible puns to an actual office without being shunned. She is currently writing a novel, but getting distracted by short stories—each threatening to become a novella. If you have the power to convince the book-buying public that novellas are the next big thing, please get in touch.

Christy Dunsmore has thirty-five years' experience in the art of avoidance. Bitten by the writing bug in elementary school, she chose not to be a writer because it wasn't too practical. She studied microbiology. This led to a BFA, which led to a career as a copywriter and illustrator, which led to owning a design/build firm. Eventually, she studied creative writing at UBC and SFU, filing all work in The Drawer. Finally embracing the impractical, Christy is now completing her first novel, and—when she's not writing—she teaches art.

Jo Dworschak is a writer, broadcaster, and performer. She is writing a non-fiction book, "Families Across Canada," about an epic road trip with her teenaged son. The story follows their 7,821-kilometre journey along the Trans-Canada Highway from St. John's, Newfoundland, home to Vancouver, and captures encounters with families they meet on the way. While at home in East Vancouver, Jo produces and hosts the hit game show *Story Story Lie* and co-hosts Co-op Radio's queer show, *Fruit Salad*.

Rebecca Fleck is working on a memoir about her extended travels through Central America, China, and India. A native Vancouverite who enjoys photography, watching movies, and occasionally belting out a Patsy Cline song at karaoke, she has lived and worked in Japan, Australia, and New Zealand. Rebecca climbed a live volcano at sunset in Antigua, got shanghaied in Shanghai, and volunteered in Mother Teresa's homes in Kolkata.

Stephanie Gray is a writer of fantasy fiction and the occasional short film script. She is the author of the self-published e-book *Lockhart and Teague: The Empty Chest*, the first in an epic fantasy series depicting the ongoing adventures of two guys in the steampunk city of New Artax.

Alyssa Hanada has been a storyteller for as long as she can remember, and has a background rooted in technical writing and journalism. She lives in Portland, Oregon, with her husband and two young boys. She previously participated in the prestigious and intensive Tin House Writer's Workshop in Portland and has spent the last ten years working as a grant writer for non-profits in her community. Most recently, she has been a participant in SFU's Writer's Studio Online, where she is at work on her first novel.

Lynn Harrison is an executive coach with over thirty years' experience working with leaders in a broad range of organizations. She is passionate about helping leaders create environments in which people thrive. Her doctoral study, "Perfect Storm: A Systems View of Abrasive Leadership," involved interviews with executives formerly perceived to be highly abrasive and shed light on the experience of the alleged perpetrator—a perspective which has received little attention in workplace-bullying research. Lynn is co-author of *Taking the Stage: Breakthrough Stories from Women Leaders* and has written various articles about coaching and leadership.

Urith Hayley, born in Panama, has been living in the Greater Vancouver area since 1977. Her love of writing had taken a backseat to an accounting career until last year, when she began the Writer's Studio.

Jennifer Heron grew up in New Westminster and developed a love for nature and the outdoors at an early age. In her day job, she is an endangered-species entomologist with an interest in the conservation of native bees and hot-springs species. She enjoys writing policy, and more recently she's been working on writing projects centring on her experiences as an entomologist. She spends much of her time chasing insects or thinking of ways to fund travel adventures to look for more insects.

After earning a BA (art and design) and EDM (art), **Cynthia C. Huij-gens** worked for many years in museum education sharing her passion for art and antiquities with visitors and schools. After arriving in Cairo on a resident visa in 2011, she began a five-year journey to embrace and understand a country in the midst of profound transition. The first draft of her manuscript for upper-middle-grade readers, entitled "The Novice Collector," was completed in Egypt. Cynthia attended VCFA Novel Retreat 2015, and was selected for AWP's Writer to Writer Mentorship Program the following year. Cynthia currently lives in Brussels.

Lis Jakobsen is a former public-relations consultant who has clocked in a lot of commercial, non-profit, and government job-related writing over the years. Now retired, she has found her way back to her fabled hometown, Hamilton, Ontario, and turned her hand to other fictions.

Leslie Jenneson grew up in Hope, British Columbia, and grew to love poetry through the music her parents listened to—most notably the music of Van Morrison, Bob Dylan, and Cat Stevens. She holds an honours degree in theology, philosophy, and ancient Greek from Ambrose University. Leslie spent most of her twenties writing prayers and liturgy for a small church in downtown Calgary. She now works as a cook and brewery assistant in Vancouver's Downtown Eastside, and continues to write poetry. Her poems explore themes of mortality, loss, questions of God, and the fleeting nature of memory.

Josh Keefer was born in Vancouver. He currently works as a cook in North Vancouver, and writes fiction in his spare time.

Chelene Knight was born in Vancouver and is a graduate of the Writer's Studio for poetry and fiction. In addition to being a workshop facilitator for teens, she is also a regular literary-event organizer and host. She has been published in various Canadian and American literary magazines. Chelene is currently the managing editor at *Room* magazine. *Braided Skin*, her debut book (Mother Tongue Publishing, 2015), has given birth to numerous writing projects including her second book, *Dear Current Occupant* (forthcoming with BookThug in 2018). She's now working on her novel, "Junie", set in the Hogan's Alley of 1930s–50s Vancouver.

Scott Lear has been a scientific writer for twenty years as a professor in health sciences at SFU. Two years ago, he began to explore the enjoyment of creative writing, and is thankful for being in the Writer's Studio to improve his art. Living in Vancouver with his encouraging wife and two kids, he also enjoys swimming, cycling, and photography.

Kathryn Lee has been a children's librarian for twenty years, and enjoys writing in her spare time. In her approach to both her work and her writing, she likes to misquote G. K. Chesterton: "Children want justice, but adults want mercy." She has recently finished the first draft of a mystery/romance novel for teens, and is currently working on a collection of interconnected romance/break-up stories for adults. No matter what she is writing, Kathryn hopes that all her characters get their fair share of justice and compassion.

Tatiana Lee is a fiction writer and poet living and working on the beautiful B.C. coast. When she is not capturing her lucid dreams in poems or stories, Tatiana is enjoying the great outdoors with her young family in tow. This unpublished, emerging writer looks forward to sharing her work with the world.

Adriana Louis is Dutch by origin, international lawyer by trade, and a recent graduate of the Writer's Studio at SFU. She spent almost two years in Uganda, working on transitional justice and refugee-rights issues, and uses this experience to write about Uganda's road to recovery and Kampala's infamous nightlife.

As a writer, **Patrick Lucas** enjoys exploring issues of identity, sense of place, intercultural experiences, and conscious travel in both fiction and non-fiction. His work has appeared in the *Vancouver Sun*, *Matador Travel*, *FreeHub Magazine*, *Pink Bike*, and *Reconciliation Canada*. Patrick is also a storyteller, and has appeared at the Vancouver International Mountain Film Festival, the Flame, World Storytelling Day, and Sam Sullivan's Public Salon.

Paolo Marcazzan left Italy twenty years ago to make Vancouver his half-home. He's dabbled in chemistry and science, but words and blank pages remain his primary source of perplexity. While trying to figure out how the two go together, he volunteers with youth, and uses paper for inking anything but words. Someday soon, he will travel Argentina, top to bottom.

Graham McGarva enjoyed a forty-year career as a city builder, balancing the poetry and mathematics of architecture, including planning and building much of the vista from his family's False Creek home. Poetry was often a useful tool in the tight-rope walk of community transformation, performed for communities and their city councils. Arriving in Vancouver in 1973 as a hitchhiker from the U.K., Graham founded VIA Architecture in 1984, gathered civic, provincial, and international architectural awards—including election as Fellow of the RAIC—before returning, in 2016, to his focus on poetry and community advocacy.

Tara McGuire leaped gratefully into writing from a thirty-year career in radio broadcasting. Her plan to create lighthearted, humorous works of fiction changed abruptly in the summer of 2015 when her twenty-one-year-old son died of an accidental overdose. Since then she has written on grief for various publications, including her own website taramcguire.com. Tara's prose and poetry will be part of perhaps the saddest book ever written—an anthology of stories by parents on the losses of their beautiful children. She lives with her husband and daughter under the tall trees of North Vancouver.

Alissa Messner is an editor in Edmonton, Alberta, and has worked in publishing and government. Her joys in life include cats, reading science non-fiction (preferably about cats), watching sports, eating brie, and cats. Plus, cats.

Sharon Miki is a hapa Japanese-Canadian fiction writer, born and raised in the suburbs of Vancouver. During the day, she is a freelance copywriter and editor; by night, you can find her devouring novels, running long distances, or writing short stories by (LED) candlelight. She is currently this close to completing her first novel.

Thomas Onstott is a native of Colorado, but now lives in Nashville. He works as a certified registered nurse anaesthetist (he passes anaesthetic gas for a living). He holds a bachelor of science and doctorate in nursing from two fancy universities (if you are into that kind of thing). At first, he started writing to entertain himself, but then he realized he could entertain other people too. He especially enjoys reading and writing for his daughter.

Viola Prinz lives in Perth, Western Australia. The author of self-published chapbook, *Speculative Mining* (2015), she has had poetry published in various literary journals, including *oratorealis* and *Primo Lux*. Formerly educated in architecture, she is also a cellist, freelance designer, and artist.

Neha Puntambekar is a freelance writer from Mumbai, currently living in Barbados. Her work has appeared in various publications, including *wsj India*, *Hindustan Times*, *Elle India*, and *The Indian Express*, as well as online. She is currently working on her first novel.

Shilpa Raju is an engineer by degree and a writer by choice. She's an active blogger with a website, Lass in a Mess, where she recounts her tales and experiences based on her observations. Shilpa is a graduate of the Writer's Studio at SFU, where she had the opportunity to interact with bestselling authors of international renown. She also holds a diploma in creative writing from Indira Gandhi National Open University. Her previous publications include articles for her college magazine and short stories for local newspapers. Jane Austen, J. K. Rowling, and Jodi Picoult are her biggest literary influences.

Christine Leviczky Riek is a poet and photographer from Surrey, B.C.

Born and raised in Saskatchewan, Canada, **Amanda Deitz** has always loved creating stories—especially serials. Her writing career began in 1998 when she was selected to appear alongside twenty-four peers as a monthly contributor for the "Minus 20" column in the *Regina Leader Post*. Since that time, she has self-published four books, a novella series, and has been featured in several newspapers. In 2007, she took home the Saskatchewan Reader's Choice Award for her serial drama, *Longer Than Life*. She lives in Saskatoon with her husband and daughter and works as a paralegal.

Natasha Sanders-Kay writes poetry and prose with an eye toward gender and social justice. She is managing editor of *subTerrain* magazine, and serves on the board of the Magazine Association of B.C., through which she is spearheading an initiative around inclusiveness in publishing. She's also worked with various arts, feminist, and anti-violence organizations. Natasha's writing has been published in Langara's *w49* (after winning second prize in Langara's Writing Contest, fiction category), in the poetry zine *Parachuting Past Patriarchy* (from GSWS students at SFU), and in *subTerrain*. She holds an honours degree in women's studies from SFU, and lives in Burnaby.

S. L. Shields left her native Winnipeg for Canada's gold coast several years ago. Since then, she has made a name for herself as a small-business owner as well as a contributing writer for *Sound Phrase & Fury* magazine. Her newly adopted city of Vancouver is never short on inspiration, and has pushed S. L. into the world of fiction writing.

Leslee Silverman is a prairie girl who recently escaped from directing theatre and entered the dangerous pantheon of writing. She loves words. Leslee has never been certain where bathos ends and pathos begins in her work. She has been unsuccessfully trying to avoid first-person narrative all her life, for which she blames Sophocles. Leslee was honoured with a Governor General's Performing Arts Lifetime Achievement Award in 2012.

Michelle Stack, PhD, is an associate professor and public commentator on education. Her research interests include media coverage of mental health and illness, university rankings, the role of media in the policy-making process, community and youth engagement, social justice, and equity in education. She also consults with school districts and non-profits on equity issues. In addition to being an academic, Michelle has dipped her toe in stand-up comedy and improvisation. She didn't think she wanted to become a YA author, but the SFU writing program changed that.

Neda Tanha is an artist, writer, and advocate for youth. She was born and grew up in Iran. She believes that through spiritual and material education, one can overcome the ignorance that is the root of all prejudice. Denied her right to a secondary education by the government, simply due to her faith, she pursued her education through the underground university, BIHE. She immigrated to Canada in her mid-twenties, and currently resides in Abbotsford with her husband and two daughters. She is now working on her first novel, which reflects her own beliefs and experiences with education.

Thi Tran is a Vietnamese, Canadian-born writer and artist. She discovered her love of storytelling while studying theatre at UBC. A lot of her work at TWS in the non-fiction genre examines her childhood growing up in East Vancouver with a single mother/refugee parent. She works with crisp memories, faint blurry ones, the ones that occupy the senses and body, and the memories that live in that inexplicable, mysterious place. Writing is one of ways in which she tries to make sense of it all. She's a cat mom, textbook Virgo, and West Coast junkie.

Barry Truter has been a traveller much of his life, having lived in places as varied as India, Hong Kong, Fiji, the U.S., and England, before landing in Canada. As a musician and writer, he enjoys connecting with audiences through songs and stories that celebrate the intimacy and diversity of human experience. His work is inspired by travel, personal experience, historical events, and social issues of the day. Leaving behind earlier careers as seafarer and IT consultant, he appreciates the opportunity to deepen his writing practice within the supportive community of the Writers Studio.

Kurt Trzcinski is an ecologist that has studied many organisms and ecosystems, and is currently studying woodpeckers. His poetry ranges from short outpourings of love and anguish to longer cycles of poems centred on our relationship with nature.

Born in Ottawa, **Cara Waterfall** has lived and worked in Europe, Asia, and Africa. Shortlisted for *FreeFall Magazine*'s 2016 Annual Poetry Contest and PULP *Literature*'s 2017 The Magpie Award for Poetry contest, her poetry has been featured in *The Fiddlehead* and *oratorealis*. A graduate of Queen's University and the London School of Journalism, she works as a freelance writer and with The Muse Group—an organization that aims to create professional development opportunities for low-income women in Côte d'Ivoire.

Leslie West is originally from Coquitlam, B.C., and has been studying creative writing at Douglas College and Vancouver Community College for four years. She is fascinated by the everyday stories that surround us, and by the complexity of human relationships. She writes short stories and is currently working on a novel. She now lives in East Vancouver.

Michael Zibauer is a teacher and writer who dabbles in multiple genres, including screenwriting, fiction, and poetry. He lives in the Vancouver, B.C. area, enjoying the sights, scenes, and surroundings of the beautiful Lower Mainland. While in the Writer's Studio, he thoroughly enjoyed working on "The Barmaid's Adventure," and adding it to his expanding portfolio of writing. Michael would like to thank all those who have collaborated with him during the program, and wish them good luck for the future.

In Memoriam

Cullene Evelyn Bryant
June 4, 1941 – April 23, 2017

The Writer's Studio
2010 Narrative non-fiction group
2012 Poetry and lyric prose group
2013 – 14 Co-host of TWS Reading Series
2014 Prose Graduate Workshop
2015 Poetry Graduate Workshop

Connie Howard
July 19, 1956 – November 15, 2016

The Writer's Studio
2016 Narrative non-fiction group
2016 Winner of the TWS Emerging Writer Scholarship

Production Credits

Publisher
Andrew Chesham

Managing Editor
Janet Fretter

Editorial Team

Section Editors
Rebecca A. Coates – Speculative
  and YA Fiction
Alessia Yaworsky – Fiction
Lindsay Kwan – Poetry and
  Lyric Prose
Nikki Hillman – Non-fiction

Copy Editors
Stephanie Candiago
Elecia Chrunik
Rebecca Fleck
Stephanie Gray
Graham McGarva
Thi Tran

Production Team
Emily Stringer –
  Production Editor
Reese Kim Carrozzini
Taylor Reynolds
Neda Tanhar

Acknowledgments

The students of the Writer's Studio would like to thank their mentors for the guidance and insight they have provided. We would also like to extend special thanks to the mentor apprentices for their support throughout the year.

We extend our gratitude to Cottage Bistro (4770 Main Street) for graciously hosting our monthly reading series.

Joanne Betzler and Grant Smith's continued support of our program and the anthology has allowed us to make the *emerge* book launch a fun and lively event. As well, Grant's Spring session on business and tax planning for writers has helped prepare our community for the business of writing.

We would all like to thank Vancouver's local independent bookstores for selling *emerge*. We urge our readers to support the booksellers that support local writers.

We would like to thank John Whatley and SFU Publications for co-publishing *emerge*. Once again, their generous support has enabled our alumni and students to work together on the production of this book.

Finally, the Writer's Studio and the *emerge* production team would like to thank our Managing Editor, Janet Fretter. Janet has managed our publication since 2014, keeping us motivated, on task, and on schedule. Janet, thank you for your hard work and passion for this anthology. We have enjoyed every moment of working with you.

Elzevir A*a* Q*q* R*r*

The interior of *emerge* is set in DTL Elzevir. Originally created in the 1660s, Elzevir is a baroque typeface, cut by Christoffel van Dijck in Amsterdam. As noted in Robert Bringhurst's *The Elements of Typographic Style*, baroque typography thrived in the seventeenth century and is known for its axis variations from one letter to the next. During this time, typographers started mixing roman and *italic on the same line*. The Dutch Type Library created a digital version in 1993 called DTL Elzevir. It retains some of the weight that an earlier digital version, Monotype Van Dijck, possessed in metal but had lost in its digital translation.

The interior of *emerge* is printed on Rolland paper, produced by Rolland Inc, Canada. The cover for *emerge* uses Kalima CIS paper, made by Tembec Inc, Canada. Both papers are Forestry Stewardship Council (FSC) and Sustainable Forestry Initiative (SFI) Certified, and are acid free/elemental chlorine free.